Rennie's Way

Rennie's Way

VERNA MAE SLONE

With a Foreword by Wade Hall

Illustrations by Len Slone

THE UNIVERSITY PRESS OF KENTUCKY

Portions of this book appeared earlier, in a slightly different form, as *Sarah Ellen*,
copyright © 1982 by Verna Mae Slone, published by Pippa Valley Printing.

Illustrations copyright © 1982 by Len Slone.

Library of Congress Cataloging-in-Publication Data
Slone, Verna Mae, 1914-
    Rennie's way / Verna Mae Slone : illustrations by Len Slone.
        p. cm.
    ISBN 0-8131-1855-7 :
    1. Girls—Kentucky—Fiction.   2. Young women—Kentucky—Fiction.
3. Family—Kentucky—Fiction.   4. Mountain life—Appalachian Region—
History—20th century—Fiction.   5. Appalachian Region—Fiction.
I. Title.
PS3569.L6746   1994
813'.54—dc20   93-39379

Foreword _____

WADE HALL

For two hundred years and more, Eastern Kentuckians and Southern Mountaineers have been recorded and distorted by writers from the outside who have visited for a few days or weeks, observed the "picturesque" mountain people and their "quaint" culture, and hurried back to their desks in New York or Boston or Chicago to write their stereotypes. Fortunately, the region has lately been raising a homegrown crop of talented writers who see their native land and people from the inside out. Numbered among these recent writers are James Still, Harriette Arnow, Jim Wayne Miller, Wilma Dykeman, Cormac McCarthy, Heather Ross Miller, and Al Stewart. To this list should now be added Verna Mae Slone, an eighty-year-old native of Knott County, Kentucky, and the author of four books about her home country, including *Rennie's Way*, a revised and expanded version of a novel entitled *Sarah Ellen*, published in 1982. Perhaps more than any of these better known authors, Mrs. Slone has lived the life she writes about.

It is 1917 in the Eastern Kentucky mountain community of Lonesome Holler, and twelve-year-old Rennie Slone's mother has died. Suddenly, Rennie's hope of completing elementary school in Lonesome Holler and going on to high school at the Caney Community Center is ended. She is left to housekeep for her father and care for her infant sister, Sarah Ellen. Her father, an Old Regular Baptist preacher, is "a silent man who spent all his time serving the Lord" and very little serving his family. He is not much different from other men in Lonesome Holler, where women learn early that they are born to work, to wait for, and to wait on their menfolks. Out of necessity and custom, Rennie is transformed from a carefree girl into a child-woman. It is a duty she assumes without hesitation: "Now she was a woman with a child to raise, a home to run. But she was from sturdy stock; not once did she even think about not doing her duty."

Drawing on her own experiences, family stories, and first-hand observations, and using the shaping power of her imagination, Mrs. Slone has written an engrossing chronicle of Rennie's maturation as a surrogate mother and an independent woman who sacrifices her youthful dreams for her sister and ultimately finds fulfillment as a single woman. It is a story that rings as true as the dinner bells that alert the people of Lonesome Holler to dinner or danger. It is an autobiographical novel that combines the freedom and flexibility of fiction with the authenticity of fact. It is a genre that Mrs. Slone calls "faction."

Rennie's way is initially based on her late mother's ways—how to cook and wash and clean and sew and grow a garden. Her mother had been a proud and resourceful woman who kept her family together when her husband was wrongfully sentenced to prison for making moonshine. "Ma weren't like Pa," Rennie rightly observes, as she follows in her footsteps. But as she matures Rennie becomes her own woman, separate even from her mother's influence and from well-intentioned people who pressure her to live their way. She becomes determined to live her life her way. She devotes herself to nurturing her baby sister, whom she rears as her own daughter. Her ways begin to seem odd to the community, especially her lack of interest in boys, but she continues in her own way, never wishing to influence anyone else's. Indeed, she is able to live most of her life comfortably within the boudaries and traditions of Lonesome Holler.

In fact, Rennie has a keen sense of tradition and the past. She is like her great-grandmother Kate, who has said that "the only way to know yerself is to know yer forefathers. Yer history is a part of ye." She has also heeded Kate's words about family pride: "Never be ashamed of yer folks because they were poor. Always remember it took very brave people to come here—people lookin' fer freedom and a better life, not only fer themselves but fer the childern and grandchildern that would follow 'em." Rennie, therefore, respects the ways of her people, even her callous, domineering father, whose insensitive behavior sometimes gives a new definition to "tough love."

Rennie is, above all, realistic and stoical. She knows and accepts the limits of her life. In her words: "It's only in story books that the mystery is solved and that the boy gets the girl and they live happy ever after. This is real life. In real life everthin' don't turn out the way we want it to." But Rennie is not bitter about her lowered expectations. The omniscient narrator tells us her mind: "Rennie liked her life just the way it was. Why was everyone trying to get her married? She liked being her own boss. Why was it so hard for people to believe she liked being alone, just her and Sarah Ellen?" Then her sister grows up and goes away to school to fulfill Rennie's dream. Although Sarah Ellen will eventually return to the mountains as a teacher, Rennie knows that she herself is destined to live most of her life alone. Rennie's way has led, as she puts it, to being an Old Maid. More importantly, however, her way has been a pilgrim's progress of love and sacrifice.

As she walks through the pages of Mrs. Slone's novel, Rennie becomes a fully fleshed and vibrant, three-dimensional character. With her back stiff and her head high, she dominates the book. But she is surrounded by other major and minor figures that deserve notice. In addition to her sister and her parents, there are these: her cousin and soul mate Johnnie, who conceals his deep and abiding love for Rennie; the passionate and self-destructive Hank, Rennie's second cousin who falls in love with Sarah Ellen; Old Kate, a wicked and hateful recluse who is reputed to be a witch; Richard Tate, the young teacher who needs only small encouragement to propose to Rennie; Miss Rose, the tireless nurse from the Community Center whose interest in her patients extends beyond medicine. And finally, there is the real-life Mrs. Alice Lloyd, the reformer from Massachusetts who moved to Caney Creek with Puritan zeal, bringing improved educational opportunities and social services. Indeed, Mrs. Slone, who was a student at the Caney Creek school in her youth, has given us a remarkable and sympathetic portrait of Mrs. Lloyd, her school, and the benevolent impulses that motivated her. This loving disciplinarian wanted to help people help themselves, and she "not only reached out a helping hand, she stood by their sides and helped them push."

As a realistic writer, Mrs. Slone knows that life is a mix of sunshine and shadow, and in the novel she presents a balanced picture of Kentucky mountain life during the first third of the twentieth century. When there is humor, it is inherent in the character or situation. When violence is called for, she includes it. But whether she is describing an idyllic pastoral scene, the vengeful slaughter of horses, a mining tragedy, or a man's unspoken love for a woman, she is always in control of her material. This is how, for example, her narrator depicts a deathbed scene that a lesser writer would have reduced to maudlin sentiment. Rennie's dying mother has just asked her to read from the Book of Psalms: "Rennie got the Bible and began to read. On and on she read. She thought her mother had gone to sleep. Finally, when she laid the Bible down she looked at her mother's face and saw that all the pain and suffering had gone, replaced by such a peaceful look. Then she realized that her mother was dead. That was the last she remembered. From far away she heard a bell ringing. Aunt Nance's voice. A baby crying. The smell of camphor. . . . Rennie never looked at her mother again."

Rennie's story is told in a simple but lyrical style appropriate to the material: "The days on Lonesome Holler came and went with very little change. Old folks died; babies were born. Winter came, followed by summer." When the characters speak, they talk in a readable and believable mountain dialect. Unfamiliar words or forms are easily understood in context. Such words as "renched" for "rinsed," "ruck" for "raked," "brought-on person" for "outsider," and "feller" for "boyfriend" give the book an authentic sound and substance. In fact, in this book the strange people with the funny accents are not the mountaineers. Rennie may admire Mrs. Lloyd and the work she and the other brought-on people at her center are doing, but she doesn't like the way they talk: "Their speech was so harsh it grated on her ears like metal."

Furthermore, the author uses folk customs not as static museum exhibits but as vital parts of mountain life. The narrative is spiced with thrash cures, bean-stringings, huckleberry pickings, graveyard memorial services, folk games and rhymes, molasses stir-offs, bee-tree robbings, ginseng gatherings, pie suppers, and newground workings—even a bedbug extermination. All of these folkways are introduced as naturally as the seasonal changes. After all, they are the ways of real people who get embarrassingly real bedbugs in their cornshuck mattresses and hold community workings to clear off a neighbor's overgrown farmland. They are real people who tie white rags over their churn tops while the milk is clabbering, who place tobacco crumbs in the quilt box to discourage varmints, and who rob downy milkweed pods for pillow stuffing.

What Mrs. Slone's book reveals to us of later generations is a community of hard-working people who grow or make most of what they need to live, with nary a welfare office in sight. Their lives of self-reliance are not unlike those praised by another Kentucky writer, Wendell Berry, who, even as we approach the brave new world of the twenty-first century, believes that a return to a right relationship with our mother earth will make us more content and fulfilled.

Mrs. Slone presents also the dark side of Lonesome Holler. People live a hardscrabble life and, then as now, suffer from poverty and ignorance. But almost all of her people would "amen" the words of Rennie's beloved cousin Johnnie: "I have all I want in this world—a place to stay, plenty to eat, a chance to work and pay my keep, and a fiddle to play in my spare time." All in all, Mrs. Slone has given us a book that is like one of her quilts—a work of art carefully crafted out of bits and pieces of real life. This book is, indeed, a family heirloom.

In her preface the author writes that "those of us old timers who remember the good old mountain days should make it our business to preserve the memory." Like a family or community quilt, a good story "preserves the memory." But this story does more. It has created a heroine who deserves to stand in the company of such strong and loving women of American fiction as Hawthorne's Hester Prynne, Henry James's Isabel Archer, Willa Cather's Ántonia Shimerda, John Steinbeck's Ma Joad, and Harriette Arnow's Gertie Nevels. If Rennie Slone is not in the same room as these more famous women, at least she dwells in the same house of fiction.

Furthermore, this novel is an important addition to the library of American feminist fiction. Without contriving to be politically correct, Mrs. Slone has profiled two women—the fictional Rennie Slone and the historical Alice Lloyd—who are models of strength, endurance, and determination. The ultimate value of this book, however, has nothing to do with current political or literary fads. It simply does what good fiction always does. It creates a believable world that we can enter and care about.

Finally, this story belongs on the shelf of great love stories— not the ones in which lovers get married in the end, but a higher kind that is based on duty and compassion and sacrifice— or, as Rennie says, "a friendship love," which "can go as far and as deep as marriage love"—and maybe, she implies, can last even longer. Rennie's way has been a life of such love for her sister Sarah Ellen and her cousin Johnnie. When Johnnie marries, she realizes that their relationship may change, but she accepts it. As Rennie knows, the quality of love is always determined by the lover. After Sarah Ellen leaves home, Rennie is truly sad and lonesome, but she reasons that she still has a good life to live and "lots of things" to do. While she was in school in Cleveland, Sarah Ellen received many vivid letters from her sister in Kentucky, and she thinks: "Rennie should write a book. A letter from her is just like settin' on the porch and talking." Well, Rennie did write the book. It's called *Rennie's Way* and it contains "the sweet and sad memories of Lonesome Holler."

Preface _____

I have written this book in the simple language of mountain people, telling it the way I would have talked to my neighbors. In a sense it is not fiction. Mrs. Lloyd, Caney Creek, and the Community Center are real. Lonesome Holler could be any one of the small streams that make up Caney Creek. Our family name, Slone, accounts for a large portion of the population of Knott County, Kentucky. All the other names are fictitious, though almost all of the incidents that are disclosed in this story really did happen to folks I know.

It is not inconceivable that a girl of twelve could take care of her baby sister and keep house for her father. It has happened and still does. Mountain children learn early to help with the family chores. They are proud to feel a part of the family. The parents are very considerate, never asking for more than the child is capable of doing.

That John Slone would accept his sentence of ten years in prison without trying to prove himself innocent is typical. For Susan to accept the bank officer's decision to repossess her property without recompense or the insurance due her is also true to life. Mountain people have been and still are being defrauded in these ways. Lack of education and lack of money for lawyers have always led them to believe that the "war was lost before the battle was begun," so they just accept things as a matter of course.

In the last thirty or forty years things have begun to change, but I can't say that it's all for the better. The old way of life is gone, never to return. We should bury it, of course, along with our dead. But those of us oldtimers who remember the good old mountain days should make it our business to preserve the memory.

To the memory of my husband
Willie S. Slone

1 _____

Rennie sat before the dying fire, elbows on her knees, chin cupped in her hands, hunched over like an old crippled woman. Only her face showed that she was a child of twelve. She was so tired, bone-tired, completely exhausted. Not the kind of tiredness that would go away after a few hours' rest, but a dullness that enveloped her spirit and soul. Hope had been crushed from her being, leaving only an instinct to survive and an inherited stubbornness to fulfill one purpose: to push all memories of her mother out of her mind. To shut out everything. But she knew she could not allow herself this one comfort. Now, more than ever, she needed to remember everything her mother had taught her. She had paid too little attention to her mother when she was alive. Now her mother was gone, and Rennie had to drag up from her memory all the things half-buried in her mind, to keep alive a picture of her mother to pass on to Sarah Ellen. It would be all Sarah Ellen would ever know of her.

Five weeks before, her mother had placed the small bundle in her arms. "I'm givin' ye this baby fer a birthday present. She jest missed havin' the same bornin' day that you got by one day."

This had made Rennie happy, until she saw the tears in her mother's eyes. Looking back, she realized her mother had been trying to tell her that she knew she wasn't going to get well. Her mother had known for a long time; there had been so many things, so many times—unnoticed then—that now came crowding into her mind. Pa thought Ma's death was caused by "that fumblin' old granny woman." Rennie knew her mother's heart had been bad. Too many years of hard work had weakened her body. The extra strain of childbirth had broken it.

Today had been a very long day for Rennie—getting up before daylight, fixing breakfast for Pa, washing the dishes, milking the cow, and coming back from the barn to find Pa already gone. He never told anyone when or where he was going or when he would be back. He was a silent man who spent all his time serving his Lord, never seeing his own family's need. Rennie was used to staying by herself, so she didn't really mind. She knew not to question her father's ways. And there was no need to ask for his help anyway.

Her first morning chore had been to fill a glass mason jar with milk; this would be kept cool in the spring for Sarah Ellen's bottle. The rest of the milk she put in the churn, tying a nice white rag over the top and leaving it to sit on the hearth so that by the next morning it would be turned, ready to be churned into buttermilk and butter. Just as she got the bottle filled, Sarah Ellen awoke, crying for attention. Rennie put the bottle on the fireboard to keep it warm. With the baby under her arm, she got clean clothes and a diddie from the quilt shelf.

"Now here, Sarah Ellen. I know ye're hungry, but first things first. Ye can enjoy yer bottle better if ye have a dry bottom, and believe me, ye're one wet baby."

Rennie sat before the fire with the baby on her lap and changed her clothes and held the bottle. She loved to feed the baby. "Poor little thing, asleep agin' her bottle's emptied. Wonder if she sleeps too much. . . . But I hain't goin' worry long as she keeps growin' like a pig."

After putting Sarah Ellen in bed, this time in Pa's place, Rennie gathered up all the dirty clothes. First she changed the sheets and pillow slips, then the towels. Some of Pa's socks she found under his bed; she had to use the broom handle to get them out. Today she would wash up all Ma's things and put them away in the small trunk in the loft. Ma had asked that her dresses be cut up and sewn into clothes for Sarah Ellen. Maybe Rennie would do that later, but for now she would just put them away.

She spread out one of the dirty sheets on the floor, dumped everything else on it, tied the corners together, and carried the bundle to the porch. She took another look at the baby to make sure she was all right, then went outside to build a fire. In one corner of the yard a hole had been dug and each side of it lined with rocks that were now black from past wash days. Close by, a large mink kettle lay upside down. Rennie placed the kettle on the racks, ruck out the cinders from the hole with a hoe, brought a shovelful of fire from the fireplace, and put the red coals under the kettle, put wood on them, and hurried to fill the kettle with water. When she had helped Ma do the wash she had carried the water up all the way from the creek, but today she would draw water from the well. It was harder work, but being closer to the house she would be able to hear if the baby cried.

While waiting for the water to heat, she went back inside the house, made up Pa's bed, swept the floor, took out the cinders, and put more wood on the fire. By the time she was ready to begin her wash, the sun was peeping over the mountain top, taking the chill from the air. It would be a nice day for washing clothes. Later on, when winter set in, she would have to do the washing in the kitchen, heating the water in a tub on the stove and putting other tubs on chairs. It made a mess to clean up.

Using the lye soap sparingly, Rennie rubbed the clothes one at a time on the washboard and put them through two waters, as Ma had taught her. She boiled the white things in a little lye and more soap, rinsed twice, and blued the sheets and pillow slips, making starch from flour and water strained through a cloth. By the time the shadow cast by the old oak tree was level with the door, all the clothes were on the line. Rennie watched the wind toss the sleeves of her Mother's dresses. "As if," she thought, "they knew to be wavin' good-bye to her."

Then Rennie sat for a while, looking into the fire and trying not to remember. She had only a few moments to rest; there was still much work to be done. Pa would be home soon. Sarah Ellen would have to be fed again. Rennie raised her head and looked around the room as if she were seeing it for the first time. In the back were the two large beds, their wooden headpieces reaching almost to the low ceiling. In one corner was Ma's spinning wheel. A large homemade cedar chest took up all the room in the other corner near the beds. Against the wall stood the quilt shelf, filled with homemade quilts and blankets. Over one bed were several wooden pegs driven into the logs for clothes racks. On one of these hung the wool yarn—red, yellow, and two shades of brown. It was the only bright spot in the house. Ma had meant to use it to knit Rennie a scarf and tam to wear when she began school at the Community Center. Now there would be no scarf, no tam, nor would she be going to school.

Rennie had first seen the set in a Sears Roebuck catalogue. Ma had bought magazines from the lady at the Center and used them to paper her house, pasting them up on the inside walls and ceiling, a page at a time. Rennie had read each and every page, before and after they were pasted up. When she saw one with a coupon stating that a Sears Roebuck catalogue would be sent free to anyone requesting it, Rennie wanted that book more than anything in this world. Ma said it did not seem just right. If the company sent the catalogue to someone, they expected to sell you an order "and we jest hain't got nary bit of cash money." But Ma had enjoyed looking through the book just as much as Rennie, spending many hours turning the pages. Pa had laughed at them, calling it their "wish and want book." Ma had promised Rennie to make her a scarf and tam "jest like the one in the book."

Rennie had always helped her mother, but now she had a special interest in the yarn. Last spring she'd helped Pa shear the sheep. She could still remember the awful smell; she was wearing a pair of Pa's old overalls, but so much of the "taller" had seeped through from the animals' bodies while she held them between her knees! Ma had laughed and said, "Jest add a little lye and a kettle of soap could be made by boilin' them britches." The wool smelled a lot better after Ma had washed it with Fuller's soap and hung it on the fence to dry.

Rennie had gone with Ma to gather roots and bark to make the dye. Walnut bark for the brown, red sassafras for the red, walnut hulls for the black, white walnut for tan, yellowroot for the yellow. Some folks used sagegrass to make dye, but Ma had never used any of it, so she didn't try. Ma was even then so heavy with child that she had had to rest often.

After the wool had been dyed and dried again, it was straightened and combed with wooden cards, then rolled into small rolls, ready to be spun. Rennie thought the rolls looked like sheep tails, only longer. Now the finished yarn hung on a peg over Pa's bed and the hands that were to have knit the scarf

4

and tam were at rest. Tomorrow Rennie would fold the yarn in the trunk with Ma's clothes, along with her own dreams of attending the Caney Creek Community Center.

Slowly she got up and walked into the kitchen, took the front caps off the stove, returned to the grate, and took a shovel of hot coals, carefully carried them to the stove, dumped them in place, and put a few stacks of stovewood on top. Then she replaced the caps, poured water in the iron tea kettle, and set it on the stove. She took the empty bucket and went to the well for more water. While the stove was heating up, she peeled potatoes, sliced meat, and stirred up cornbread. All her motions were stiff and jerky, as if her limbs were being pulled by strings, going through the actions without a thought—a twelve-year-old child with a load that could be too much even for a grown woman. Last spring she had been a happy, carefree girl, running, laughing on her way to school. Now she was a woman with a child to raise, a home to run. But she was from sturdy stock; not once did she even think about not doing her duty. She did not question why. As long as there was breath in her body she would keep on, with no complaints. She was needed; that was all that mattered.

That night, when she at last stretched out her tired, aching body in the bed alongside Sarah Ellen, she caught the small baby's fingers in her own childish hands and murmured, "Ye're mine. Ma gave ye to me. We're family."

2 _____

When John Slone and Mary Gent got married, he brought his wife home to live with his parents. That was mountain custom. The youngest boy always kept his old folks as long as they lived, and in return they would give him the homeplace. The sturdy old log house on Lonesome Holler had been handed down time and again. The Slones had lived on Caney ever since Little Granny Alice had brought her family from East Virginia in 1790. They were the first white people to live there, maybe the first people, period. There was no evidence that any Indians had ever made Caney their home, though maybe some hunting parties had camped there: Rennie and her cousins had found arrowheads and pieces of flint in the shallow, rocky soil on the hillside below the family graveyard.

Grandma Kate, John's mother, loved to connect her family history with the stories in Rennie's history book. "When George Washington was getting in as president, Little Granny was settling the Slones on Caney. And when Bonaparte was climbing all over Europe, Grandpa Billie was climbing all over the hills of Caney, cutting trees to build this house in Lonesome Holler. Jest think," she said to Rennie, "some of them logs could have been growin' here when Columbus came to America."

Rennie loved to look at the names in the Good Book. The black leather was frayed and the pages were yellow at the edges. It had traveled in a small black trunk on a wooden cart pulled by oxen on that long trip over the mountains. The older names were faded almost beyond recognition, but the newer names could still be read: Kate Smith Slone, born about 1820, wife of Jim Slone, born 1820. Mary Gent Slone, born 1880, wife of John Slone, born 1860. Rennie Slone, born October 4, 1905. Sarah Ellen Slone, born October 5, 1917.

"Poor old Grandma Kate," thought Rennie. All she had known about her own past was her name, Kate Smith. She had been raised by Pa and Ma Branham on Pound Ridge in Virginia.

About the time the mountains were being settled, many

families were crossing from East Virginia into what is now Kentucky. Pa and Ma Branham owned a small trading post close by the trail. They also had "room up in the loft" where tired, weary travelers could bed down for the night. Almost all these pioneers learned, sadly, that they had started out with more household plunder than was wise to bring along. They were glad to exchange these extras for a night's lodging and maybe a little salt, sugar, coffee or tea. Pa and Ma had no children of their own. Although they met many strangers, they were still a very lonesome couple.

It was early November in 1823. The Branhams thought they had seen their last travelers for that year; soon the snow would have all the trails covered. One evening, nearly dark, they saw a caravan climbing slowly up the hill along the path leading to their house. Pa Branham always said, "The sight of them poor folks would have been funny if they hadn't looked so pitiful like." The one and only wagon was being pulled by what must have been the milk cow. A woman was struggling along with a large bundle, followed by a gang of young'ns, one about half grown, the others all smaller. Ma Branham had gone to meet them, for she saw they needed help. The stranger, seeing Ma's smiling face and outstretched arms, meekly handed the bundle over to her without a word. Before you could say "scat" they were sitting around the table eating a hot meal, and Ma Branham was scurrying about urging more food and refilling glasses with milk as they became half-empty. She apologized for not having more food, though the table was full.

After supper the Smith family told their story. Mr. Smith had gone ahead a few years before to stake a claim and build a log house on a boundary of land, a grant given to him by the government. He now had the house finished and enough of a crop planted and gathered to see his family through the winter. By a chance traveler he had sent back word for his wife and kids to join up with the next group of people heading west and come join him in the new home.

Everything had gone wrong. First the children had taken measles. Then, by the time they were well enough to travel, it was early fall. All the other locals had gone on without them. And then yesterday their one mule had died, forcing them to hitch their milk cow to the wagon. It was too far to turn back now. There was no place and no one to go back to: other folks now lived in the rented house they had left. These were strange times; people were brave but often foolish.

Next morning when the Smiths were ready to resume their journey, the cow could not get up. There was no way they could take the wagon, and all of them had to walk. Kate, the youngest, was too small to walk the many miles, yet she was too heavy to be carried. It was after much talking and crying that Mrs. Smith was persuaded by the Branhams to leave Kate with them for the winter. She or her husband could come back in the spring to get her and the wagon and the cow. Pa Branham took the small girl and went to the barn to gather eggs while the rest of the Smiths, with what they could carry on their backs, faded into the distance. They were never to be heard from again. Ma Branham said she felt they had all been killed by Indians or died from exposure. She knew Mrs. Smith would have come back for her baby had it been humanly possible.

If Ma had foreseen how things would turn out, she would have tried to find out more about the Smiths, but now, try as hard as she could, she could not even remember their first names. So many folks traveled through that way. The Branhams could not write and kept no records. All Ma could tell Kate later was that Kate had cried for many days for someone called Tad. Ma didn't know if that was the child's brother or a dog.

Kate had never given up hope that someday she would learn something about her kinfolks. For years, every time she met someone named Smith, she would ask if they knew a Tad Smith. Kate loved the Branhams as her own, but she still wished to know more about herself. Maybe that was why she cared so much about the history of the Slone family. Years and years later, talking to her own grandchildren, telling her stories over and over so they would remember, she declared, "The only way to know yerself is to know yer forefathers. Yer history is a part of ye."

Afterwards she would take her grandchildren up to the

head of Lonesome Holler to show them an overhanging cliff and the cave where Little Granny Alice Slone had lived with her husband and four sons that first winter until they built their log house. The rocks were still black from the cooking fire. The logs and brush used to barricade the entrance had long been decayed. She told her grandchildren, "Never be ashamed of yer folks because they were poor. Always remember it took very brave people to come here—people lookin' fer freedom and a better life, not only fer themselves but fer the childern and grandchildern that would follow 'em. Remember 'em for what they were. They did the best they could with what they had, and they deserve to be praised, not belittled."

Mary Gent was only fourteen when she married John, thirty-four-year-old son of Kate and Jim Slone. She knew he didn't love her; mountain people didn't even use the word love when referring to the relationship between a man and his wife. Someone might say he was "a fool about her" or "he thought a lot of her." Of course many couples did love each other, but it was not spoken of lightly. Mary knew John only needed someone to look after his parents, who were getting too old to wait on themselves. Mary loved old folks, and one couldn't help but love Grandma Kate, who turned all the household chores over to the younger girl but insisted on helping a little herself. Grandpa Jim spent all his time playing his fiddle. Mary loved nothing better than to listen to those old ballads and often joined in, singing as she hurried around the house cooking, sweeping, doing the washing, or making up the beds. They often sang around the fire in winter or around a gnat smoke outside on the porch when the weather was warm.

Mary was very happy. Only one thing bothered her. Year after year passed and still she did not get pregnant. Grandma Kate, who had been a granny woman all her life, could not understand. She was proud of her own record: she had caught nigh onto a hundred young'ns. "I have never lost nary mother ner child," she'd say. She could tell you the name and age of every one of them from memory, though she kept no records of the ones she helped bring into the world.

Then in the spring of 1905, it happened. Mary first noticed it when she was making lye soap; the smell made her sick. She had been mistaken so many times she was almost afraid to hope, but as spring turned into summer she knew this time it was true. Yet she didn't tell John or the old folks. It was a secret she didn't want to share just yet. And then, before she could tell, something happened.

John's brothers Bill and Tate made moonshine. No one talked about it, but everyone in the family knew. Grandma Kate and Grandpa Jim didn't approve, but they kept their mouths shut.

It was the first really warm day that spring. Mary was singing as she walked back and forth across the kitchen, putting away the milk and washing the dishes. She hurried so that she could get outside. Talking the old folks into taking their chairs outside to enjoy the evening breeze had been easy. Coming to the door, she saw Grandpa had been tuning his fiddle and was now ready to play.

"What shall it be, Mary, my gal?" he asked.

"Oh, 'Barbara Ellen,'" she answered as she looked anxiously down the road. John had gone to the store earlier in the afternoon. He should have been back by now.

And then they heard it. Grandpa dropped his fiddle bow; Grandma clutched her hands together over her heart, her lips trembling as she said, "Oh, no." Mary listened. There it was again: the nearest neighbor's dinner bell sounding three long rings—a pause—and two short rings, over and over again: the signal. Grandpa said just one word—"Revenuers"—with a whole lifetime of hate and resentment rolled into it. He spit it out as if it left a bad taste in his mouth. As Mary grabbed a hold of their own dinner bell rope, she saw John come riding fast. Jumping from the mule's back at the gate, he ran into the house shouting, "Keep ringin' until someone up the creek answers." She heard him get the gun from the pegs over the door and run out the back way. It seemed like ages until she heard the answering bells. Dropping the rope, she went to put up the mule, taking his bridle and saddle off and putting him in the stall. She would come back later to feed him; he had been ridden too hard to eat yet. She came back to the house to find that the old folks had gone inside. Grandma was on her knees. Mary wondered if it was right to pray for someone who was breaking the law, but she whispered, "Please, I hope no one gets killed." Mary knew it was no use asking the old folks to go to bed. In the kitchen she rebuilt the fire in the stove and put on a boiler of coffee.

It was almost two o'clock the next morning when she heard someone at the door. Big Jed stood there, his hat in his hands, tears in his eyes. "Well, Bill and Tate got clean away. They caught John. There was a lot of shootin'. One damn revenuer got killed. Those law men had left their hosses at the foot of Bald Hill and walked the rest of the way up the holler. Someone must have tipped 'em off. Went right straight to where the boys was set up. Bill or Tate, one, slipped back and killed their hosses, cut ever' last one of their throats. Never seed such a mess—blood all over the place."

As he paused for breath, Mary cried, "But why did they take John? He's a preacher. Everbody knows he don't make moonshine."

Big Jed wiped his face with his old red handkerchief and answered, "Well, I don't clearly know, but he did have a gun and he was caught at the still. He'd gone to warn his brothers. They had John handcuffed and was walkin' when they passed my house. They stopped and asked fer to get somethin' to ride, and I told 'em, 'I would shoot my old mule right dead before yer eyes 'fore I'd let one of ye get on his back.' But when I seed John was kind of favorin' his right leg, I offered to take him in on my mule. I guess they thought I was tryin' to fool 'em and get John away from 'em. I would, had I got a chance, but they kept their guns on us clear all the way to Hindman. I told John I'd bring ye word. Hate to tell ye, but it shore looks bad fer him."

"But John's a preacher. Never made a drop of likker in his life. Won't even taste of the stuff." Mary couldn't believe it had happened.

"I know that," Big Jed said. "Everone on Caney knows John's a born-again man, but he did have a gun. John claimed he never fired a shot, but the law man said the gun had been fired and a man had been killed. I think they was madder over the hosses than anythin', though."

"I recollect John shootin' at a chicken hawk jest before startin' fer the store. He probably went on without cleanin' his gun."

"It was them no good sorry jerks over on Pigeon Roost what told on my boys," Grandpa's voice shook. "They been mad ever since I voted agin Ben in that last school 'lection. Don't look like anyone would get that mad over a little biddy school 'lection."

Mountain people seldom cry. They hide their grief in work. Mary and the old folks' hearts were broken, yet their lives would go on as before. It was many weeks before the fiddle was taken down from its peg on the wall. No songs were heard coming from the old log house on Lonesome Holler for a long while.

Mary took the old folks to see John while he was still in jail at Hindman. But they were to see him no more when the law took him on to Catlettsburg. John asked his family not to try to make that long trip. There was nothing they could do for him. His sentence was ten years in prison at Frankfort.

As for Bill and Tate, it was a long time before anyone knew where they had gone. One day when Mary made her weekly visit to their homes, she found them empty. Somehow the men had gotten word to their families to meet them some-where. A few months later a pack peddler stopped at the old house on Lonesome Holler and told Grandpa Jim, "There was some folks in West Virginia, said if I ever passed this way to find out how you folks were and to tell you they were all right." That evening Grandpa took his fiddle down and played while Grandma sang "Barbara Ellen."

On October the fourth, after eight hours of hard labor, Mary gave birth to a little girl and called her Rennie. When she was one year old the flu epidemic hit Caney, and Grandpa Jim and Grandma Kate, along with twenty other folks, died. Although Rennie had the flu, it didn't hurt her much. Mary had it and recovered, but it left her with a bad heart.

Every six or eight months Mary received a letter from

John—just a few words telling her nothing. She always answered, but there was little she could tell him. The days on Lonesome Holler came and went with very little change. Old folks died; babies were born. Winter came, followed by summer.

3

The first winter after the old folks died, Mary was too busy to get lonesome. All the neighbors up and down Lonesome Holler had chipped in and helped out. One man dug and hauled coal for her. He also cut and dragged in enough wood to do her for the winter, and in payment he used John's mule to haul his own wood and coal. Another neighbor milked and fed the cow and took a share of the milk in return. Come spring, someone would do her plowing if they too could use the mule. Mary knew she could raise enough food for herself and Rennie if she just stayed well enough to work, but she would still have to have cash money for taxes and shoes. Grandpa Jim had gotten a small war pension, just a few dollars each month, which had once been enough, but now that source of income was gone. Mary could exchange eggs and dried roots for her coffee, sugar, and salt at the store, but she really didn't know what she would do when her taxes came due. Would her farm have to be sold? In this her neighbors could not help her. Many times she lay awake far into the night thinking, "What will I do? Please, God, show me a way."

Her prayer was answered in a very unusual way. Mary had heard of how a Mrs. Alice Lloyd had come from Boston and established a school called the Caney Creek Community Center. Mary herself had never visited the school, but she had talked with neighbors who had. She had watched the strange-looking men and women riding past her home on their way to the Center with their beautiful horses and loud, squeaking saddles. Mary blushed when she saw the women riding astraddle, wearing pants. She also felt insulted when they laughed. Didn't they know it was bad manners to laugh and talk when passing someone's house? The strangers would have been surprised had they known someone was peeping at them from a crack in the door.

It was late spring, a beautiful sunshiny day. Mary had finished her garden work, and the corn had been hoed out of the first weeds. Now she had a few days for spring housecleaning. "Believe I will sun all of Grandpa and Grandma's wearin' things and the new quilts," she told Rennie. So, going up into the loft, she brought them all down and began hanging them on the yard fence, the porch railing, and anywhere she could find room. She kept stepping back to admire the pretty bright colors of the Double Wedding Ring, Rose of Sharon, Dove of Peace, Drunkard's Path, Nine Patch—all such beautiful pieces of art.

"Hello," the man said.

Mary jumped. She had been so busy she hadn't heard the riders.

"Sorry to have startled you. Please forgive me. I'm Mr. Scutchfield. May we come in, please?"

Mary looked up. At the gate stood four horses with riders, one man and three ladies.

"Shore." At last she began to recover her voice. "Come on in, get ye a seat, if ye can find room here on the porch. I'm sunnin' my quilts and things."

"We saw those beautiful quilts from the big road. That's why we stopped. Hope you don't mind."

"No, I don't. Get down and set a spell." Mary really didn't like talking to these strangers, but good manners and custom demanded it of her. She felt ashamed, not knowing why, and angry at herself because she did.

The riders dismounted. While the man hitched their horses to the fence, the three women came in.

"I'm Mrs. Goodman," one lady said. "We wanted a closer look at those quilts. They're so beautiful. That's really why

14

I'm here in the mountains. I wish to buy some Appalachian handcrafts, and these are magnificent. Mr. Scutchfield is from the Caney Community Center. He's been kind enough to go with us to look at some things. These are just great." Mrs. Goodman talked on as they crowded around the quilts. The ladies sighed and "ah'd" as they turned them over, feeling them, pinching the material.

"I guess they smell somethin' awful now," Mary said. "But agin' evenin' the sun and air will have 'em all nice and fresh smellin'. I put some 'backer crumbs in the box where I keep 'em," she added as one of the women sneezed.

"I'll give you ten dollars each for these quilts, and I'll buy every one," Mrs. Goodman said.

"Well, I 'spect ten dollars is more cash money than I ever had at one time in my life, but I can't sell these quilts. Ye see, they belonged to John's mother. She made 'em and she's dead now. They're to be my little girl Rennie's when she gets growed up and marries. Ye jest don't sell somethin' like that, no matter what." Mary tried to keep the angry tone out of her voice. "But I have one in the house almost finished. I'd be more than glad to let ye have it, when I get it done."

Mary went inside and returned with a beautiful Lone Star in red, yellow, and blue and spread it out on the porch. The ladies moaned with awe.

"How long would it take you to finish it?"

"I could get it done agin' Friday. All I like is jest the bindin' around the edge. See here?"

"Well, I'll give you ten dollars now and pick it up Friday."

"No," Mary replied. "I'll sell ye the quilt, but I don't want ye to pay me now. Ye give me the money when ye get the quilt. I don't want pay fer somethin' before I've finished it."

"How long does it take for you to make a quilt like this?"

"I guess about six or eight weeks, if I set my mind to it. I never did pay any attention to how long I worked on one. I jest sewed a little whenever I had the time and the quilt scraps. I have to store-buy the linin' and thread. Course, I jest work at them in the winter."

"Could you make me, say, four more in the next four or five months?"

"No, it's crop time now. I have to raise my corn and garden stuff, and then, come fall, I have to put it all away. Only time I can get time to sew is wintertime."

"Well, will you promise to make me some this winter? I guess I'll have to settle for that."

"I would be glad to, if I can get hold of the stuff to make 'em. Ye see, it's jest me and my baby here, and I can't hardly leave, even to go to the store."

"What if I send you the cloth, cotton, and thread, and pay you eight dollars each?"

"I shore will. I'll make all I can. I'll try to make ye four or five this winter. I'll be more than glad."

"Then it's settled. But I still can't understand the folks around here. Everywhere I go I get shown such beautiful work, and the women keep saying they need money. They agree that I offer a fair price, but they don't want to let their quilts go."

"Well," Mary tried to explain, "I guess when ye sew somethin' like a quilt, ye kind of put yer heart into it, and it's like sellin' a part of yerself. Ye want yer family to have it to keep when ye're gone, like I still have Grandma's—and someday they'll be Rennie's. That way she won't never forget Grandma."

After discussing the pattern, color, and so on, the ladies and Mr. Scutchfield left. He was to pick up the Lone Star on Friday.

Thus Mary's money worries were over. The quilt money would pay the taxes and buy Rennie some shoes. Mary could have her own shoes half soled again, too. From then on she and Rennie would live good, as long as she stayed able to work. If she got sick, she knew her neighbors would have a workin' for her and help her out of a hard place.

For the next seven or eight years Mary made Mrs. Goodman three or four quilts each winter. Mr. Scutchfield brought Mary the material, picked up the finished quilts and paid her, and mailed them up North. Every Christmas Mrs. Goodman sent Mary and Rennie a present—hard candy, pretty ribbons for Rennie's hair, bright colored buttons. In return Mary sent her jars of jelly and boxes of nuts gathered in the hills behind her home.

Mary now had more money than she had ever had in her life. She sold the mule because she could pay someone to plow and dig her coal. She grew her own food. She felt very thankful.

From her first day at school, Rennie thought of nothing else. Mary was glad she loved to learn, but she missed her so much. Everything was so quiet and lonesome there on the hill without the laughter of her small child. There was a knothole in one of the planks on the porch; Mary knew that when the shadow cast by the sun reached it, it was four o'clock and Rennie would be on her way home. Trying to keep busy helped some, but the days were so long. Again and again she would glance at the knothole. How slowly the sun crept across the floor when it looked like rain! When it rained hard, Mary would walk out of the hollow to walk back with her child. Most of the road was only a path around the hill or along the creek bed; a washout could be very dangerous.

Mary heard from her neighbors that you could get used clothing from the Caney Community Center in exchange for foodstuff. One day she picked some green beans and carried them in a coffee sack to the Center. She made the trip with a friend, who had a load of mustard salet. The other woman knew the way, having been there before. They went first to the kitchen, where a sign said "Hungry Din." The kitchen was twice as large as Mary's whole house, and the stove, big as a pig pen, was so hot the air in the room was almost unbearable. Those poor cooks! How could they stand it? Kettles as big as wash tubs that took two women to lift on and off the stove. So much food the smell made you sick.

One of the cooks checked what they had in their sacks and wrote something on a piece of paper.

"This is your due bill. Take it to the Exchange. The girl there will pay you," she explained. A boy came and took their bags of beans and greens to a storeroom under the kitchen. After he'd brought back their sacks, they went along a path behind the dining room. Mary peeped through the windows and saw rows and rows of tables, each covered with a black oilcloth and set with twelve plates. When they got to the building with a sign that read "The Exchange" over the door, they met other women, some of whom they knew. Everyone carried on small talk until a girl dressed in the school uniform—a white skirt and middy-blouse—came and opened the door. She gave each one a box to look through. Those who found something they wanted or could use held onto it and returned the rest to the box. The school girl priced what they had chosen and marked it on their due bill. Mary found a few things she thought she could use. Most were very worn; they all smelled old and musty.

At first she was reluctant to wear the used clothing. What if it had belonged to someone now dead? Would people sell their dead folks' clothes? These strange people had strange ways, and they talked so funny it was all Mary could do to keep a straight face when talking to them. The clothes did not seem so bad after they'd been washed, and after wearing them a time or two Mary felt more comfortable in them. But she didn't think she would go back again.

The Center gave Mary a dream, though. When Rennie had finished her eight grades in Lonesome Holler, Mary wanted her to go to school at the Caney Community Center.

When Rennie was ten years old, her father came home from prison. From then on things began to change.

4

In the yard of the old log house there stood five old apple trees, aged and gnarled yet still fruitful, with their apples and leaves giving shade and comfort as well as rusty beauty. Under one, Rennie had built a playhouse furnished with flat rocks covered with sheets of green moss. The table was set with broken pieces of old plates and bowls, cared for as treasures. An empty peach can was the water bucket. Here Rennie spent many hours with her rag dolls, rebraiding their yarn hair and washing their clothes. Her mother had made the dolls from quilt scraps, using as a pattern an old doll that was now in the little black trunk in the loft.

Mary came from the kitchen with a bowl of scraps for the hen and chickens. The hen was tied to a nail in the wall of the house, under which she could keep her little brood safe at night.

"Ye were a foolish old hen," Mary said as she crumbled the cornbread on the ground just out of reach of the hen. "Ye stold your nest out too late in summer. Now yer chicks may not make it through the winter. I'm jest wastin' the feed I give 'em, but I'll help ye."

"Rennie," Mary called. "Come get yer bonnet if ye want to go with me to gather milkweed pods."

"Ma, I'm comin'."

"Bring yer dolls in as ye come. If'n ye don't, that ar' old dog'll tear 'em up." As the girl passed her in the doorway with an armload of dolls, her mother patted her on the head and said, "Ye're a good housekeeper. Someday ye'll make some man a good wife."

"No, Ma. I hain't never goin' to marry. I'm goin' to stay with you fer always."

Mary only smiled. Funny to be talking this way to a child. They had been very happy here alone together. "Get ye a poke and ye can get ye some pods to make a bed fer yer dolls. I'll give ye some scraps and ye can sew them yerself. Time ye was learnin' to sew."

Soon Mary and Rennie were down in the lower pasture. The past week had been very hot. The milkweed pods were bursting open, just right to gather. If left any longer the nice fluffy seeds would be blown away. A rain now could ruin them.

"Ma, ye got aplenty of feather beds and pillers. What fer ye want to get these?"

"Well, ye never know. They jest might come in handy sometime when we have company. Er someone might get their house burnt up and we could help 'em out by givin' 'em some pillers. I jest hate to see anythin' go to waste."

They had almost filled their bags when Mary looked up and saw Big Jed riding up the path to their house. When he saw them he called, "I got a letter fer ye. 'Spect it's from John. It was down to the post office, and being I was comin' this way I thought I might jest as well bring it along."

Mary walked over to the fence as Big Jed rode to where he could hand her the letter without getting down from his horse.

"How's yer folks, Big Jed?" Mary asked.

"Tollable, tollable. I'll wait 'till ye read what John has to say 'fore goin' on. Allus thought a lot of John."

With hands trembling, Mary tore open the letter. She had received very few letters from John lately. He could not write very well himself, and like all mountain men he didn't like to ask someone to write for him. His stubborn pride wouldn't let him ask for a favor. The note was very brief. "I am getting a pardon, be home September 24." Today was the twenty-third.

"Oh, Rennie, yer father is comin' home."

Turning to Big Jed she said, "Thanks for bringin' me such good news. I must hurry and get the house cleaned up, cook plenty of good food. Folks will be droppin' in to see him.

"Oh, Rennie, yer father is comin' home. I can't believe it—after all these years he's comin' home!"

By nightfall Big Jed had carried the news to everyone up and down Lonesome Holler.

Rennie had not missed having a father. Mary had talked very little about him. The children at school knew where he was, but it was accepted as a matter of fact. Rennie tried to think about the fathers in the homes she had visited, silent working men who took no notice of their children except to tell them to "be good and don't bother." Rennie didn't believe she was going to like having a father around. As she saw her small bed being carried upstairs—"Ye're a big girl now, big enough to sleep by yerself"—Rennie knew she would be lonesome up there in the loft. But she said nothing. That night she slept beside her mother in the old homemade wooden bed for the last time. Both of them lay awake long into the night.

"What's wrong with me?" Mary thought. "I should be glad that John's comin' home. Truth is, I'm scared. God fergive me, but I can't even remember what he looks like. I'm a wicked woman, Lord. I've fergotten my own husband. I've been very happy here, jest me and Rennie. We've lived better than most of our neighbors. I'm a young woman. I'll bear more childern. God fergive me, but I do so dread them pains of childbirth. John is an old man. He won't help with the work, and he'll be called on by our neighbors because he's still a preacher."

Rennie heard her mother's silent crying but pretended to be asleep. There was nothing she could do. She couldn't even understand. She knew she hated her father, and hated herself because she did.

It was almost dark the next day when they saw him coming up the hill. Climbing slowly, only a few steps between rests, he would stop, look all around as if making sure where he was, and drink up the view like a drowning man.

"Howdy, Mary," was all his mouth said, but his eyes said much more. Even Rennie could see that the suffering had left its mark. "How are ye, Mary? And this is Rennie, I guess. She looks like Ma."

"Yeah, that's what everbody says."

They went in and ate the supper Mary had prepared, as if it were just another day, as if he had never been gone.

Ten months later Mary gave birth to a little boy. John named him Owen. He lived only a few hours. Rennie went with her father to dig the grave. The baby's grave looked so small alongside Grandpa's and Grandma's. The graveyard looked different since John and his friends had spent a few days building a new fence, covering the little grave houses with new boards, and trimming the rambling roses that had rambled all over. Even some of the headstones had tumbled over. Since Grandpa had died no one had cared for the little family graveyard.

John had taken some boards from the barn loft to make Owen's coffin. Smoothing them with a hand planer, he then joined them together with nails, covered them with white cloth, and trimmed them with lace. He had gone by himself to bury the child, telling Rennie to stay with Mary, who was too sick to know what was happening. She asked Rennie over and over again why she was crying.

It was several weeks before Mary was able to get up. Rennie stayed home from school to help with the work. John never knew if she went to school or not. He just expected hot meals to be on the table and clean clothes to be there when he needed them. He felt they were his due as the head of the house. He would milk the cow or chop wood if asked, but he never volunteered on his own.

In his work as a preacher he was very faithful, attending services the first Saturday and Sunday of each month at Mount Olive, the little church on Lonesome Holler. Many nights he was away from home, going to other churches, to funerals and weddings or to visit the sick and dying. Mary didn't complain that sometimes his own family needed him. But Rennie was not so understanding. Once she said, "I thought the Bible said that charity begins at home." Mary only smiled and told her not to let her father hear her say that.

When, only a few months after Owen's death, Rennie suspected her mother was pregnant again, she hated her father even more. "I'll never marry," she vowed.

During the winter the roads were too bad for travel. Every day some of John's fellow preachers and other men of the church would visit him. They'd sit in a circle around the fire, chewing their tobacco, spitting into the cinders, discussing but never agreeing on church work or what the Bible meant or didn't mean. Sometimes the arguments would get so heated that a man would leave, slamming the door as he stomped out. But in a day or two he'd be back.

There was no room around the fireplace for Mary, so she would keep a fire going in the cookstove. There would always be a large iron kettle on the back of the stove filled with shucky beans, dried apples, pumpkin, or cushaw. She and Rennie would stay in the kitchen. Sometimes she would iron, heating the flatirons on the stove and smoothing the clothes out on a quilt on the dining table. Sometimes Rennie would play with her dolls; other times she would read. A few times she listened to what her father and the other men had to say. Once they were talking about Mrs. Lloyd and her school.

"I don't think a woman should try to run a school. That's man's work."

"Yeah, and don't the Bible say to beware of strange women? And she shore is a strange woman."

"Did ye know she gives the boys presents—ye know, pencils, candy, er gum—if they'll wear a tie, and ye all know it's a sin to wear a tie. Pride, that's what it is. She is a haring our young'ns to sin."

"Well, people off from here wears ties. They don't think it's a sin," said John. "As good a man as ever I saw come to see me when I was in the pen, and he wore a tie. Prayin'est man I ever seed."

"That don't keep it from bein' a wrong. Jesus didn't wear a tie, God didn't make Adam a tie. It's jest fer looks, so it's a sin."

"The teacher is learnin' our young'ns that the earth is round, and it hain't so, fer the Bible plainly says, 'There are four angels standing at the four corners of the world.' So how can it have corners if it's round?"

"Yeah, and those teachers also say that the earth goes around the sun. That's agin' the Bible, fer it says, 'The sun rises and goeth down and hastens back to its starting place.' Did not Josaway demand that the sun stand still? These teachers of Mrs. Lloyd's is destroyin' the very souls of our young'ns."

"Yeah, I'm afraid she is c'ruptin' our folks. We will jest have to pray a little harder and learn 'em the truth at home. Don't the Bible also tell us, 'Bring them up in the way they should go, and when they are old they will not depart from it'?"

"Them women with their bobbed hair and wearin' britches plagues me when I meet 'em. If I was to catch my old woman er one of my girls like that, I would beat the hide off her."

John was out front chopping wood the day Mr. Scutchfield came.

"Hello, I'm Mr. Scutchfield. I've come to see Mary about the quilts. You must be her husband, John."

"Yeah, that's who I be, but I don't know what ye mean about the quilts."

"Well, you see, Mary has been making quilts for some of my friends up North. I pick them up and send them."

Mary came to the door. "Howdy. Won't ye come in and set a spell?"

"No, I haven't any time for a visit, but thanks anyway. I just stopped by to leave an order for two more quilts. A Day's End and a Drunkard's Path. Do you think you can finish them by December? They're to be Christmas presents."

Before Mary could answer, John said, "She won't be makin' any more quilts fer sale. I'm home now and she don't have to work anymore."

"Please, John," Mary began. "I do so love to sew, and I've given my word."

"No more quilts," John said. He went back to his wood-chopping without looking at the other man. As far as he was concerned the matter was closed.

"Let me know if you change your mind," Mr. Scutchfield told Mary as he rode away. "Those ladies sure were counting on those quilts for Christmas."

Mary went over and began picking up the wood John had chopped. "We really do need the cash money fer taxes and shoes." For once there was anger in her voice.

"Are ye questionin' yer husband, Mary? Don't the Bible say a man should be the head of the household?"

"Where will ye get any work? Ye're too old fer the mines."

"God will provide. Don't the Bible tell ye to submit to yer husband? Trust me."

In the fall, when the tax collector came around, John sold

24

ten of Mary's laying hens. Mary knew they needed the extra eggs to buy salt, sugar, and coffee at the grocery store. This time she didn't question him; she had resigned herself to his ways. That winter Mary didn't eat eggs. Neither did Rennie find her usual boiled egg in her dinner pail. John didn't notice. He still ate two every morning.

5

The summer before Sarah Ellen was born, Mary wasn't able to do all the work. Rennie stayed home from school to help her.

"I wish ye didn't have to miss so much school," her mother said.

"I don't give that no never mind," Rennie assured her.

By early September Mary's feet were swollen so badly she could no longer wear her shoes. Instead she wore a pair of John's old socks. She lay in bed most of the time or sat with her feet propped up on a chair. She had put away all the garden stuff, filling all the glass jars, wooden barrels, crocks, and churns with fruits and vegetables. The potatoes, both white and sweet, still had to be dug. Mary was worried because John had to pull the fodder and cut the tops by himself. She just knew he would "never in this world get enough." Rennie offered to work with her father, but he told her, "Stay with yer Ma. She needs ye. If ye need me if'n yer Ma takes sick to have the baby, ye ring the dinner bell."

"I know Pa, I will."

One day Mary asked Rennie to go up in the loft and bring down the box in which she had put away Owen's clothes— long white dresses trimmed with handmade lace and edged with featherstitching, belly bands made of unbleached muslin, tiny undershirts. Some of the clothes had been in the family for generations. Some had been Rennie's.

"We'll wash these today," Mary told Rennie, "and have 'em all nice and clean fer the new baby. Ye carry a lot of water because baby clothes have to be renched a lot of times. All the soap must be got out so it can't hurt the baby's tender skin."

Almost every day one or another of the neighbor women would stop in to see Mary, talk a while, and help Rennie with the work, whatever she was doing. One day Aunt Nance, John's sister, came. She brought two old worn-out sheets and gave them to Mary. "I jest thought ye might could use these. They jest about done their do in this world but will make good diddies fer the young'n."

"I'm much obliged to ye. I'll tear them into squares and hem 'em. Give me somethin' to do this evenin'. I do so hate to jest set here like a bump on a log, seein' Rennie do all the work. She works so hard."

One day Uncle Tom and Big Jed came along to get John to go to church with them. Uncle Tom wasn't really Rennie's uncle. Everyone on Lonesome Holler called him that. The church was so far away they would have to go on Friday and not get back until Sunday.

"I can't leave my home now, Mary expectin' any day and my fodder needs pullin'. I get along so slow by myself."

"I think I'll jest stay and help ye save yer fodder and not go to the meetin' after all," Uncle Tom told him.

"I 'spect I will, too," Big Jed added. "They's more ways to serve the Lord 'sides goin' to church and preachin'."

Rennie was awakened from her sleep one night by the bell being rung by John. She knew it meant her mother was sick. She put on her clothes and went downstairs. Her father was already dressed and holding a lighted lantern.

"Some of the women will soon be here," he said. "Jest as soon as they hear the bell they'll come. You stay with yer Ma while I go catch the mule."

Rennie went to the bed where her mother lay. "Anythin' I can do to help ye, Ma?" she asked.

"Yeah. Jest set here and hold my hand like I do yers when ye're sick," her mother told her with a smile.

Aunt Nance was the first woman to arrive. She told Rennie it would be better if she didn't stay with her mother while the baby was being born. "Ye're too young."

"Let her stay," Mary said. "She's twelve years old. That's almost grown up."

It was late next day before the ordeal was over. Rennie had hidden herself in the barn loft, but she could still hear her mother's screams. "A breech birth," Aunt Nance, had said. Rennie had cried and cried. "I hate Pa, I hate him," she said over and over.

Aunt Nance came to the barn and yelled. "Come and see, Rennie. It's a girl."

When Rennie first saw her mother, Mary was so white Rennie thought she was dead.

"No, she's jest asleep," Aunt Nance told her. "I gave her some hot tottie. It'll make her sleep and rest fer a while."

Mary was never able to sit up, although she lived for over a week. One evening John went to the store while Rennie finished the chores. After washing the dishes, she came and sat by her mother's bed. "Anythin' I can do fer ye, Ma?" she asked.

"Yes, read me somethin' from the Good Book."

"What ye want me to read?"

"I want to hear ye read the Psalms."

Rennie got the Bible and began to read. On and on she read. She thought her mother had gone to sleep. Finally, when she laid the Bible down she looked at her mother's face and saw that all the pain and suffering had gone, replaced by such a peaceful look. Then she realized that her mother was dead. That was the last she remembered. From far away she heard a bell ringing. Aunt Nance's voice. A baby crying. The smell of camphor. . . .

Rennie never looked at her mother again. She knew when the women came and bathed and dressed the body. She even told Aunt Nance where to find Mary's new dress. Uncle Tom brought a long hickory stick and measured Mary before sawing the planks for the coffin. Rennie heard the ringing of the hammer as the nails were driven into the planks. She listened from where she lay on her bed in the loft.

That evening all the neighbors came. Some stayed all night, singing one song after another, all lonesome and sad. Rennie didn't think she could ever sleep again, but sometime during the night the physical need for rest overtook her young body and blissful sleep came at last.

No one except Aunt Nance could understand why Rennie refused to go to the grave where Mary was buried.

"I must stay with Sarah Ellen," she told her father.

"It jest don't seem right somehow fer none of her kin to be there."

"I jest can't bear to see my mother put into the ground. She would understand. She knew how much I loved her."

6

Everything had gone wrong that morning. Rennie had planned on doing the family wash, and now it was raining. She lay there in bed listening to the musical splattering of the softly falling rain, glad she had remembered to bring in the stove wood that Pa had chopped. She was also glad that the night before she'd set the washtubs under the leak of the house to catch water for washing. She had to remember, when she got up, to cover the tubs with boards, so the fry chickens wouldn't fall in and drown. There was no danger yet, though; the chickens wouldn't come out as long as it was raining.

Someone had come for Pa during the night. Rennie had heard them ride up, but it was the smell of carbide that fully awakened her. The man had emptied his lamp in the fireplace and refilled it as Pa put on his clothes and went to get his mule. There had been a cave-in at the mines. Men had been killed. John was needed to make coffins and preach funerals. Rennie knew he would be gone for several days. She hated to hear about the poor men but was glad to be alone. Her father helped her so little and demanded so much. She had no reason to be afraid—if she needed anyone all she had to do was ring the old dinner bell. The neighbors would hear and come, day or night.

Sarah Ellen was still sleeping. After getting dressed, Rennie took her milk bucket and started for the barn. The rain had become just a heavy mist. Old Bossie was not in her stall. Pa had left the barn door open again. He had been in a hurry, but he should have remembered. Walking through the wet dog fernel weeds that surrounded the barn, Rennie went around to the back, where she saw a break in the fence that told her what she already suspected.

Rennie didn't like leaving Sarah Ellen alone for so long, but she had to go up the hill near the barn so as to see down the road. From there, she saw something moving along the creek bank, but it was hard to make anything out in the fog. She went back to the house, made another check on the baby, and then left her milk bucket, put the cat out, shut the door, and went out after the runaway cow.

Old Kate lived just down the hill from the Slones' log house. Rennie had never liked to pass her house; some folks said she was a witch. Rennie didn't believe in witches, but Old Kate wasn't friendly. Once, when Rennie was coming home from school, she had watched the old woman put a cat on her chop block and cut its head off with a broadaxe because it had killed a small chicken. Rennie still shuddered when she thought about it. Bravely, though, she stopped to ask Old Kate if she had seen Bossie. Old Kate was coming from the back with a bucket; when she saw Rennie she began to run, her long wet dress tangling with her legs as she hurried toward her back door. Rennie didn't understand. Going to the back, she knocked and called. "Kate, have ye seen my cow? She got out of the lot last night and I can't find her." No one answered.

Then she saw the cow. Bossie was in no trouble; she wanted

to get home as much as Rennie wanted to get her there. Leading her along by the bell rope, she brought her through Old Kate's yard. "Hope she don't make a mess," Rennie thought. "Don't see how she could make it any worse."

A razorback hog was rooting for scraps of coal under the porch steps, making almost as much noise as the old pot-licker hound, who was straining his chain and barking loud enough to wake the dead. An old black rooster had gathered his harem of wives on one end of the porch, which was cluttered with drifts of rusty tin cans and broken fruit jars. Rennie wondered why it was that, when visitors from the Caney School came to Lonesome Holler, they always took pictures of Old Kate's house. Seemed as though they would rather have a picture of one of the nice clean houses, with their pretty vining roses and flowers. "Strange people have strange ways," she thought.

Rennie had no use for the milk bucket now; the cow had already been milked. She fastened her up in the barn because there was no telling when Pa would get around to fixing the fence.

Sarah Ellen was awake and crying.

"There's no milk fer ye, honey." Rennie felt like crying herself. "I don't know what to do." She sweetened some warm water with a little honey and filled the baby's bottle with it. After a few questioning sips, Sarah Ellen was content to drink it.

Rennie boiled two eggs and made herself some coffee. She mashed some butter into the egg yolks and fed them to Sarah Ellen. She hoped she was doing the right thing. It would be at least three or four hours before she could get any milk. She put some salt on the rest of the eggs and ate them herself.

"Well, sister, I guess we can sing the miner's song this time." Rennie sang:

> Here's the poor miner
> A pretty good man
> Brings his dinner
> In a bakin' powder can.
> A few fried 'taters,
> One boiled egg.

Been a poor dinner
If the hen hadn't laid.

Rennie knew she had to get out of her wet clothes. She couldn't afford to get sick. If she caught a cold, Sarah Ellen might catch it. Hunting for a pair of Pa's old socks, she said, "I should wear Ma's shoes. She'd want me to, but I can't jest yet. I might later." Then she whispered to herself, "Oh, Mommie, I need ye so much."

She began to laugh, a wild, hysterical sound. "Old Kate looked so funny runnin' through the rain with that full bucket of milk, tryin' not to spill it! Hope it gets flies in it before she gets it strained."

Old Kate wasn't kinfolks with anyone along Lonesome Holler. She had moved from Pike County with her husband, Uncle John, who was a black man. It had been against the law for a white woman to marry a colored man unless she would swear she had "nigger" blood in her. Uncle John had cut his arm and let Old Kate suck the blood so that she could swear it. They had been married only a few months when he was killed in a mining accident. They had no children. Everyone on Lonesome Holler had tried to be kind to Kate, but she was hateful and mean. She had disputed with all the neighbors about the line fences, about anything that came up. When she had a quarrel with a man, she would go out in her front yard, turn her back to him, and throw her dress up over her back and pat her naked hind end. This embarrassed the men, and made them very angry.

Once when Grandpa Jim was coming home from the store, Old Kate was going through this performance. Grandpa came home and told Grandma, "I'm goin' to stop that woman once and fer all." He took his old hog rifle from its peg above the door.

"Jim!" Grandma screamed. "Ye know ye hain't goin' to kill her!"

"Course not, although it might be a good thing." He went to the smokehouse and found an old salty meat skin and loaded his gun with it, tamping it in just right. Next day he took his gun with him. Sure enough, Old Kate came out and turned her dress up. Grandpa aimed at her behind and let go with the gun. When that meat skin found its mark, there came a scream that could be heard for a mile. "Bet that raised a blister as big as my hand," Grandpa laughed.

Every Friday was mill day. Big Jed had a water mill, and he ground corn into meal for all the families on Lonesome Holler. Thursday Pa brought two sacks of corn from the barn. After supper Rennie poured the corn out on a quilt on the floor. Pa read his Bible while she shelled the corn. Rennie placed Sarah Ellen, who had begun sitting up, on one end of the quilt, and gave her some of the cobs to play with. Soon she crawled over and began running her fingers through the corn, trying to bury her hands in the sliding pile of grains and laughing with glee. Rennie picked her up and placed her on top. Soon she was half buried. Rennie heard her whimper but plucked her up too late.

"Oh, Pa! Sarah Ellen has wet in the corn."

"How could ye, Rennie! Now we'll have to shell another turn."

"I never thought. She was havin' so much fun."

"Ye never think. That's the trouble with ye. Ye'll never be grown up. I'll have to go shuck some more." He lit the lantern and, taking the empty sacks, started for the barn loft, grumbling and muttering to himself.

Rennie carried the wet corn up the stairs to the loft and spread it out on the floor to dry. It could be fed to the chickens. She hung the quilt on the porch railing to dry and took a clean one from the shelf and spread it out on the floor. Later, as her father was helping her shell the second turn, he said, "I'm sorry I scolded ye. I ferget ye're only a child yerself. Ye're doin' a good job carryin' so heavy a load on such small shoulders." His kind words brought the tears to her eyes that the scolding had not.

A week later Sarah Ellen got sick. She acted hungry but took only a few sips from her bottle and then started to cry.

"Acts like her mouth's sore," Pa said. "'Spect it's the thrash."

Rennie looked inside the baby's mouth. It was red and raw.

"Better let Old Jim give her some creek water from outer his shoe. He never seed his pa, his ma was carrying him when his pa got killed. He's allus cured the thrash fer all the childern on Lonesome Holler. Jest ask him fer the shoe. Don't tell him what ye want with it. Won't do no good if ye do."

Rennie knew she wasn't going to let Sarah Ellen drink old dirty creek water, especially not from someone's old shoe. She hadn't forgotten what she had been taught in school about health. But she knew better than to try to argue with Pa.

She rushed through breakfast, milked the cow, made the beds, swept the floor, gave the dishes a "lick and a promise," and carried the baby up the hollow to Aunt Nance's.

The old woman met her at the door. "Been wonderin' when y'd get around to bringin' the young'n up to see me. I keep a watch out fer ye all. I watch ever' day for yer chimney smoke. I know when ye hang yer wash out. I told yer ma 'fore she died I would keep an eye out fer ye." Aunt Nance was one of those people who never stopped talking, never let the other person get a word in edgewise.

"I think Sarah Ellen's got the thrash," Rennie said, "and I've been so careful to show everbody that I could raise her all by myself. Now I've let her go and get sick. I'm so scared."

"Now, now, don't cry. All little ones has thrash one time or another. Hain't a thing to it, if ye can keep it from goin' through 'em."

"Do ye know a cure, Aunt Nance?"

"Well, I allus used yellerroot myself. Tastes awful. If I wasn't so stiff in my joints . . . I know jest where some used to grow up yonder on the second flat. Don't guess ye believe in lettin' her drink water out of someone's shoe. No, I didn't 'spect you did, bein' Mary's daughter. Never did hold to that myself, but they's folks that will swear right down to ye that it's the one and only way. Tell ye what. I hear they have a nurse over to the Caney school that helps folks that are sick.

Why don't ye take her over there? She come to see Uncle Ned when he got his leg broke, set that leg, put splints on it, and had him walkin' good as new in less than three months. Good as a man doctor, she is."

Bright and early the next morning Rennie found herself on the road to Mrs. Lloyd's new school with Sarah Ellen. Only her love for her baby sister could have gotten her to go see these strange people. She had never liked trying to talk to them when they had visited her mother with Mr. Scutchfield. Their speech was so harsh it grated on her ears like metal. She could understand them, but it was so hard getting them to understand her. And the perfume they used! A slight resemblance to the smell of wildflowers, only where the flower scent was pleasant the perfume was sickening. Rennie had always hidden in the back room or gone up to the loft when the strange people came to buy quilts from her mother. Even their money held their odor for days.

In spite of her worries, Rennie enjoyed her walk down Lonesome Holler. The air was just chilly enough so that a sweater felt good. The smells and sounds of spring were in the air. People were out in their gardens, hauling rocks, scattering manure or cinders, raking weeds. A few were on the hillsides, grubbing, digging up sprouts, getting the ground ready for plowing. Everyone had a kind word for the girls. Some came to the road to see Sarah Ellen. "Come in and set a spell," they said. "Be sure and stop on yer way back. Don't see why ye don't stay all night with us."

She followed the winding path down Lonesome Holler, crossing and recrossing the creek. Once she set Sarah Ellen on the bank and threw rocks in the water to use as stepping stones.

The closer she got to the school, the less she knew what she was going to do. Had Mr. Scutchfield been there she would have gone first to him, but she knew he was no longer at the school. Just outside of the community alongside the road stood an old sycamore tree spreading its friendly shade over both creek and road. Here Rennie sat down to rest and give Sarah Ellen her bottle and changed her diddie. She had brought along extra ones in an empty pillow slip. She could see some of the houses from where she sat, small-frame plank structures sitting on high posts. The outsides were covered with bark-covered slabs; each house had a creek-rock chimney.

Rennie picked up her sister and her bag, straightened her shoulders, and bravely entered the Center. Boys and girls were rushing to and fro. Everyone seemed to be in such a hurry. Everyone smiled, but no one stopped to talk.

"Hain't ye lost over here, Rennie?" It was her cousin Nell.

"Well, I hardly knowed ye, Nell. Ye look so different in that white uniform."

"It's me, all right."

"Could ye tell me which house is Mrs. Lloyd's?"

"Go up these steps and across the porch and knock on that first door ye come to. I'd go with ye, but I'm on my way to class. Be seein' ye."

"Thanks, Nell. Much obliged to ye."

Gathering all her courage, with a fast-beating heart and trembling hand, Rennie knocked on the door.

"Won't you come in, please?" a gentle voice said.

Rennie set her bundle down, opened the door, and went in. Coming in from the bright sun, she couldn't see at first. The windows were covered with dark curtains. Rennie looked around for someone. In the very back, behind a large desk, sat a small woman. There was a typewriter before her, almost hidden by stacks of letters and papers.

"Won't you please sit down?"

Rennie sank into the most comfortable chair she had ever been in in her whole life. Almost like a feather bed, she thought.

"What can I do for you?" The voice was kind. Rennie forgot all her fears.

She could see the woman must have been getting ready to go out, for she had a tam on her head and a matching scarf around her neck. Rennie caught her breath. It couldn't be, yet there it was—the very tam and scarf she had seen in the "wish book," the same color wool that was still hanging on the peg over Pa's bed.

Rennie was so startled she forgot to speak until Sarah

Ellen whimpered. Then she remembered her errand. "My sister is sick. Aunt Nance said I should bring her over here to see a nurse."

"Why did your mother not bring the baby? Isn't she too heavy for you to carry?"

"My Ma's dead."

"You mean you're taking care of her all by yourself?"

"Well, there's Pa, but he don't help much. He's a preacher and is away from home quite a lot. I don't mind the work. But now Sarah Ellen's sick. I think she's got the thrash, and I don't know what to do."

Rennie couldn't believe she was talking so freely with this strange woman. She wasn't the first person to fall under Mrs. Lloyd's spell, and she wouldn't be the last.

"The nurse is out just now. She'll be back soon. Why don't you tell me all about yourself while we wait. Why do you keep looking at my tam and scarf? I'll remove them if they make you uncomfortable."

Much to her own surprise, Rennie heard herself talking, telling all about her "wish book," the dream of coming to the school at Caney, her mother's death. Mrs. Lloyd, with her sympathetic interest, had gotten through to the mountain girl as no one else could ever have done, not even one of Rennie's own folks. She had talked to no one like this since her mother's death. Rennie didn't know it, but Mrs. Lloyd had this hold on many people. This was why she had been able to help mountain folks when many others had failed. She not only reached out a helping hand, she stood by their sides and helped them push.

"I think the nurse is back now. And Rennie, will you do me a favor?"

"Anything I can."

"Will you let me give you my tam and scarf?"

"Oh, no! I couldn't take yers. That would be like beggin' after I told ye how I wanted one."

"I would count it a great privilege to know they were worn by a brave little grown-up girl like you. Won't you please take them? It would mean a lot to me."

Rennie did. "I'll treasure 'em forever and a day."

She went through the rest of the day in a daze. Miss Rose, the nurse, assured her that the purple medicine would cure Sarah Ellen's mouth and that she would be visiting Rennie's home next week to make sure.

Pa was gone when she returned that night. He never took any notice of the baby unless she cried. This was the one time when Rennie was glad about his neglect; if he had seen the purple medicine on Sarah Ellen's mouth he would have been very angry at her for taking the baby to the nurse. Rennie didn't like going against her father's wishes, but she still thought she was doing the right thing. If Pa had asked, she would have told him the truth.

That night, as she put her sister in bed, Rennie made a vow. "Sarah Ellen,. someday you'll go to school at the Caney Creek Community Center. If it's the last thing I do, I'll see to that." Sarah Ellen only gurgled.

7 _____

So far Pa had never discussed making a garden. He had spent several days plowing the corn field until it was almost dark, coming in so tired that he went to bed without even reading his beloved Bible. Rennie always rechecked to see whether he had fastened the barnyard gate. Sometimes she felt as if she were the parent and he the child. She knew he didn't have the strength to follow that heavy plow back and forth around the hill, using his foot to turn over the iron shovel at the beginning of each new row.

Now Pa had been gone for three nights. He had gone with Big Jed and Uncle Tom to a union meeting on Brush Creek. He was supposed to be home sometime today.

"I believe I'll clean off the garden." Rennie thought. "If Pa don't mention it, I'll have to remind him to haul manure and spread it over our garden, then turn it under. He'll have to hurry. Lots of folks have already planted peas and potatoes. It's time to put out early onions."

She hurried through her morning chores and changed Sarah Ellen and fed her. She fastened the cat upstairs, not wanting to have it in the room with the baby, and left the front door open so she could hear Sarah Ellen when she woke up.

First she ruck the dead weeds from the strawberry patch. Next she cut the now-dry corn stalks and carried them, an armload at a time, to a large rock pile that had been in the middle of the garden for generations. Each year, as the garden was worked, more of the plentiful small rocks all over the place had been picked up and placed in one large heap. Burning corn stalks on the pile helped to get rid of snakes.

The cabbage patch came next. Here, still standing, were the almost rotten stalks of the cabbage her mother had grown the year before. It was hard for Rennie to believe her mother had been dead for such a short while. All that seemed to have been in another lifetime, long ago.

At first when she noticed someone going along the road around the other side of Lonesome Holler, she thought it was a man, but when the rider waved to her, she recognized Miss Rose, the nurse from the Community Center.

"Rennie," Miss Rose shouted. "Can you tell me where the Halls live? Am I on the right road?"

"Yeah, go right on up the Holler. They live in the third house on the right. Quite a fer piece yet to go."

"How's Sarah Ellen?"

"Right purt."

"That's fine. I'll stop on my way back from Halls'. Jimmie Hall has a bad stone bruise on his heel."

"Miss Rose is such a good person," thought Rennie. "Wish there was something I could do fer her. I don't think I got anythin' she would have."

A loud squall from the house told her Sarah Ellen's nap had ended. The garden was all cleaned up, so she put her rake and hoe away in the tool shed and returned to the house.

"Sarah Ellen, someone is comin' to see ye. Let's get all purtied up."

The cat was making almost as much noise as the baby; when she let the cat out, it made a fast retreat toward the barn. Rennie gave Sarah Ellen her bottle, propping it up with a pillow. Then she built a fire in the stove and began dinner. She would have to go to the spring for water. Pa was supposed to be home by dinner, and Big Jed and Uncle Tom would probably stay for dinner. So Rennie cooked a large kettle of potatoes, warmed up the leftover shucky beans, peeled three large onions, and baked a pone of corn bread.

She was just taking dinner up when Miss Rose returned.

"Did ye find the place?" Rennie asked. "Ye've not been gone long."

"Yes," the nurse answered as she dismounted. She tied the mule up to the hitching block and came in. "But Mr. Hall wouldn't let me see the boy. In fact, he wouldn't let me come in. He threatened to set the dogs on me if I didn't leave at once. 'There's nothin' to havin' a stone bruise,' he told me. 'Had 'em all my life. Just stick your heel in a fresh cowpile while it's still warm. That's all I ever done.' Rennie, do folks really do that?"

"Yeah, reckon so. Course, my Ma didn't. She allus used a pollus made from sugar and turpentine. Some say a piece of fat salty meat is good. But if ye don't go barefoot, ye don't get stone bruises in the first place, Ma allus said."

"Rennie, a stone bruise is a kind of boil. If it's not treated, it could become infected and cause blood poisoning. The boy could die. I want to help these people so much, but my hands are tied. Oh, well. Let's have a look at Sarah Ellen."

"Won't you eat dinner with us?" Rennie asked.

"Sure, thanks. I'm as hungry as a bear."

Rennie set two plates and dished up a bowl from each kettle, opened a jar of apple butter, and filled two glasses with milk. Ordinarily she would have been too shy to ask one of the strange outside people to have dinner with her, but Miss Rose had been so kind. Soon they were eating and having as much fun as if the older woman had been another mountain girl.

After dinner was over, Miss Rose offered to help with the dishes, but Rennie wouldn't hear of it. Rose had learned during their talk that Rennie loved to read, so when she left, she promised to return soon and bring some books that she would be glad to loan. "They're just lying there, gathering dust," Rose said. She would have liked to give the books to Rennie, but she had been in the mountains long enough to know about stubborn mountain pride. She knew that if Rennie accepted the books as a gift she would have to give something in return, even if it meant disfurnishing herself of something she needed. But to loan and "barry," that Rennie would understand. It was a way of life Rennie had been brought up with. No one refused to loan a neighbor anything—a cup of sugar, a few matches, a mule to work or ride, farm tools, even clothes.

After Miss Rose had gone on, saying that she had some more folks to visit before returning to the Community Center, Rennie sat on the porch and waited for her father. She saw him and his friends coming in time to have their dinner on the table when they arrived. The other two men hitched their mules up to the block while Pa went to unsaddle his and turn him loose in the pasture.

The men washed their hands and faces in a basin on a bench outside the kitchen door, then dumped the water they used in the back yard. After speaking "Howdy" to Rennie they talked among themselves. She kept watch, and as each cup of coffee became half-empty she refilled it from the pot on the stove.

Rennie could tell from their talk that they had had a good time. The three-day gathering of people from all over the county had met on Brush Creek; there were three delegates from each church. It had been three days of singing and praying and preaching. They had spent each night with a different Brush Creek preacher, but all three had stayed together.

After eating, they sat on the porch, leaning their chairs back against the wall, chewing tobacco, spitting over the porch railing into the yard. It was almost dark when the men left.

Rennie and Sarah Ellen had gone to bed early. Pa sat for a while reading his Bible by the light of the coal oil lamp. As he got ready for bed he said, "Well, Rennie, I see how ye finally got around to cleanin' the garden off. Been wonderin' when ye would. I'll clean the chicken-house and barn out to'mar and spread the manure around the garden. Should have it ready fer plantin' by the end of the week. Don't know jest where the signs are; I'll have to look that up in the Almanac. Are ye asleep, Rennie?"

"No, Pa, jest layin' here thinkin'."

"Well, think ye can plant the garden all right?"

"'Spect so."

The next day Rennie went up in the loft to look for the garden seeds. Again she was reminded of what a short time her mother had been gone.

It was very dark in the loft. There was no window to let in light. Rennie stood there in the darkness for a while, waiting for her eyes to adjust, taking in all the smells that brought back so many memories: drying apples, cushaws, beans, nuts stored away for winter, strings of popcorn and hot peppers hanging from pegs in the rafters, the musty smell of old clothes. On one side was the bed where she had slept when her mother was alive. She went over and opened the little peep-hole, a two-foot opening in one end of the loft, far up under the eaves. The shutter, made from split boards and now smooth from use, hung on hinges made from two worn-out shoe soles. The latch, a small piece of wood called a button, turned on the nail that held it in place.

As Rennie stood there looking out, she could see far up and down Lonesome Holler. She thought of why this little peep-hole was there; it did more than let light and air into the loft. When the old house was first built, there was still great fear of Indians. From this vantage point, a visitor could be spotted long before he got close. In later years it was revenuers that were watched for.

Once, when great-great-grandfather was a boy, he had shot and killed a "panter" from this door. His father had gone to Lickin' Creek to gather salt, leaving the mother and small children alone. All night the panther circled the house, climbing over the roof while the frightened people stayed awake keeping a large fire going in the chimney. Just before daybreak, the animal crawled into an old hollow stump that had been in the yard as a watering trough. With a pounding heart, the twelve-year-old boy climbed the stairs, loaded his father's old hog rifle, softly opened the little door, took careful aim, and ended the life of the black panther.

Rennie pulled the open wooden box over near the door so she could see. Inside were old cracked fruit jars filled with seeds. The smaller ones—cabbage, tomatoes, pepper, and parsnip—were bundled in small squares of cloth torn from worn-out clothes and tied with a string from the same cloth. The seeds had been saved, dried, and put here by her mother. There were tears in Rennie's eyes as she untied the strings, looking for what she needed now. She replaced the others to be used later. In each bundle, in her mother's handwriting, was scribbled the name of each on a small piece of paper torn from a brown paper bag. There were a lot more seeds than she would need. Mary had always loved to have a plenty so as to give some to her neighbors should they need any.

When Rennie came back into the kitchen, her father was cutting potatoes, slicing them carefully so that each piece would have at least two or three eyes. "I think a peck of 'taters will be enough to plant now, jest a few to gravel on. I'll plant the real patch somewheres in the corn field."

Rennie waited until her father had plowed two long "furs" in the garden. Then she took the bucket of cut potatoes and dropped two pieces at a time, about two feet apart, along the trench left by the plow, and gently stepped on each one. Later she used a hoe to drag soil up in a hill over them. Then she planted a few rows of peas. A few hills of 'tater onions came next. Along one side of the fence were some old, half-buried washtubs filled with rotting manure and rich soil; there she planted tomatoes, cabbage, and pepper. Later, when the plants were large enough, they would be dug up and set out in rows.

Rennie loved the smell of the freshly turned earth, the feel of it against her bare feet. She would stop frequently to lean on her hoe and just suck in the smells of spring by the lungful. She didn't think of what she was doing as work; it was something she enjoyed to the very depth of her soul. For generations, year after year, her womenfolks had made a garden here in this same earth, and now she too was a part of that life. To plant and grow food for your body was as natural as breathing. It was so much a part of her life that she didn't think about it or ask questions. She just enjoyed it. Had a stranger passed by, he might have thought that he had seen a deprived little girl doing work that was drudgery. He would not have understood—nor could Rennie have explained.

8 _____

For a few days after the garden was planted Rennie didn't have much work to do. Pa was still breaking ground for corn. Miss Rose had left the books she had promised. Rennie hurried through her morning chores, then made a pallet for Sarah Ellen by placing a folded quilt on one end of the porch, and sat beside her and read. Every now and then she checked to see how far the sun had crept across the floor; she mustn't forget to have dinner ready when Pa came in. She didn't think he would approve of the books she was reading; he would say reading was a waste of time, unless she read the Bible. But Rennie knew there couldn't be too much wrong in enjoying *Little Women*, *Ivanhoe*, and *Uncle Tom's Cabin*.

One morning, when she gave Sarah Ellen her bath, she noticed small red spots on the baby's legs and arms. When Pa came in from work she showed them to him.

"What do ye think it is, Pa? Could it be measles?"

"No, it's not measles. They come in splotches. I'm afraid we got chinches on our beds. It sure looks like bedbug bites to me."

Rennie exclaimed in horror, "Where on earth could we have got bedbugs?"

"Well," her father answered, "I jest might have brought 'em back with me from Brush Creek. I don't like to talk about anyone, but one place we stayed the night shore had bedbugs. They almost eat me up alive."

"What'll we do?"

"I'll stay at the house to'mar and help ye. I don't think they've got enough start to have gotten into the walls. It won't be too much of a job to get the beds cleaned up, but if we have to tear all that paper from the walls, we shore will have a job on our hands."

Rennie couldn't go to sleep thinking about those bugs. She felt as if they were crawling all over her. How could she keep Old Kate from finding out? "If she does," Rennie thought, "she'll tell everyone up and down Lonesome Holler, and I'll be so plagued I'll jest die from shame."

After breakfast the next morning Rennie got a clean quilt from the chest in the loft for Sarah Ellen's pallet. Then she carried all the quilts, sheets, pillows and feather beds out into the back yard. Everything that could be washed had to be boiled in water. Pa emptied the shuck mattress out behind the barn where maybe, just maybe, no one would see him burn the shucks. While Rennie washed the ticks, he would prepare clean shucks by breaking out the hard stems and shredding the rest with a table fork.

The wooden slats and springs were doused with hot water. Rennie stuck first one end of the slats into the tub of hot water, then the other.

Pa made a shuck brush and poured some lamp oil into an empty peach can. He brushed the sides and corners of the iron bedsteads with the oil. Going over and over again, he turned them around so as to get at all the spaces. He examined the walls behind the beds but could find no evidence of the hated bugs. He tried to comfort Rennie by saying, "It's no shame to get chinches; it's jest a shame to keep 'em."

"I jest hope we're gettin' rid of 'em fer once and all." To herself she thought, "I shore hope Miss Rose won't come today."

By nightfall the beds were set back up. Only the smell of kerosene reminded them of their misfortune, and that would linger for days. Each morning for many weeks Rennie examined the corners of the beds looking for the dreaded bugs, but she and her father had done their work well. Rennie wondered if Big Jed and Uncle Tom had also brought back the unwelcome visitors from Brush Creek. From now on she would see that her father changed his clothes in the barn if there was any question of where he had spent the night.

Every Sunday her father went to church. When her mother had been alive sometimes she and Rennie had gone with him. One Saturday evening Pa told Rennie, "I wish you and Sarah Ellen would go to meetin' with me. I'm goin' to take the wagon. Uncle Tom's family is riding with us. He's goin' to bring his mule over early tomorrow to huck in with mine. There'll be plenty of room. It's a memorial meetin' over on

Steer Fork, at the Amburgey graveyard. Ye should get out more. There's goin' to be dinner on the grounds," he added.

"Yeah, I believe I'd like to go. Good thing I washed our best clothes this week."

It wasn't quite daylight the next morning when Uncle Tom showed up riding his mule bareback with the rig on it. Rennie and her father were ready. While Uncle Tom hitched up the wagon to the two mules, Rennie got Sarah Ellen ready; she filled two bottles with milk, wrapped them in some extra diddies, and tied them up in a pillow slip. Rennie sat on the wagon seat between Pa and Uncle Tom and held Sarah Ellen on her lap. When they got to Uncle Tom's house, Aunt Jane and her four grandchildren were waiting by the side of the road. Rennie gave her place on the seat to Aunt Jane, who insisted on holding Sarah Ellen. Rennie got in the back with the others. Some old quilts made a nice place to sit. Rennie felt good being with young folks again. They talked and laughed as the wagon jolted and bumped over the rocky road. Before they arrived at their journey's end they'd picked up more people.

Although they were early, a lot of people were already there. The graveyard was about halfway up the hill. The menfolks left the wagon alongside the road and took the mules down near the creek and hitched them up beside several other mules, just far enough apart so they couldn't kick each other. The shade of the creek willows was cool. The womenfolks and young people began to climb the hill. Someone had cut a path through the weeds and scrubs to the graveyard. A stand had been built near the lower side—an open shed with a board roof, a floor of sawed lumber, benches along three sides, and a table in the center covered with a white cloth that was stiff with starch and ironed to perfection. On the table sat a bucket of water and a dipper. Around the stand were split logs laid across each other to form seats. The preachers and church members would sit on the stand. The rest of the congregation would sit on the logs or on the grass.

Many of the graves were decorated with crepe paper flowers. Some were covered with white sheets, and some of the sheets had beautiful embroidery work—flowers, birds and words of love—stitched into them.

Aunt Jane was still holding Sarah Ellen, so Rennie walked around the graveyard and read some of the names. There were little gravehouses covering a few of the graves. She peeped through the latticed sides; dried Princess Feathers and Fall Roses were still there, crumbling into dust. There was one new grave covered with oilcloth pinned down with rocks.

As the singing began, Sarah Ellen awoke and began to cry. Rennie went to get her from Aunt Jane and took her to one of the many shade trees. She sat down on the grass and gave Sarah Ellen her bottle; Rennie wanted to be close enough to enjoy the singing. She loved those old gospel songs. They were all sad and mournful, but beautiful. She loved to hear how someone gave out each line before it was sung—there were few song books. Many of the preachers knew the songs by heart. Many could not read.

Rennie loved the singing but she didn't care much about the sermons. She had heard over and over, again and again, how you must be born again. Rennie couldn't understand why, if you could know when you were a sinner, you couldn't know when you were a Christian. When one preacher said that a woman who bobbed her hair or wore pants couldn't go to heaven, Rennie thought of Miss Rose, who had short hair and wore riding britches. She was so kind, spending all her time helping people without receiving any pay. She just had to be headed to heaven.

There were five preachers who took part in the service. The first one just spoke a few words and then knelt and led prayer. Everyone on the stand got down on their knees; everyone else bowed their heads. On and on he shouted in a loud voice, asking for mercy, sometimes calling the name of someone he hoped God would heal or turn from his wicked ways. Rennie wished he would thank God for some of the many gifts that had been bestowed on them—the songs of birds, the flowers, the pretty fluffy clouds against the blue, blue sky.

The preachers stood up, one after the other. Some mentioned the names of the folks buried in the graveyard, bringing tears and loud moans from female relatives. If a preacher got carried away and preached too long, someone would start a song and "sing him down." Sometimes one of the women would jump to her feet, clap her hands, and shout her praises to God. Over and over again they would shake hands with each other, often hugging and kissing.

After the meeting came to a close, white cloths were put on the benches and the food was brought out. Everyone had brought something. Rennie had a dozen boiled eggs and a jar of her mother's pickled beets. She knew someone else would have brought shucky beans, and the beets would go well with the beans. When everyone had eaten, the men and boys gathered under the trees and the older women sat on the grass. Aunt Jane again watched Sarah Ellen while Rennie helped the younger girls clean up and put away the food. Everyone sat around a while waiting for their dinner to settle, discussing the weather, and catching up on the news.

When Rennie came to get Sarah Ellen from Aunt Jane she passed a group of women. One woman remarked to another, "Hain't that Preacher John Slone's girl?"

"Yeah, that's her," answered the second woman.

"Well, preacher or not, it looks like his girl has got her a bastard," the woman said, making sure she spoke loud enough for Rennie to hear.

Before Rennie could reply, Aunt Jane jumped to her feet. "You dirty-minded hypercrit. That's one of the best little girls in these hills. That's her little sister she's raisin' all by herself, and doing a right smart of a good job! Her mother died last fall, leavin' that little baby, and Rennie would not hear of anyone else keepin' her sister."

"I'm sorry. Please forgive me, child," said the woman.

Rennie couldn't answer, she was too near crying. She took Sarah Ellen to the wagon and climbed in and sat there until the others came. Somehow she had outgrown all the other girls of her age and didn't like to listen to their chatter about boys and everything else.

9

Pa was getting along so slowly with his plowing that Rennie was afraid he wouldn't get the corn planted in time. Again and again he would be asked to come to someone's home to faith doctor the sick or hold prayer. He never worked on Saturday but went instead to church with Big Jed and Uncle Tom. The Old Regular Baptists had a meeting on both Saturday and Sunday once each month, neighboring churches using a different weekend. Rennie hated herself for not wanting her father to spend so much time doing the Lord's work. But if Pa didn't raise enough corn to feed the mule, cow, and chickens and to make their own bread, she just didn't see what they were going to do. Her father was too old to keep going on this way.

Time and again Rennie went to Aunt Nance's for advice. Once the older woman kept Sarah Ellen at her house all day, but Rennie missed the baby so much she refused to let Aunt Nance take her after that. Some days she would put a folded quilt on the ground under the apple trees and let Sarah Ellen play while she worked in the garden, but soon the small child began to crawl off. When Rennie found her trying to put gravel in her mouth she knew she had to do something else with her during the day.

Miss Rose came by several times to bring more books and magazines and to pick up the ones Rennie had finished. Sometimes she wouldn't have time to stop and would just wave as she hurried by. Rennie thought it would be wonderful to be a nurse and be able to help out. If someone like Miss Rose had been with Ma when Sarah Ellen was born, Ma might still be alive. Rennie had finally gotten Pa to see that Miss Rose was not like other brought-on people. He no longer complained when she came to visit or take a meal.

It was late one Sunday evening, almost on the edge of dark, when a rider came up the path to the Slones' house on Lonesome Holler. You could tell he was a stranger by his clothes, yet he seemed to know just where he was going. The two girls and their father were sitting on the porch. The young man rode up, hitched his horse to the fence, and came up the steps.

"Howdy. You must be Uncle John, and this is Rennie, I 'spect."

"Ye've got the advantage of me," Pa said. "You know me, but I can't say as I ever saw you before in my life."

"Ye've seed me plenty of times, and I recollect you. I'm yer brother Tate's boy. John—named after you, I was—but they never call me anythin' but Johnnie."

"Well, well, well. What a ye know! Come in, come in. Have a chair. Rennie, go get him somethin' to eat."

"First I'd like to put my mule up, if ye have somewheres I can stable him fer the night."

"Shore. I'll go with ye and show ye the way."

Rennie hadn't seen her father so pleased about anything in a long time.

Soon they were all around the table. Johnnie kept eating and talking while the others sat spellbound. He told them that when Tate and Bill and their families settled in West Virginia near a coalmining camp, they took the name Smith.

"Uncle Bill and Aunt Sally still live there," Johnnie said. "Two of their children are still at home with them. All miners, just kind of livin' hand-to-mouth. Pa, he died jest a few years after he got there; never did take to minin' much. I believe he was so homesick he jest gave up. Ma, she raised us young'ns by takin' in washin'. All the mine bosses' wives and the company doctors' wives got her to do their washin'. They didn't pay her much, but it kept the wolf from the door. Me bein' the only boy in the family. . . . The girls helped what they could till they got married. Fer the last five years there's just been Ma and me. I never liked workin' in the mines. I love the smell of outdoors. I guess I'm jest a farmer at heart. Two weeks ago Ma died. Wish I could have brought her back here to bury her, but I knowed it was too dangerous. She'd told me so much about y'all and this old house I believe I could've come here in the dark."

"Grandma Kate would shore have been pleased had she knowed y'all went by the name of Smith."

"Yeah, I know. And one of my sisters named her first born Tad. Uncle John, why didn't ye get a good lawyer? Ye could have proved ye didn't kill that man. There was no use ye havin' to go to prison."

"I know. But ye see, I knowed if I brought all the proof, the law would hunt fer Bill and Tate. As long as there was someone to punish, they were all right. My brothers had families to raise, and me, at that time, I had no young'ns and didn't know I ever would, so I jest kept silent and went on."

"Yeah, that's what our folks allus thought and that's one reason why I'm here. If ye can use a big stout miner that don't know anythin' about farmin', I'm willin' to learn. All I own in this world is my mule and saddle and what I have in my saddle bags. What ever happened to Pa's and Uncle Bill's farms? I guess they were sold fer taxes?"

"No, there's an old man, one of these furners comes from up North. Well, he come lookin' fer a place to stay durin' the summer. Mary told him about y'all's house and told him he could stay there if he paid the taxes. He comes ever' summer. Stays to hisself a lot. Says he's writin' a book and don't talk to people very much. He fixed up that old place, and it looks right smart."

Pa yawned. It was way past his usual bedtime. "Guess we'd better go to bed. Johnnie, ye can sleep up in the loft; there's an extra bed up there."

"Thanks, but it's bound to be awful hot up there. Jest give me a quilt and a piller and I'll bed down in the barn loft on the hay. Come cold weather I'll move in upstairs."

Johnnie may not have known much about farming, but he took to it the way a duck takes to water. With the two mules spelling each other, in no time at all the corn was planted—twice as much as John had first planned on. Johnnie also helped Rennie with the feeding, carried in all the water, and chopped the stovewood. Sarah Ellen took to Johnnie right off. He would toss her up in the air, let her ride on his shoulders, and keep her laughing.

Rennie loved to hear him play his French harp. John had told him not to play it in the house because, as an Old Regular Baptist preacher, he was "agin' music."

"But Grandpa played his fiddle in the house, didn't he?" asked Johnnie.

"Yeah, but it was his house then. Now it's mine."

"I wish I could have seed Grandpa's fiddle. Pa allus told me that Grandpa had asked fer it to be buried with him."

"Yeah, he did, and I think that was blaspheming," said the preacher.

They were at the breakfast table when this conversation was going on. After John left, Rennie said to Johnnie, "Come up in the loft. I have somethin' to show ye." He followed her up the stairway and watched as she pulled the little black cowhide trunk from under the bed. Its rusty hinges squeaked as she lifted the lid. She took out a bundle and put it on the bed. Carefully she unwrapped the fiddle. As she handed it to Johnnie his eyes sparkled. He took it from her as if she had given him the most precious thing in the world.

"But I don't understand," he said. "I thought it was to have been buried with Grandpa."

"No, when Grandpa and Grandma died with the flu, Ma was real sick. Grandpa had always said he wanted it to be buried with him, but with Ma bein' too sick to say a word, none of the neighbors knowed. When Ma got better, she let it hang there on the wall until jest before Pa came home. Knowin' how he felt about music—it bein' a sin and all— she jest hid it up here in this old trunk. Ma weren't like Pa."

"Oh, Rennie, it must have been so ordered by the powers above! I have so longed to have a fiddle!"

"Pa heard ye say that he would shore say ye was blaspheming," Rennie said, laughing.

"What he don't know won't hurt him. Music is beautiful. All good and perfect gifts come from God, and it's a God-given talent. I won't play around Uncle John, but I'll drive them animals crazy while I'm learnin' out there in the barn. Ye wait and see."

Johnnie had said he was going over to see the old home-place where he had been born the next day after he first came to Lonesome Holler, but, what with helping Uncle John and finding the fiddle and all, it was over a month before he got around to going. Early one morning he came in from milking the cow and found Rennie just finishing her dishes. "I'm goin' over to our farm today. You and Sarah Ellen want to come along?" he asked.

"Well, I wasn't planning on doin' anythin' that won't wait until to'mar. I don't care if I do go. I'll be ready in two shakes of a sheep's tail and one of 'em's already shuck."

Rennie fixed an extra bottle for Sarah Ellen, tied some diddies in a pillow slip, and filled an empty lard bucket with beans and cornbread for herself and Johnnie. It was just about a two-mile walk if they went up the hill where his father and uncle had had their moonshine still. They found the place all grown up, but you could still see a clear spring of water near the opening to a small cave. The rocks that had been used to make a furnace were all that remained, and they were tumbling down. The clay used to stick them together had been washed away by rain.

"Shore was a nice place fer a still," Johnnie said with admiration in his voice.

"Ye're not thinkin' of moonshinin' are ye?" Rennie asked anxiously.

"Course not. I hate the stuff. What fer would I want to risk my hide? I have all I want in this world—a place to stay, plenty to eat, a chance to work and pay my keep, and a fiddle to play in my spare time. Guess I'll have to work some come fall to buy me some new clothes. Hain't goin' to let that worry me none now, though. I'm shore somethin' will come along. Allus has."

As they went along the ridge they noticed huckleberry bushes on both sides of the path loaded with green berries. "We'll have to come back in a few weeks. These berries will be ripe by then. Nothin' in this world's better eatin' than huckleberry dumplin's. Can ye make 'em, Rennie?"

"Yeah, shore. Course, I hain't learned how as good as Ma."

"I think ye do jest fine bein' as young as ye are. You must get out, go places. This fall I'm goin' to take ye to a bean stringin'. I'll get me a girlfriend, and maybe ye'll see some boy ye'll like quite smart."

"Oh, no, I'm too young fer a boyfriend, but I'd love to go with ye if Pa will stay with Sarah Ellen."

When Johnnie finally got to his old place, he couldn't believe his eyes. He'd been very young when he had been taken away, but his mother had talked about it so much he thought he could remember. But this was not the old tumbling-down shack that he had expected to find. There was a new board roof, glass windows with pretty white curtains, and the planks of the porch were painted. The clay between the logs was whitewashed; a new fence surrounded the flower-filled yard; there were even split-rock steps.

"And ye say this brought-on feller has been livin' here?" he asked.

"Yeah, a old-like man, never talks much. I met him in the road one day walkin' from the store, and when I spoke 'Howdy,' he jumped as if I had scared him half to death. I could hardly keep from laughin' right in his face."

Just opposite the house on the other side of the road stood an old sycamore tree. Here, in the pleasant shade, the three travelers had their picnic. Rennie had not had so much fun since her mother's death. Their joyful laughter soon brought the stranger to his door. Seeing them, he came over to where they were.

"What are you doing here camping on my property?" The words were harsh but there was still some kindness in his voice.

"Well," Johnnie began, "ye see, this is really my property. I was born in that house and I jest wanted to come back and see it."

"Oh! Well, I'm glad to meet you. I guess someone has told you, then, how I've been paying the taxes and spending my summers here. Hope that's satisfactory with you. You're not wanting me to leave, are you?" There was fear both in his voice and in his face.

"No," Johnnie answered. "I'm more than pleased with the arrangement. Ye shore have purtied the place up right smart."

"Yes, I love living here and I'm glad to meet the owner. I would love to meet and talk to the people of Lonesome Holler, but so far no one has ever invited me to their home. I haven't even been asked to attend their church."

"Oh," Rennie interrupted him. "Ye don't have to be asked. Just come on. Around here, ye'll be more than welcome, jest come on any time. Folks may be jest a little stand-offish at first, but once they learn ye, it's all right. We all been thinking ye just didn't want to have any truck with us folks."

"Well, I guess strange people have strange ways."

"That's what Pa allus says."

10

It was one of those beautiful mornings—the sky so blue, just a few puffs of clouds—as the sun came slowly over the edge of the hills, drying dew from the ground, inching its way across Lonesome Holler.

The day before, Johnnie had told Rennie that the huckleberries were ripe enough to start picking. Pa had promised to stay home with Sarah Ellen. Last washday Rennie had saved the rinse water and had cleaned all the empty glass fruit jars. She had asked Miss Rose if she wanted to go with them. They would be taking a jug of water and some grub and would stay out all day.

"Rennie, do you think it's safe to go so far back in the hills?" the nurse had asked. "Folks are saying over at the Community Center that there has been a bobcat roaming the ridges."

"Oh, don't pay that no never mind; people allus start some sort of talk like that so as to scare the women come berry-pickin' time. It's the moonshiners what does that. They's afraid someone might run upon their stills. Johnnie will be with us, if it will make ye feel any better. He can take Pa's gun."

Johnnie had not wanted Miss Rose to go, saying he didn't like brought-on people. When Miss Rose stopped at the house, Johnnie always made himself scarce, going out the back door as she came in the front.

"Oh, ye'll like her once ye learn her. Jest wait and see."

They were all ready to go when Miss Rose rode up. Rennie had on an old pair of Pa's overalls, the legs rolled up, and an old shirt, and her hair was tied up in a red kerchief. She had told Miss Rose to wear old clothes. The nurse thought her riding britches and boots would be just fine. She had also brought her safety kit.

"It's better to be prepared," she explained. "One of us might get a snake bite."

Johnnie stalked along ahead of the girls, carrying the gun and other things. They went by the cave where the Slone brothers had been caught making whisky. "It's such an ideal place. Why hasn't someone else used it?" Miss Rose asked Rennie.

"Well, fer one thing, it's considered bad luck to set up where someone's been caught, and a lot of folks say the place is hanted. Folks swear right down that they have seed a man riding a horse with no head. The horses that the reve-nuers rode in here had their throats slashed."

"You don't believe in ghosts, do you?"

"No, my mother learned me better. But there are plenty of folks what do."

By now they had reached the top of the hill where the huckleberry bushes were. It was nice and cool in the shade.

"Now, let's all stay in hollerin' distance of one another. No one get lost," Johnnie cautioned. "Pa allus said, should any of us ever get lost in the hills, first, do not get scared. Set down and rest, and then go downhill until ye find runnin' water. Follow it the way it's runnin' and ye'll sooner er later come to a house where people live."

"That's a great idea," thought Miss Rose.

At first they could hear the plunk, plunk of the berries as they were dropped into the tin buckets. Rennie showed Miss Rose how easy it was to get a handful by gently pulling your open fingers along the stems. "Ye'll never get yer bucket full jest pickin' one at a time."

Johnnie went farther along. The girls stayed close to the path, talking up a storm. They saw two more folks also picking berries. Rennie knew them, a man and his wife who lived on the other side of the hill. She hollered, "Howdy! Are ye findin' any berries?"

"Yeah, there's a plenty everwhere ye look. The huckleberries shore hit this year!" the woman answered. The man only nodded. The two turned and began picking their way back the other way. It wasn't good manners to join in. Anyway, Johnnie and Miss Rose were strangers to them.

"Come see us, y'all," the woman hollered to Rennie.

"Y'all stop sometime when ye pass," Rennie replied.

By noon all the buckets were full. They found a large mossy rock and sat there to rest, eat, and drink. The water was warm. "But it's wet," Rennie said. There were large slices of ham, chunks of cornbread, a boiled egg for everyone. Miss Rose's contribution was three now-melted candy bars which they laughingly licked from the wrappers.

They all drank water from the same jar. This raised Johnnie's estimation of Miss Rose. "She's not so stuck-up after all," he thought to himself.

She thought, "I don't believe I ever ate a dinner that tasted so good. This mountain air and eating like this sure gives you an appetite."

From where they sat, Miss Rose could see far down the valley—on this side Lonesome Holler, on the other, Goose Creek. From some of the houses she could see smoke rising from the kitchen flues, a signal that dinner was being prepared.

"Where is the Community Center from here?" she asked.

"Over that way. Can't see it from here. It's between them hills right there," Rennie pointed out.

"I don't see how you all can keep up with where you are in these hills. I could get lost, I'm sure. I'm just now learning how to follow one road. I'm always having to ask directions."

"Well, I 'spect it would be jest as easy fer us to get lost was we in the streets of yer town where ye was raised."

"I guess so. I'd never thought of it that way. I feel guilty for taking this day off from my work, but I certainly have enjoyed myself."

Rennie said, "This *is* our work, but if ye get pleasure out of doin' somethin', it makes play out of it."

"You're very young to be so wise," Miss Rose said. "Many people live their whole lives without learning that."

Johnnie took out his French harp and began playing. The girls sat there listening. Suddenly Miss Rose pointed and whispered, "Look! Beside that rock. See the fox?"

"Johnnie, ye've called the varmits out from their holes with yer harp playin'," Rennie laughed.

The fox came from behind the rock slowly and went around the hill dragging one leg.

"Oh, the poor thing. See, it's been hurt." Miss Rose was upset.

"Oh, no." Johnnie told her. "It's not crippled at all. Had it been, it would never have let itself be seen. We're jest too close to its den, and it's got young'ns here under some of these rocks. By makin' like it's hurt it thinks we'll follow it. This way it could lead us away from its den. Watch." He jumped up and ran at the fox so quickly that the startled animal dropped on all four feet and dashed from sight. Miss Rose laughed. Rennie said, "Well, let's leave so she can come back to her little ones. It's time we go home, anyway."

The buckets that had been full when they set them down now were missing an inch or so of berries.

"Has something been in our berries?" Miss Rose asked.

"No," Rennie explained, "They've jest settled down. The weight squished the bottom ones. We'll pick a few more on our way home."

"I'd rather pick huckleberries than blackberries," Johnnie remarked as they gathered up their things. "It takes longer, but ye don't get eat up by chiggers."

"What are 'chiggers'?" Miss Rose asked.

"It's a little small red mite that makes a big itchy welp. It gets on your legs and arms," Rennie explained. "Grandma said it was a no see 'em but big feel 'em bug. Remember how Grandma spelled huckleberries, Johnnie?"

H.U. huckle, B.U. buckle, H.U. huckle I
H.U. huckle, B.U. buckle, huckleberry pie.

And you remember post office:

P, round O, cruckled S, T, O, F double time, I C E.

She had a rhyme for Mississippi, too, but I can't remember it."

"I can't either, but I remember the one she allus said when we were hoeing potatoes:

> I'm a careless potato and I care not a pin
> how into existence I came.
> If you plant me dill-wise or dribble me in,
> to me it's exactly the same.
> The bean and the pea make more lofty attire
> But I care not a button for them.
> I beautifully nod with my white flower
> While the earth is hoed up to my stem.

Sarah Ellen was asleep when they got home, and Pa was sitting on the porch reading his Bible. Miss Rose insisted that Rennie keep her berries. "You keep them and I'll be around this winter to help you eat them."

"Is that a promise? Please take a few fer yer supper. A bowlful with sugar and milk is awful good."

"Well, I guess so, I never had huckleberries. We have something similar we call blueberries, which are a little larger in size. I've had so much fun today. Thanks for asking me."

Rennie was very busy all afternoon canning the berries. The kitchen was hot from the fire in the stove. She was proud of the thirty-two quarts of berries and the kettle of dumplings, which had turned out just fine for supper. Johnnie and Pa both said they were delicious.

"Now," Rennie asked, "Johnnie, don't ye like Miss Rose?"

"Well, she's all right fer a brought-on person. But I feel better around people of my own kind."

11 _____

John had sold the sheep, saying there was no need to keep them, as Rennie had never learned to spin. The money he received for them paid the year's taxes. He gave Rennie two dollars and told her to buy shoes for herself and Sarah Ellen. Rennie had taken two of her mother's dresses to Aunt Nance; the older woman had promised to make a dress for Rennie and something for the baby with the cloth. Rennie felt bad about cutting up her mother's things, but Aunt Nance reminded her that that was what her mother had told her to do. Miss Rose bought the shoes for them when she went to Hindman that weekend. There was also enough money for some stockings—one pair for Rennie, two for Sarah Ellen. This was the first store-bought hose that Rennie had ever owned.

That evening, after doing up the work, Rennie dressed up in all her new things and came out on the porch, where Johnnie and Pa were sitting.

"All dressed up and nowheres to go," said Johnnie.

"Ye shore look purty, honey, but don't get stuck-up. Ye know pride is the snare of the Devil. Ye look like yer Ma first time I ever saw her."

"Say, Rennie," Johnnie went on. "I heard down at the store that Sol and his wife Sally was planning on a bean-stringin' this comin' Friday. What ye say we go?"

"Can we, Pa? Will ye stay with Sarah Ellen?"

"Well, if nothin' comes up, I will. Johnnie, will they be any drinkin' there?"

"If I see anyone takin' one drop I promise I'll bring her home."

"So now ye have somewhere to wear yer new rig," her father smiled.

Rennie hoped all week that no one would come with business for Pa. Friday afternoon she hurried through her work and had supper an hour early. She couldn't believe her ears when Pa told her to leave the dishes, that he'd wash them. Johnnie wanted them to ride one of the mules, but Rennie thought it would be more fun to walk. It was only a mile.

"Ye'll need the lantern; it'll be dark agin you come back. Better check and see if they's enough lamp oil in it," Pa said.

Rennie had stuck two of Ma's darning needles in a flannel cloth and put them in her pocket. Johnnie had tied his fiddle up in his old work shirt. Pa still didn't know he had it.

"Guess I'll get a chance to try my music out on real people. The pigs and chickens are gettin' used to it by now."

"First time I heard ye out there in the barn I thought Old Kate's cat had got into the hen roost."

"Oh, I'm not all that bad."

"Jest joshin'," Rennie said.

Early as they were, they found a crowd gathered. Several mules were hitched up outside the yard along the fence. There were two wagons.

Johnnie stopped in the yard where the men were. Rennie went on into the house, a small one-room cabin. Sol and Sally had not been married long. There were perhaps a dozen women sitting on the sides of the two beds and in chairs along the wall. In the middle of the room was a large pile of green beans on an open quilt. Rennie saw there were two or three girls about her age that she'd gone to school with.

"Well, I guess there's enough here fer us to begin," said Sally. "All you women get a chair and a lapful of beans. The men will be in directly. I barried about everbody's chairs around here, but some of ye will still have to sit on the floor."

All the younger women sat down around the quilt and began snouting the beans, throwing the strings in one place on the quilt and the finished beans in another. Everyone was talking, catching up on the news. As the menfolks came in, they paired off in couples, a husband or boyfriend getting beans from his partner's lap. While the others worked, Johnnie played his fiddle.

"Never thought I would hear anyone play like Grandpa Jim Slone again," one old man said. "I can shut my eyes and not know the difference."

"Yeah, he shore has the same touch," his wife whispered.

> Bile them cabbage down,
> Bake that hoecake round.
> Only song that I can play
> Is bile them cabbage down.

That one was followed by "Sally Goodin," then "Arkansas Traveler."

"What about 'Old Joe Clark'? Ye learned that one yet?" someone asked.

Johnnie's answer was to play it. Many of them joined in the singing.

"Well, here's one I think fits the occasion. Out in West Virginia, where I growed up, they called shucky beans leather britches, so here's the tune."

"Don't know as I ever heard that un, but I have heard dried beans called leather britches before," Sol said as Johnnie paused before singing.

> Some folks say a preacher won't steal.
> I caught three in my cornfield.
> Uncle John had a bushel
> Uncle Tom had a peck
> Big Jed had a roastin' ear
> Tied around his neck.

By then there was a large mound of beans ready to be strung. Rennie threaded the two darning needles from a large ball of twine.

"How long ye want the strings?" she asked Sally.

"Twice around," came the answer. So Rennie caught the end of the thread between her fingers and thumb, brought it around her elbow, back to her hand, and again around and back. Someone cut it for her with a knife and handed the rest to someone else.

She called, "Come on, Johnnie. Time to quit playin' and go to work. Here, I have a string all ready for ye."

The young man placed his fiddle on a shelf on the wall, came and sat down by Rennie on the floor, picked up a handful of beans, ran the needle through one, pulled it along the twine to the end, wrapped the thread around the bean and tied it, and then put three or four more beans on the needle, criss-crossing them and stringing them like beads. All the other folks who had brought needles were doing the same. As the strings were finished, Sally took them and hung them from pegs Sol had driven into the logs along the side of the house. Here the beans would hang until they dried.

Although everyone was now working at the beans, the entertainment didn't stop. Some people told jokes, some stories. Many had heard the stories before but they listened and enjoyed them. These people had a knack for making a tale sound good no matter how many times it had been repeated. A few new riddles were told and passed on.

Johnnie was the life of the party. "I want to tell ye somethin' that happened to Uncle John, Big Jed, and Uncle Tom last year when a washout caught 'em over on Clear Creek and they had to stay about a week before they could get home. Well, you know how Old Regulars are about chicken and dumplin's. Uncle John can look at a big fat hen and guess into two how many dumplin's she'll make. Everone thinks when a preacher eats with ye, ye jest got to have chickens. If them poor hens had any sense, they'd take to the hills when they saw a preacher comin'.

"But let me get back to my story. First night they stayed with these folks, there was a big kettle of chicken and dumplin's, which looked pretty good fer dinner—but not so good when they come up cold fer supper. Next night they went to another house; this time it was fried chicken. The third night it was an old rooster so tough ye couldn't stick a fork in the gravy. By this time they had had their fill of chicken and craved somethin' else, but the waters hadn't gone down enough for 'em to come home. Big Jed said, 'Let's wait until we see the smoke comin' from the stovepipe, give 'em time to have supper on the table, then go in.' The folks asked 'em in to eat, but would ye believe it—it was another kettle of chicken, a hen that had that day got her head caught in the fence as she flew over and hung herself. 'It must have been so ordered,' the old woman said as she welcomed the three preachers to eat. 'Will one of you say grace, please?' she asked. Uncle John said:

> We have had them hot
> We have had them cold
> We have had them young
> We have had them old.

We have had them tender
We have had them tough—
But please, dear Lord,
Don't you think we've had enough?

The house rolled with laughter. The beans were finished; everyone began to get ready to go home. Some of the little children had gone to sleep, so their parents had to gather them up. Everyone was asking each other to go home with them, knowing they wouldn't go—but mountain manners demanded the invitation be given.

"I hate it I can't let ye have a dance," Sol told them, "but ye can tell I hain't got no room. I promise ye next year I'll have another room added onto my house, and ye can dance all night, ye can dance fer who laid the chunk."

"Don't look like that's all ye'll have added by next year," someone said. Sol laughed and Sally blushed.

Rennie and Johnnie were the first to leave. It was a really dark night. The path led under the trees; they couldn't have seen had they not had their lantern. Johnnie walked ahead, swinging the light around. As they crossed the creek, Rennie's foot slipped from a stepping stone, and if Johnnie hadn't caught her she would have fallen into the water.

As they stood there laughing, Rennie said, "Oh, Johnnie, ye're so good to me. Ye seem like my brother."

"Yer brother! I wish I wasn't yer cousin." Too late he saw he had said the wrong thing.

"Why, Johnnie. Why don't ye want to be kinfolks with me? Am I such a bother?"

"No, Rennie. I'm very glad to live with y'all. Ye jest don't understand. I sometimes forget ye're only a child, what with takin' care of Sarah Ellen, keepin' house, and doin' all this work. Please forget what I said. Someday, when ye're older, then you'll know what I meant."

"Ye're jest like Pa. That's what he allus tells me when I ask him somethin' about God er the Bible. 'Wait till ye're older, then ye'll understand.' How do ye know I won't understand if ye won't even tell me?"

"Ferget it. We're home now."

65

There was no light in the house. Johnnie went in with Rennie and held the lantern for her until she found the lamp. Johnnie lit it with a match from his pocket and without speaking went on through the room and out the back door.

Rennie whispered, "Be careful with that lantern out there in the barn. Don't set somethin' on fire."

"Oh, heck, ye're not my Ma."

Rennie couldn't for the life of her tell why he was so mad.

Oh, well, maybe she *was* too young to understand a lot of things. As she got in the bed beside Sarah Ellen she found that Pa had not taken the child's clothes off. She even had her shoes on. Very carefully, so as not to wake the baby, she removed them. Rennie whispered to herself, "I'll jest let her sleep in her clothes. It won't hurt nothin' this one time."

She lay there a while, thinking about the bean stringing. She decided that Johnnie must like Pa a whole lot. You just don't josh about your kinfolks like he did unless you think a lot of them. If you don't like them, you just don't have any truck with them.

"I wonder what he meant about not wantin' to be my cousin."

12 _____

By the middle of June, Rennie's garden began to come in. There had been green onions, lettuce, mustard, and radishes before then. She had gathered them when they were very small and had washed, drained, cut, and mixed them together in a large bowl. Just before they were to be served she killed them by pouring hot grease over them.

After the first of July, Rennie was kept busy for five or six weeks putting away the fruits and vegetables as they became ripe. There didn't seem to be enough hours in the days. She even begrudged having to rest on Sundays. While she was making kraut from the cabbage, some of the tomatoes became overripe; these she cooked, ran through a sifter, and made into tomato juice, which she canned. While working up the tomatoes, some of the cucumbers became overgrown; they were saved by salt pickling. The corn too was ready to be canned and salt pickled.

The early beans had gotten too full to can or dry for shucky beans. Rennie pulled the dead vines up, carried them to the shade of an old apple tree that stood in the yard, and, while she relaxed, pulled the pods from the vines. Later she would scatter them out on the floor of the loft. During the winter, when she had more time, she would shell them for next year's seeds and for soup beans.

Just behind the house was an old coalbank opening where the Slones had dug coal for their fires for many years. Here, just inside, John had built a small platform to hold the pickling barrels. Rennie had filled one with sauerkraut, one with beans, and one with roasting ears of corn packed in salt water. On top of each she had placed a large, clean-scrubbed creek rock wrapped in a clean cloth. On top of the rock she had put several pods of hot pepper to keep the gnats away. An old quilt made a covering. The air was cool, but when winter came the food would not freeze. A few weeks before, Johnnie had helped his uncle mend the hoops on the barrels and fill them with water to soak, so as to stop the leaks.

Rennie had worked very hard, and yet she had not filled all the glass jars, and there were still the apples to put away.

She would not try to make any jelly or apple butter because, for one thing, there was no money for sugar. The late patch of beans she could dry. The cushaws and pumpkins could be dried during the winter. A stick tied above the open fireplace could be strung with rings cut from cushaws and pumpkins and left to dry. She had almost a bushel of dried apples, and the onions had been pulled and were in the barn loft. Johnnie told her she had enough food to winter a large family, but still Rennie worried. She knew she didn't have as much put away as her mother had always had. "I want to have a plenty," she sighed.

It was during the first week of September and they were at the supper table when Johnnie said, "Rennie, do ye think ye could gravel us a mess of sweet 'taters? If so, I'll get out early and kill a few squirrels. I shore am par'sel to sweet 'taters and squirrel gravy."

"I 'spect so. I saw where the potato ridges was sort of breakin' in a place er two. Come to'mar I'll take a table fork and see what I can find."

"I'll also look some more fer a bee tree." said Johnnie. "I know there's one somewheres up on Dead Man's Ridge, but I hain't spotted it yet. The bees have been waterin' here in the creek jest above the house, and they allus fly in the direction of that ridge."

"Be careful, son." John cautioned. "Don't get too close to someone's still. They might mistake ye fer a law man."

"I think I know where everone around here is moon-shinin', and I allus stay clear. If I was to get too close they would fire a warnin' shot. I'd know when to make myself scarce."

So Johnnie had already gone to look for squirrels the next morning when Rennie got up to start the day's work. There had been a slight rain during the night, but now the sun was up, bright and warm. After getting all the morning chores out of the way, Rennie gathered the last of the peaches and was sitting on the porch peeling them when Miss Rose stopped by. When she saw the rag doll Sarah Ellen was playing with, she asked, "Where on earth did you get such a beautiful doll? I never saw anything like that in my life."

"That's one my mother made fer me," Rennie answered. "If ye think *that's* purty, ye jest ought to see the one she used fer a pattern—Grandma Kate's, the one she had with her when her mother left her with the Branhams."

"Do you mean your mother took the other doll apart and cut a pattern?"

"Oh no, Ma would never have done that. She jest looked at Grandma Kate's and made mine like it."

"That's remarkable. Your mother was really talented."

"Yes, often she would look at a dress pictured in a catalogue or magazine and cut one fer her er me."

"Rennie, you're always talking about your father's folks, the Slones, yet you never mention your mother's family. Who were they?"

"The Gents, from yound side of the hill."

"Are they still alive, your grandfather and grandmother?"

"'Spect so. Ma had three sisters and two brothers older than her. She got married before they did. I remember her sayin' they had to dance in the hog's trough at her weddin'. I guess she had a passel that was younger than she was, but she never talked any about 'em."

"But don't they ever come to see you and Sarah Ellen?"

"No. They never even came to see Ma when she lay a corpse."

"Did your father let them know?"

"If you mean did he send them word, no, but ye know how news travels here in the hills. They heard all right."

"There are some Gents that bring their kids to the Community Center. They must have more money than most folks around here—ride fine horses, have nice saddles, and they dress well. Could that be your folks?"

"'Spect so. Ma allus said her folks had a plenty. But if they didn't want to have any truck with her, she didn't want any with them. Ma had good learnin'; she was almost a school teacher. She was the one that learned Pa to read, after they was married. They must have been some trouble between Ma's folks and Pa, but no one ever told me what it was. If Ma had wanted me to know she would have told me."

"I'm sorry. Please forgive me. I shouldn't have asked so

much, anyway. It's none of my business. May I see that doll of your grandmother's?"

"Shore. Ye watch Sarah Ellen and I'll go fetch it. Can ye stay fer dinner? We're goin' to have squirrel gravy and sweet 'taters, if Johnnie ever gets back with them squirrels."

"Oh, he's already back. I saw him down by the spring as I rode up. I guess he was skinning them. Rennie, I get the impression that Johnnie doesn't like for me to be around."

"It's not that. It's jest because ye talk different from all of us. He likes ye. I guess while he lived around the minin' camps, so many people made fun of him, the way he talks. He jest feels so plagued. I tell him you hain't like that."

"Well, if you think it's all right. I haven't anything I have to do just now."

In a few moments Rennie brought back the doll.

"Guess it smells awful, bein' put away so long. If ye'll set here with the baby, I'll jest get these peaches on to cook and go gravel them sweet 'taters."

"I'll be more than glad. That way I'll feel like I'm earning my dinner—although watching Sarah Ellen is more fun than work."

When Rennie came back from the garden, Johnnie had the squirrels in a kettle on the stove. She washed the potatoes and put them in a pan in the oven to bake. While everything was cooking she put the cooked peaches in jars and sealed them, leaving out a bowlful to cool for their desert. When the squirrels became tender she thickened a small bowl of milk with flour and poured it into the broth, stirring it with a long-handled spoon. It wasn't long until everyone was around a table set with greenbeans, sliced tomatoes, cucumbers, onions, peppers, a pone of cornbread, and a pot of coffee.

"I can't get over it," Miss Rose said. "You mountain folks have so much to eat, yet you raise it all yourselves."

"Not the poor, starvin' people ye expected to find?" asked Johnnie.

"Not at all."

"It wasn't that way fer many of the folks that lived at the minin' camps in West Virginia. They bought old, dried-out loaf bread, condensed milk, and food in tin cans. Sometimes I'd get so hungry fer a good square meal I'd almost cry. Uncle John and Rennie couldn't run me off if they tried."

"No danger of that," John spoke up. "Ye more than pull yer weight around here."

"He shore has helped me out," said Rennie, "gettin' all the wood, carryin' water fer me to can and put away grub fer winter."

"Rennie's the one that's worked like a mule around here," Johnnie said.

"Well, let's quit this braggin' on each other and wash up the dishes. Then I'm goin' to rest all the rest of the day. I'm so full I don't think I could jump from a snake."

"I second that," was Miss Rose's comment.

For the next few weeks Johnnie and his uncle were busy saving fodder. They also cut some tops. It would take a lot to winter two mules and the milk cow. Every chance he got Johnnie went looking for the bee tree. He always came back with a few roots of ginseng. After he washed them, he strung them on a twine and hung them out on a nail behind the stove to dry. He had gathered some of the bright red berries and planned on planting them come spring. By the first of October the ginseng leaves had turned yellow and were much easier to find.

One morning at breakfast Johnnie asked his uncle, "Do ye care if I take both mules and go help old man Reece with his cane patch? He asked me yesterday. Said he couldn't pay any cash money but would give us a barrel of molasses."

"Shore, that would be jest fine. I wish I was able to go to work with ye. The girls and I may come over later to eat some 'lasses foam. But Johnnie ye don't have to work fer us this way."

"I'm part of the family, hain't I? I shore want to help all I can. I'd like to make some cash money. I've pondered and pondered and I can't come up with a thing. I know I'm not goin' back to the mines."

Rennie spoke up. "Miss Rose said they was going to start a mail route up Lonesome Holler. Someone would be hired fer the mail boy."

"I already looked into that. I'm too young. I talked with the man at the post office. Ye have to be twenty-one before ye can bid."

"What about Pa? Couldn't he bid and let you carry the mail?"

"Ye've forgotten my prison record," John said.

"Well, I guess that's out," Rennie said as she got up and began to clean off the table. "But somethin' will come up. Allus does. Wait and see."

Pa was true to his word. One afternoon he took the girls over to old man Reece's to the stir-off. A lot of other folks were already there, some to help, some only to eat 'lasses foam. The air was a mixture of odors: the delicious smell of hot molasses, smoke from burning wood. There were shouts urging the mules on, laughter, and calls for more cane as the hungry burrs crushed out more and more of the sweet juice. Yellow jackets buzzed everywhere. When one little boy slipped and fell into the stink hole, his mother took him to the creek and washed him off and hung his clothes on a limb to dry. While he ran around in his birthday suit, everyone was filling up their buckets and jars with molasses to take home. Rennie fetched some for supper and poured it over butter and hot pancakes, which Pa called flitters—a thin dough made from flour, salt, soda, and milk, fried in bacon grease. The rest she fried next morning for breakfast in a skillet with a little lard and a pinch of soda.

When Johnnie brought home his barrel of molasses he stored it in the smokehouse. He told Rennie, "They shore will make the sweet 'taters and cushaws taste better. But I still want some honey fer our biscuits and butter, come winter."

"Ye work too hard," she said.

"Not work when ye enjoy doin' it," he answered.

"I found the bee trees," he announced the next night at the kitchen table. "Get some empty lard cans ready and sharpen yer axe, Uncle John. I want ye to come with me. I found three trees. I know two is on our land, but one I'm not sure of. It could be on Old Kate's side. I don't want to tangle with her."

"Maybe she'd let ye cut it fer half," Rennie said.

"No, better not. The least ye have to do with that woman,

the best," John answered. "I'll go with ye to'mar. Hunt us up some old rags to burn, Rennie. If I had some gums made I would try to save the bees, but we'll leave enough honey fer them to survive the winter."

Rennie watched her father and Johnnie as they climbed the hill. The young man, carrying the axe and the lard cans, went ahead; Pa followed with a bundle of old rags. Every now and then Johnnie would stop and wait for John to catch up with him. They would rest a while and then go on. "Pa's getting old," Rennie said to herself. "Him and Johnnie thinks a lot of each other."

When John saw the first bee tree, he said to Johnnie, "I don't think it would pay us to cut this one. The weevils have got in it."

But the next one, an old hollow oak, looked fine. They put some of the rags in a hole at the base of the tree and set them afire.

"Don't want to use too much smoke; jest enough to quiet the bees. Don't want to ruin the taste of the honey."

When Rennie heard the ringing sound of the axe she knew they were cutting the tree.

"I never saw so much honey in one tree in my life," John said when he examined the fallen tree.

Johnnie had cut the tree in such a way that it fell on some small brush, thus breaking the crash. Hardly any of the honey was spilled. John cut the cone, filled with precious sweetness, careful not to get any that was filled with young bees.

"Some folks like bee bread. I don't. Do you?" he asked.

"Leave it fer the bees," Johnnie said.

"Poor Ma," John remembered. "She shore could eat more honey than anyone I ever saw. Once she ate about four pounds and then told Pa, 'It was kind of strong tastin'.'"

"I've heard my father laugh about that," Johnnie told him.

They almost filled one of the cans; the other can ended up about one-third full.

"This is mostly all lin honey, the best kind," John said. "Shore will be good with hot biscuits and butter."

"It's good like this," Johnnie answered as the warm golden liquid ran down his fingers. He licked it off. "Wonder what prim Miss Rose would say if she saw me now," he thought. "Wish Rennie could have come with us."

"We've got enough honey to do us. No use goin' to see about the other tree. May be on Old Kate's land, anyway," John said.

He's tired, Johnnie thought.

They cut two short, stout saplings and ran them through the rings on each side of the lard cans. Johnnie put the heavier one over his shoulder.

"We better get away quick. Them bees will soon be comin' to."

"We've left enough honey fer them to rebuild, if some fox don't find the tree first."

"I allus feel bad about robbin' poor bees that way, after they've worked so hard all summer storin' up fer winter," said Johnnie.

"Never thought of it that way," his uncle answered. "Jest thought it was God's way of feedin' us."

Every day Johnnie went to the mountains he brought back several bushels of black walnuts. Rennie helped him remove the soft outside layers of hulls, staining her fingers dark brown.

"Ma used walnut hulls to make brown dye," Rennie told Johnnie.

"I can see why," he said, trying to wash his hands clean.

"Wash the dishes a time er two and ye'll get rid of it," she laughed.

"No thank ye. I'll jest let it wear off by itself."

Pa watched Sarah Ellen so Rennie could go with Johnnie to gather chestnuts and hickory nuts. She would have liked to ask Miss Rose, but knowing how Johnnie felt, she didn't mention it.

"Would love to have some hazelnuts and chickepins, but hain't run across any yet."

"Used to be a chickepin tree in the yard, over to yer folks' old house."

"Yeah, I know. I looked for it. Must have blowed down."

"'Spect so, but we've got more nuts now than we need."

"Remember, we didn't raise very much popcorn this year.

Them nuts will be awful good to crack and eat while settin' around the fire this winter. And what about putting some in the molasses when we make stiff jacks?"

"Hadn't thought of that. Let's get a plenty."

Day by day Johnnie's strings of ginseng got longer and longer. "Hope I can get enough to buy me some new shoes and a bow fer my fiddle."

Rennie would stand and admire the rows and rows of filled glass jars in the small closet beside the chimney with the pride of an artist. Red beets, tomatoes, yellow corn, green beans, white kraut, and pink peaches. She saw them as a job well done.

"Agin' we get our 'taters dug, we'll have all the grub we need," she told Johnnie.

"Not quite. We still hain't got no hog meat. Shucky beans hain't no good without hog meat. I think there's a gang of wild pigs over on the Nealy side of the Hollybush ridge. Ye remember them caves, jest above that first flat, Uncle John?"

"'Spect so. I used to traipsey these hills when I was young, jest as you do now."

"Well, I believe some old sow has birthed her litter there. They's about five, maybe six, purty good sized shoats, and I'm aimin' to get me one er two. They should be gettin' kind of fat by now on mast."

"Ye make shore they don't have any markin' on their ears. If ye should kill another man's pigs he'd never fergive ye. If they're weaned from their mother without bein' marked, then they're counted as wild pigs."

"I'll make shore. I'll go layway them and watch. I'd like to catch one alive so as we could fatten it with corn. Make the meat taste a lot better."

Next morning found Johnnie in a tree just above the opening of the small cave. As light began to break over the hilltops, he heard a grunting and squalling. Looking down, he saw three pigs—about sixty or seventy pounds each, he guessed—poking their snouts out of the cave. They turned their heads first one way and then the other, sniffing the air. Then, with a squall, they rushed down the hill.

Johnnie had seen that there were no markings on their

ears. Now he still had to make sure there was no mother pig with them. He sat still. Soon two more pigs came rushing out and took out after the first. He had seen enough.

Next day Johnnie and his uncle repaired the old log pig pen.

"Countin' yer chickens before they're hatched, hain't ye?" Rennie teased.

"No, countin' my pig before it's caught. But I'll catch it. Ye jest wait and see."

"Ye must be very careful, son. A pig can snap a man's leg er arm off with them tush and can do almost as much damage with its hooves."

"I'll take care."

Johnnie had watched the pigs for several days, keeping well out of their sight, letting them get used to his smell. Just below their bedding place were several chestnut trees; here they stopped each morning, after eating all they could find. Then they scattered on around the mountain, foraging as they went, until late each evening, when they would visit these same trees again, gathering the few nuts that had fallen during the day. It was their last stop before bedding down for the night in the cave.

Johnnie had taken the mule and sled as far as he could along the old haul road and had left them there and gone on. He climbed the tallest chestnut tree and shook down a lot of nuts. He made a large loop on a rope, placed it among the fallen nuts, tied the other end around a good-sized sapling, and hid behind a tree to wait. It wasn't long until the pigs came.

At first he thought they were going to pass up his trap. But then one came over and with a grunt and a squeal began chomping the nuts. Johnnie watched carefully. When the pig placed both its front feet inside the rope loop, quick as a wink, Johnnie gave a jerk. The squealing pig was caught around the middle. The hours and hours of playing cowboy with the other boys around the mining camps in West Virginia now paid off. The pig squealed and jerked so that Johnnie feared it would kill itself, but after an hour or so it became weaker and weaker until there was no fight left in it. He quickly tied its legs together and, making a muzzle with the rope, pulled it over its mouth. He was almost as tired as the pig when he finally got it in the sled and turned toward home.

Rennie and Sarah Ellen were asleep when he arrived, but Uncle John was up. With a lantern, he helped Johnnie get the prisoner in the pen. There the pig lay, full of fear and fright, only his eyes showing any life. John reached through a crack between the logs and cut the ropes.

"I hate to spoil a good plow rope, but it can't be helped. I'll splice it back. I'm proud of ye, son."

"I'm not proud. I wish there was some way to live without takin' the life and freedom from somethin' else."

"The Good Book tells us that man was given domenion over animals, and was not Peter told to slay and eat?"

"I still don't like it, but come the first cold spell and I'll go back and kill another. You have the water hot while I'm gone. I'll tell Big Jed about the others; 'spect he might want 'em. Two will be enough fer us."

"Yeah, no use takin' more than we need."

13

By her first birthday Sarah Ellen could almost walk by herself. She pulled herself up and began walking around chairs and things. Rennie was afraid that she would fall and get hurt.

Johnnie said, "Let her alone. A few bumps won't hurt her. Ye can't protect her all her life. Ye're worse than an old hen with one chick."

Johnnie was grouchy these days. He still hadn't found any work. The cold nights had forced him to move from the barn into the room up in the loft. He had brought his fiddle with him and hid it in the little trunk under the bed, but he wouldn't play it even when Uncle John was away from home.

Mr. Spradlow, the brought-on man who rented Johnnie's folks' place, had gone back up North for the winter. Before he left he brought Johnnie the key to the door, asking him to watch out for his belongings and giving him permission to go in and stay whenever he liked.

One day Johnnie, Rennie, and Sarah Ellen went over. It was strange and scary going into a stranger's house with him not there. There were shelves and shelves of books. Rennie would have liked to read them all. An old-fashioned talking machine stood in one corner.

"Do ye know how to play this thing?" Rennie asked.

"Yeah, the bank boss at the mines where Pa worked in West Virginia had one. One day his son asked a lot of us kids to come in and hear it. Here, I'll show ye how it works."

He cranked up the handle, opened the lid and put on one of the few records he found on a shelf. When the music started and a voice began to sing, Sarah Ellen looked around to see where the person was. Finding no one there, she reached for Rennie and hid her face in her sister's dress.

"What kind of music is that?" Rennie wanted to know.

"I think it's a piano. I'm not shore."

"Well, shut it off. I don't like it anymore than Sarah Ellen. I don't see how anyone could enjoy that."

"Yeah, I know. Strange people have strange ways."

Rennie went into the kitchen. What an array of pots and pans! And a cabinet full of plates and bowls, and a drawer full of forks, spoons, and gadgets.

"Why would one person want so many dishes? There's enough here to feed a workin'."

Johnnie built a fire in the grate. They ate the lunch Rennie had brought at the pretty little table with the bright, flowered oilcloth cover.

"This is fun," Rennie said, "but to'mar we must dig the rest of the 'taters."

"And after that I must go try to find me some work. I need some cash money. I hear there was a man over on Irishman Creek wantin' men to help make staves. Guess I'll mosey over that way and see. I ought to go back and see my folks before winter sets in."

"We better be gettin' back. Time we rest a while, it will be supper-gettin' time. Be dark before ye know it."

They stopped on top of the hill. Sarah Ellen had gone to sleep. They stood there looking over the mountains. As far as the eye could see the rolling hills went on and on until they met and blended with the blue sky.

"I don't guess there's a place in the whole world as purty as this. I've never seen any other places, but they jest can't be too many that are this purty.

"Well, I guess home is best, no matter where home is."

"Johnnie, it sure was a lucky day fer us, when you became a part of this family. Ye shore have helped us out a lot."

"I've done no more than my duty. I don't see you laying down on yer job either."

"Oh, let's quit braggin' on each other before we get stuck-up on ourselves. Let's go home."

The next few days were very busy ones. The sweet potatoes were dug and poured out on the floor of the porch to dry. Later they were wrapped in paper and put into barrels. The Irish potatoes were buried in holes dug in the garden, covered first with dry grass, then with a mound of earth, and then given a roof of split boards to keep out the snow and rain.

Johnnie waited until Uncle John returned home from one of his many trips before he went to see about a job at the stave mill. He took a change of clothes with him in the saddle bags. "If I'm not back in a week, ye'll know I've found work. We still must get in wood and coal fer winter."

"It's not yer place to do all the work," Uncle John told him.

"Well, I eat and sleep here, same as anyone else. Leastways, I'm more able than you are. If I get a job er not, I'll see there's enough coal and wood fer winter."

Three days later Johnnie was back. Miss Rose had stopped by to leave Rennie some more books and magazines. Now that the garden had been taken care of, Rennie found a lot of time on her hands. With justified pride she showed Miss

Rose all the food she had canned, dried, and put away—the nuts, and apples for snacks.

"We shore have got a plenty. The only thing that worries me is milk. There won't be any milk fer Sarah Ellen. Our cow will soon be dry till she drops a calf in February. Ye know, they used to tell us that cows pawed up the baby calves from out of the ground. How silly! None of us children believed it, but we never let on that we knowed better."

"Won't some of your neighbors let you have milk for Sarah Ellen?"

"Yeah, Aunt Nance has two cows. I thought I would offer to milk fer her this winter in return fer some milk. I know she's gettin' old and has a hard time gettin' around."

When Johnnie saw Miss Rose on the porch with Rennie he went the long way around to put his mule up. Rennie knew he had not gotten the job.

Rennie asked Miss Rose to stay for supper.

"I really would like to have supper with you, for that food at the Community Center leaves a lot to be desired and you have such delicious meals, but I know that Johnnie goes out of his way to avoid me. I don't like to put him in an awkward position."

"Oh, his bark is worse than his bite. He's disappointed because he can't find work. He needs some cash money."

While they were at the table eating fried potatoes, canned greenbeans, homemade sausage, apple butter sweetened with molasses, and corn bread, Miss Rose told Johnnie, "They're looking for someone to haul coal for the school. Would you like that job? You have two mules."

"No, I don't want to work for them brought-on people."

"Their money's jest like anyone else's," said John.

"Yeah, but they don't treat ye the same. Allus lookin' down on us, as if we was trash."

"I'm a brought-on person, as you call us, am I not?" Miss Rose asked.

"You said it, not me," Johnnie snapped.

"Be careful, son," John warned. "I don't want anyone insulted at my table."

"Sarry." Johnnie pushed his chair back and stomped upstairs.

At the mouth of Lonesome Holler, where it entered Caney Creek, stood the Hall's Grocery Store, an old log house. The front was the store; a small lean-to at the back was the living quarters, where Long Bill lived. Over the store was the post office of High Rock, entered through a boxed-in stairway in one end of the store. Long Bill was both the grocer and the postmaster. The mail was delivered only twice a week, Tuesday and Friday. Groceries were brought in once a month from Paintsville. Long Bill picked them up at the Wayland depot. Hall's Grocery sold a lot more than groceries: hardware, nails, ploughshares, hoes, dry goods, oilcloths to cover tables, sewing material, lace, buttons, needles, thimbles . . . you name it, he had it. If you couldn't make or grow yourself what you had to have, then you bought it at Hall's. A large barrel of salty crackers, a showcase full of stick candy, strings of rock candy, Long Tom chewing gum. The scents of ginger and other spices blended with the smell of leather saddles and shoes.

Long Bill not only ran the post office; he bought and shipped out hides—horse, cow, possum, mink, fox—and dried roots— ginseng, yellowroot, puccoon, snake root, sassafras. The people from surrounding hollows could bring their surplus eggs and butter and exchange them for other things. Once a week someone from the Community Center came and picked up the eggs and butter, paying Long Bill in cash.

The morning Johnnie brought his ginseng to Long Bill's, Old Kate was there, bringing some of the same roots. Johnnie had run across her several times when he was out sangin', but he had tried to avoid letting her see him. This morning he passed Old Kate as she came out the front door. She had a large coffee sack full of groceries on her back and a frown on her face that would have turned a churnful of buttermilk, Johnnie thought.

Long Bill had a puzzled look on his face. "I can't understand it," he said.

"What?" Johnnie asked.

"Ah, never mind. What do ye want?"

"I have some 'sang roots to sell ye."

"All right, pour 'em here on the scales and let's see. Well. Looks like there's a little over three pounds. Ye shore have been busy. Three pounds and two ounces. Seem about right to you?"

"Yeah, that's what I guessed, give er take a few ounces."

"That will come to two dollars and twenty-one cents. Want cash money er goods?"

"Give me two dollars. I want to order me a new fiddle bow from the Sears Roebuck catalogue. And give me twenty cents' worth of that silk ribbon fer a hair bow for Rennie. Get me a peppermint stick for Sarah Ellen fer the other penny."

"What color ribbon?"

"Green. That will look purty in her reddish-brown hair."

Long Bill had Old Kate's ginseng roots in a pile on the counter. He poured them into another pile nearby. He kept looking at them.

"Johnnie, which one of these piles do ye think should weigh the most?"

"About the same, I guess. What I brought in might be a few ounces more."

"That's what I thought. I've been weighin' roots all my life and I thought I could prit nigh guess how much there was, but this stuff Old Kate jest sold me beats all get out. It comes to over four pounds. Thought my scales had torn up on me."

"It looks dry enough," Johnnie said.

Long Bill took out his knife and cut into one of the dried roots, dropped it, and tried another.

"Well, I'll be dad-burned. Look what that old witch has done. She's filled these roots full of sprigs er iron tacks. No wonder they weighed so much. She pushed the sprigs into the roots when they was green, and then when they dried up, ye couldn't see 'em."

"Well, I never in all my life," laughed Johnnie. "What are ye goin' to do?"

"I'm jest goin' to ship 'em along with all the rest. If she can fool me, I can fool them folks off yonder that buy these roots. That old coot. What a scream." As Johnnie was leaving, Long Bill called, "Say, Johnnie, a teacher from down at the grammar school said fer me to pass the word along that he was goin' to have a pie supper Saturday night fer all the children that go to the Lonesome Holler School. Pass the word along. You and Rennie might want to come."

"Shore will, and thanks, Long Bill."

"Don't mention it. And no use to ask ye not to tell about the spiked ginseng. Too good a story, and the laugh's all on me."

Again Miss Rose was having dinner with Rennie and Sarah Ellen.

"I eat here so often I feel as if I should pay you board," she said.

"We're much pleased to have ye," Rennie assured her.

"What is a pie supper?" asked Miss Rose. "I don't like to appear dumb, but I never heard of a pie supper."

"A pie supper is where any girl er woman that wants to fixes a box of grub—two of each thing, ye know, two pieces of chicken, two of pie, and whatever—and she puts them in a purty box all fancied up and takes it to the school on the given night. The boys and men bid on them and whoever's box they get, they eat with the girl what fixed the box. It's supposed to be kept a secret whose box is whose, but the girl allus lets her boyfriend know which is hers. And there's allus a lot of other fun—ye know, music, games, and jokes. The money is used to buy things fer the school. This time it's a Christmas party fer the kids."

"I thought the Community Center sent presents to all the schools."

"They do send some things, and we're thankful to 'em fer what they send, but it's not all that much. And anyway, we had pie suppers long before there was a Community Center."

"How much do these boxes usually cost?"

"Not much, around a quarter. Our folks don't have much cash money. Unless a girl has two boys both wantin' to be with her—then it's fun. They keep tryin' to outbid each other. It's a strict rule that ye must share ye box with the one that finally buys it."

"Sounds like fun."

"Why don't ye fix a box and come?"

"Would I be welcome?"

"Are you kiddin'? Ye know everyone would be pleased fer ye to be there. And ever box means that much more money to buy things fer the children. That's all the Christmas some of 'em have."

Again Pa stayed with Sarah Ellen so Rennie could go. Johnnie took his fiddle and the lantern. Rennie filled her shoebox with goodies and tied it with a piece of the green silk ribbon. There was already a crowd of folks gathered; some of the men had built a fire in the school yard. There was just enough nip in the air to need some heat. Inside, the women and children were gathered around the old pot-bellied stove. Lighted lanterns hung from the rafters.

"I see old man Bob Tut is here, and I bet he's drunk as usual. They say he's already lookin' fer a third wife," Johnnie told Rennie.

"Why, Aunt Liz hain't been dead much over a month, and who would have him, what with them twelve children of his'n?" Rennie answered.

"Well, if I see him makin' sheep's eyes at you, I'll bust him one," Johnnie teased.

Rennie placed her box on the desk with a stack of others and went to look for Miss Rose. She found her with a group of older women. Rennie was pleased to see they were talking very freely with her. Most of them knew her because she had visited them as a nurse at one time or another.

Soon Mr. Slone, the teacher, walked up behind his desk and rang the small school bell. All the men came in and laughingly sat in the much-too-small seats. As he held up each box Mr. Slone made some funny comment about it, and then the bidding started. He began by asking a quarter. When a husband bid for his own wife's box, no one bid against him, but when the box was a young girl's the price would sometimes go up, five cents at a time. A few boxes brought fifty cents.

When he came to Rennie's, he said, "Now here, boys, is a very nice one. Don't guess it means anythin' but the ribbon on the box is jest like the one in a certain young girl's hair. What am I bid?"

"Twenty-five cents," said Johnnie.

"Thirty," came from the back of the room. All heads turned as Joe Smith raised his hand. Johnnie looked at Rennie. Her face was as red as poor Joe's.

"Okay?" Johnnie asked quietly, and Rennie nodded yes.

Miss Rose's box was last. "Here's one looks awful good to me. Heavy too. Come on, men, there's a lot of ye that don't have a box. What am I bid?"

"Fifty cents." It was old man Bob. He pulled himself up, eyes red and blurry, tobacco juice dribbling from his mouth. Miss Rose stifled a cry by placing her hand over her mouth.

"Sixty," shouted Johnnie.

"Seventy-five." A large squirt of tobacco juice hit the floor.

"One dollar." Everyone gasped when Johnnie spoke.

"One dollar and a half."

"Two dollars."

Rennie knew that was all Johnnie had.

"Take it," Bob answered, and sat down.

Everyone paired off and began eating. Miss Rose and Johnnie sat at the desk behind Rennie and Joe. After everyone had finished, Johnnie played some on his fiddle. Some of the people joined in his songs.

As they were going out the door, Miss Rose whispered to Rennie. "Tell Johnnie I thank him very much."

On their way home Rennie said, "I didn't think ye liked Miss Rose."

"I don't," Johnnie said, "But I jest couldn't see her havin' to share a box with that dirty old widd'er."

"But that was the money ye'd saved fer yer new shoes and yer fiddle bow."

"I know. But Grandpa got a whole lot of music from that old home-made bow of his'n, and I don't 'spect I would care much fer a store-bought one, anyhow."

14 _____

The long winter days found Johnnie more restless than ever. Now that it was too cold to stay in the barn he couldn't play his fiddle. One day he came home from Long Bill's store with a large paper box. He cut a big square from one side and drew a fox-and-goose game chart. With two red grains of corn for foxes and twenty-two white for geese, he and Rennie played for hours. Every night after she had washed the supper dishes and cleaned the table they would place the board between them, and while Pa read his Bible they would enjoy their game. Johnnie was better with foxes, but Rennie always won if she had the geese.

One night Rennie was in a thoughtful mood. "I seem to have a dread on me. I jest know that somethin' dreadful is goin' to happen. Everthin' has jest been going too good. What with catchin' the pigs, findin' the bee tree, my garden growin' so good, none of us being sick . . . we have jest been havin' too good a'luck."

"God is bein' good to us," Pa said.

Johnnie added, "And we've all worked hard. Everbody could have plenty if they were willin' to work hard."

"God helps those that help themselves." John returned to his Bible.

"I still think everthin' has jest been goin' too good," Rennie sighed.

"Well, not everthin'," Johnnie smiled. "I remember a few burnt pones of cornbread and two er three kettles of scorched beans. And it shore was not good luck fer that old possum to kill over half yer fryin' chickens before I caught him."

"Yeah, and what about the sled turnin' over with yer last load of pumpkins and cushaws jest as soon as ye come around the high point behind the barn? I swar', I didn't know what had happened—them things come bouncing down the hill. I thought it was rainin' pumpkins," Rennie laughed.

"Well ye could say it was good luck that it was a load of the puny ones, the last ones on the vine that didn't have time to get full-grown. I was jest bringin' 'em in to feed the cow and pig."

Johnnie was glad he had gotten Rennie to laugh. He didn't

want to admit to her that for some unknown reason he too had been lonesome that night. "Guess I should go home and see how my folks are," he thought, though he knew he felt more at home where he was needed.

The next day Rennie had just hung her last batch of clothes on the line to dry and had returned to empty the water from the washtubs when she happened to look down the road and see someone coming, riding fast. It was a stranger on a strange horse. Something was wrong, but she knew he wasn't stopping at their gate when he didn't slow down. She watched as he turned in at Aunt Nance's and saw the old woman come out to the gate as he dismounted. It was too far away to hear what he said, but Aunt Nance's screams were loud.

"Oh no! No! God have mercy on me, help me, oh Lord."

Rennie didn't know what to do. Johnnie and Pa were both gone, Sarah Ellen was asleep; she couldn't leave home. She ran to the bell rope and began ringing it. Maybe some neighbor would hear.

"Okay, where are ye, Johnnie, when ye're needed? Why hain't ye at home now? What must I do? Aunt Nance needs someone with her. What must I do?" She heard Sarah Ellen crying. The bell had awakened her, but Rennie didn't stop ringing. She saw Old Kate come out in her yard, turn and go back inside. "A fine neighbor *you* are," Rennie thought. She could still hear Aunt Nance, even over the noise of the bell. It was only a little while—but it seemed like hours to Rennie—before men and women began to respond to the bell from up and down Lonesome Holler. They came, some with little children, some walking, others on mules. In no time at all a large crowd was gathered at Aunt Nance's. Rennie didn't know when the stranger left. One neighbor woman stopped on her way home to tell Rennie what had happened.

"It was their oldest girl Susan's man and boy. Both got mashed up in the mines last night."

"Joel hain't much older than me! We went to school together."

"Yeah, I know, but he was helpin' his Pa load coal, over at Harlan. I would have stayed with Aunt Nance," the neighbor went on, "but they's a plenty with her, and I recollect I had a kettle of beans on cookin' I had to get back to before they burned up and set the house on fire."

That evening Rennie took an apple pie and some baked sweet potatoes to Aunt Nance's. The house was full of people, and everyone had brought food. Rennie placed hers on the already loaded table and went to sit on the side of the bed where her aunt lay. She took the older woman's hand.

"Aunt Nance, ye must bear up. Susan and her young'ns are goin' to need ye."

Next day Johnnie helped some other men dig the graves while Pa and Big Jed took two wagons and went for the bodies. It was almost dark when they passed. Rennie watched. The two coffins were in Pa's wagon. Susan was on the seat with Pa, holding a small child in her lap and very pregnant with another. In Big Jed's wagon five or six more children rode on quilts in the back, and two almost grown girls rode in the seat. Had to be ten or twelve children in all.

It was a week after the funeral that Susan asked Pa and Johnnie to go to Harlan to get her house plunder. There was nothing else for her to do but move in with Aunt Nance. Again Big Jed went with them. Late next day they returned with empty wagons.

"The bank boss had nailed up the house," Johnnie explained, "sayin' he was holdin' everthin' in payment fer what Susan's husband owed the company store. I begged him to let me go in and get the childern's clothes, but he said no, that the debt at the store was much more than what the stuff would bring. 'I have lost money on them,' the boss said. 'They have lost their lives. Don't that mean anythin' to ye?' I said. That man has a bank full of money, but he shore don't have a heart of gold," Johnnie told Rennie.

John had talked with the man in charge of the mines. There was nothing he could do. "What about insurance? Won't Susan get a pension?"

"No, she can't get anythin'. Ye see, her husband had taken the boy with him to help him load coal. The boy was under age. 'We didn't know he had his son with him; that broke the contract. The company doesn't owe them anythin'.'"

Johnnie had never seen his uncle so angry.

"I would hate to have to pay *your* debt when ye come to die."

"I'm only following orders," the boss said.

"So am I. So am I. But when the real Judgment Day comes, my Boss will be on the right side."

When everyone up and down Lonesome Holler heard, they helped with what they could. Miss Rose brought boxes of used clothes from the Community Center. Long Bill give all the children new shoes from his store.

Not long after, on a cold winter night just after Christmas, Rennie heard someone on the porch.

"It's us, Joan and Jane. Ma took bad. She's havin' her baby. Could Uncle John go after someone quick?"

Rennie opened the door. The girls were covered with snow, and were very cold and frightened.

"Pa's gone. The only granny-woman lives way over on Brush Creek. Last I heard she had broke her leg and has been laid up all winter."

"What about yer friend Miss Rose?" Johnnie called from his room in the loft, "She's a nurse. Think she could catch a baby?"

"Would ye go fetch her?"

"Already got my shoes on. You fix the lantern while I go saddle the mule."

In less than two hours Rennie heard the mules as Johnnie and Miss Rose passed the house. In a little while he returned with the other children.

"Aunt Nance said could ye bed these young'ns down somewheres. She didn't want 'em there at the house."

"How did ye ever get 'em all here by yerself?"

"Well, I guess we did more sleddin' than walkin'. Had to stop ever little while to count 'em; 'fraid I might lose one."

Johnnie was trying to joke with the children; he saw how frightened they were. "All you boys can sleep up in the loft with me. Rennie, you take the baby in with you and Sarah Ellen. Hank can sleep with Joan and Jane in Uncle John's bed. Be kind of scrouged, but it's only fer a night."

Next morning Rennie was up early. She peeled and sliced a large bowl of potatoes while the stove got hot. She fried two skillets of bacon, and after taking the meat out of one skillet of grease she poured in the potatoes. Into the other she poured a small cup of flour and stirred it with a large spoon. When the flour turned brown she added a quart of water. She wished she had milk, but water-gravy was better than no gravy at all.

When the potatoes, meat, and gravy were on the table, she put a few spoons of grease in another pan and filled it halfway with molasses. When the mixture began to boil, she put in a pinch of baking soda, which changed the thick molasses to a bright yellow foam and filled the room with fragrance. All the while a large pone of cornbread was baking in the oven.

Soon they all were around the table. "I don't know if I have enough plates to go round," Rennie commented. "Can two of ye eat from a platter? I'll feed Sarah Ellen from my plate. Joan, you let yer little brother eat with you."

"Jest give me a bowl er anythin'," said Johnnie. "I'm so hungry I could eat from the pot."

"I want us all to eat at one time. I don't like fer anyone to have to wait."

After breakfast, while the three girls washed the dishes, Johnnie built a large fire in the grate and kept the younger children amused by doing tricks with a long string: Job's Coffin, Cat's Paw, Jacob's Ladder, Baby in a Cradle. He formed each pattern by crossing and releasing the string from his fingers and sometimes by using his teeth. The young kids watched in awe. The older ones asked to be taught how it was done.

It was almost ten o'clock before Rennie heard Aunt Nance's old dinner bell. She ran to the door and listened. There was no break in the ringing. That meant the baby was born and mother and baby were both all right. If either had died or something had gone wrong, the bell would have been rung a few times, there would have been a pause, and then the bell would have been rung again.

"Okay, childern, bundle up. We're taking ye home. The old Hoot Owl has brung yer mother another baby. Ye have a new brother er sister."

All the children were eager to go except Hank, a three-year-old who now had two younger ones in his family.

"I don't want to go home. Let me stay here with Johnnie and eat 'lasses.'"

Everyone laughed.

"Why don't ye let us jest keep him fer a few days? He won't be much trouble, and ye're goin' to have yer hands full until your Ma's up and around," Rennie said.

"All right, he can stay if Ma don't care. If'n she wants us to come back and get him, we will."

Hank and Sarah Ellen got along together so well it led Rennie to say, "It's a caution to see how Hank takes care of her, and him not much more than a baby himself."

Susan named the new baby Rose, after the nurse. She told Rennie, "It shore was a good day fer all of us when Miss Rose come to the hills. When Johnnie brung her in I thought to myself, 'Why she hain't nothin' but a child herself. How can she help me any?' But law' me, child, she shore knows what she's doin' when it comes to catchin' babies. Never had an easier time with none of the rest. I shore think a lot of Miss Rose. Hope little Rose grows up to be jest like her."

15 _____

For the next two weeks Hank refused to go home. Each day Joan or Jane would come for him, but he would put up such a squall that they'd just go back home without him.

"Don't ye want to see yer new sister?" they'd ask.

Hank would stomp his foot and yell, "No, I don't see no cause fer another sister. I got too many, anyhow."

"Hank, her stay with me," Sarah Ellen would beg. "Hank, her my sister." And everyone would laugh and just give in to the two little bosses.

"He's no extra trouble," Rennie would say. "Ye wouldn't

believe how he looks out fer her, and him not much older than she is."

It wasn't long before Susan was up and around, able to stir about the house, so she came herself to get Hank. When Hank saw her coming he grabbed Sarah Ellen's hand and they ran up the ladder to the loft, where Johnnie had his bed. They crawled under the bed back next to the wall.

"I don't know what I'm goin' to do with that young'n. He won't mind me to a word that I say." Susan was out of breath from her first walk since the birth of little Rose. She dropped down into a chair and fanned her face with her bonnet, took off her coat, and stuck her feet toward the fire. "I don't know if I'm too hot to be cold er too cold to be hot."

Rennie wanted to laugh. The two little kids had sure looked funny going up the ladder, as surefooted as two little goats. "He's no trouble. We keep tellin' y'all. It's a caution to see how he takes care of Sarah Ellen. I never seed two kids take to one another like them two."

"But I don't like to stay away from any of my young'ns." Tears gathered in Susan's eyes. "Makes no never mind how many ye have, ye hain't got nary a one to spare." She wiped her eyes with the bottom of her apron. "It's all the same to their mother. He's all the man child that I've got now since Joel got mashed up in the coal mines."

"I'll see what I can do. Ye're still too weak to try and go up them steps to the loft. I know they're under the bed up there," said Rennie.

"Yeah, 'spect so. I don't seem to be gainin' my strength like I should," Susan said. "Allus before I was same as new by this time. Why, when my first one was born I was up cookin' supper the same day. And when Joan was born I hoed out a patch of cabbages next day. Guess I am gettin' old," Susan said with a soft laugh.

"How old are ye, if ye don't mind tellin'?" Rennie asked.

"Well, I don't just rightly know. Ma didn't have nary Bible in which to write down our bornin' days, but I think I'll be forty-two this next fodder pullin' time. Ma said she recollected that Pa was pullin' fodder when she took, and she had to ring him out of the corn field."

"It's too cold on them kids to stay up there in the loft. I'll go and see if I can get 'em to come down." Rennie went scrambling up the ladder. When she saw them huddled up against the wall under Johnnie's bed, she didn't know whether to laugh or cry.

"Hank, if I give ye a big jar of molasses to take with ye, will ye go home with yer mother?" pleaded Rennie.

"A real big jar like the one ye put milk in?" he asked.

"Yeah, a real big half-gallon jar like the one I put milk in."

"And can I come back when I eat it all up?"

Rennie had to laugh. "It'll soon be summertime, and you and Sarah Ellen can play together all day long."

"Will ye make Ma say that she won't whip me if I come down?"

"Yes, son, I won't say a mean word to ye," Susan called up, "and ye can come back and play with Sarah Ellen, and she can come up to our house and play with ye any time."

Rennie took a large glass jar from the side table and went to the smoke house. Inside, on a long bench, was a large barrel lying on its side. From a hole in the side protruded a round peg wrapped in a cloth covered with beeswax. With a twist, a tug, and a pull, she removed the peg from the bung-hole and rolled the barrel over on its side until a small trickle of molasses ran out. Then she held the lip of the jar under the bunghole and rolled the barrel just far enough for the thick sweet liquid to slowly fill the jar. Rolling the barrel back, she closed the hole with the peg, put the lid on the jar, and licked the spilled molasses from her fingers as she went back to the house.

Even with the cherished prize, Hank still had tears in his eyes and Sarah Ellen was bawling like a calf.

Supper had been late that night. When Rennie came into the big room she saw that Pa had put a lot of coal in the grate and had a nice roaring fire going, she knew he was thinking about sitting up for a spell and reading his Bible.

"I can get caught up with some of those socks of Pa's that I've been puttin' off fer quite a spell," she thought. "They're so near worn out they're past darnin' any longer—jest won't hold the yarn. I jest as well unravel the feet and knit back new ones. Some are too fer gone to even do that. Oh, I know what I'll do. I'll jest get rid of the feet of the worst ones and unravel the tops and make Hank a pair. That would shore pleasure him. But all of Pa's socks are such a dull gray. I wish they had been dyed a purty bright color. Pa never will wear anythin' but gray, sayin' it's sinful to wear anythin' bright. If that's so, then why did God make so many purty birds, butterflies, and flowers?"

A loud thump at the kitchen door interrupted her thoughts.

"Why in the dickens did ye fasten me out? It's cold out here, and this load ain't gettin' any lighter," Johnnie yelled.

"I didn't know ye were outside," Rennie began to explain as she lifted the latch and turned the wooden button at the top of the door.

A blast of cold air came in as Johnnie entered the kitchen. He was carrying a long white sack so full that it stuck straight out across his shoulders and had him almost bent over double.

"What in the world do ye have there? Did ye rob a pack peddler?"

"I told ye at the supper table that I was goin' to the barn and shuck the corn that we've been pitchin' back fer the seed corn." All year, every time anyone used any of the corn that was stored in the barn loft, as they shucked it, whether to feed the stock or to take to the mill to be ground into meal for bread, they pitched the largest and whitest ears in a corner to keep for the next year's seed.

"But to'mar isn't Friday, and we went to the mill last week."

"No, this is seed corn, and get out of my way so I can get this off my back. Ye never hear a word that I say to ye. Allus got a book in yer hand and yer head in the air. Totin' this on my back has begun to make me feel like a mule."

"And ye've begun to look like one, too," Rennie laughed. Johnnie went on into the big room and slid the bag of corn down in front of the fire, where John sat reading his Bible, tilted back in a chair beside of the chimney so the firelight fell on the book.

Rennie closed the kitchen door, checked the stove to make

sure there was no fire left, and checked to see if both water buckets were full. She reminded herself that she must bring one of the buckets of water and set it in front of the fire before going to bed or she might have to thaw it out next morning by heating the poker red hot and sticking it in the water, and breakfast would be late. Pa would grumble and Johnnie would tease.

When Rennie returned to the big room, she took a quilt from the quilt shelf and spread it out on the floor. Johnnie picked up the sack of corn, but before he could empty it, John spoke up.

"Take care! Take care! Don't ye know ye must never shell corn on the floor if ye're goin' to use it fer seed corn? It's bad luck. Ye must allus shell it into a basket. The bigger the basket, the more corn ye'll gather come gatherin' time." Johnnie mumbled something that sounded like a curse word.

"There's a two-bushel basket up in the loft, full of old clothes. I'll jest dump 'em on the floor," said Rennie as she turned to go up the ladder.

"I'm afraid we won't have any luck with that corn comin' up. It ort'uv been shelled on the first day of the year, but what with the granny race of Susan's and all of them young'ns of hers runnin' back and forth, it clear slipped my mind." John went back to his Bible reading, leaving Rennie and Johnnie to shell the corn by themselves.

Johnnie set his chair up close against the basket and placed one leg on each side. Taking an ear of corn from the sack, he began rubbing the kernels from the cob and letting them fall into the basket. Rennie filled her lap full of the ears of corn and shelled them the same way. When her apron was full she emptied it into the basket. They were careful to remove only the best formed grains, leaving out the nubbin ends. Later Rennie would feed these to the chickens. The only sounds were the crackling of the fire, the dropping of the corn kernels, the thumping of the cobs as they landed in the corner, and the turning of the pages of John's Bible as he struggled to read it, one word at a time. The corn cobs would be used for many things. Some would become pipes, file handles, stoppers for jugs, or coverings for the sharp end of a spindle when it wasn't in use at the spinning wheel. Others would be burned in the stove for cooking, and still others would end up in the outhouse.

"It's a pity Sarah Ellen and Hank's not here to play with the cobs. I remember havin' so much fun with 'em when I was little," Rennie broke the silence. "We'd build houses, barns, fences, hog pens, and all kinds of things with 'em."

"Well, where I grew up around the minin' camps, we never saw this much corn at one time. There was a few families that growed a little truck patch and got jest a little corn to eat fresh, and the peddlers would come around with their wagons full of garden stuff they'd raised back in the hills further away. Ma, she'd swap scrip to them fer a mess er two ever' now and then, but most allus we got our grub from the company store. Homeground meal shore tastes better than that old bolted meal, and half the time it was that old yeller meal, not fit fer a dog to eat."

"How come Sarah Ellen went to bed so early. She ain't sick, is she?" Johnnie asked.

"No, jest tired out with playin'. It was too cold fer her to get outside, and I got all my old dolls out and let her play with 'em." By now all the corn was shelled and poured from the basket back into the sack.

"And speakin' of yeller corn, I never could understand why it was that we allus pick out only the white ears to plant, yet when we gather it there'll be some yeller, a few red, and some speckled with different colors," Rennie mused.

"Oh," Johnnie laughed. "That's so we can have fun when we shuck it, specially if we have a get-together corn shuckin'. I love it when I get that first red ear and get to kiss the prettiest girl there, and the score game when ye count the points to see who wins. White ones don't count any, a red one twenty points, yeller is five, and a squewee ball, er speckled one, counts ten. It makes fun out of all that work."

"Yeah, Miss Rose says they don't do that where she come from, that when the young folks get together it's jest fer fun. I like our way best. Here we have bean stringin's, apple peelin's, corn shuckin's, quiltin' bees, hog killin's, barn raisin's, and a lot more. We even make a party out of a granny race." Rennie smiled when she said this.

"Well, I had a race shore enough when I went after Miss Rose, but I don't remember any party afterwards," Johnnie returned. "But to tell the truth, I like a candy pullin' er play party best of all."

"Oh, ye're lazy and like to eat, that's what's wrong with you." Rennie threw a small cob at him.

"I like all the games when I get to kiss the girls, like 'Kissin' the Door Knob,' 'Please er Displeased,' 'Laugh and Go Foot,' 'Who Got the Thimble,' and so on. Rennie, did ye ever kiss a boy?" Johnnie asked. Rennie blushed and answered with an angry, "No, and I never want to." Then she turned to the fireplace and picked up the flatiron she'd set there to warm.

"What in the world are ye goin' to do with that? Ye shore aren't goin' to iron somethin' tonight, late as it is," Johnnie said in a very surprised tone.

"I'm goin' to wrap it up in a old rag and let ye take it up to put in yer bed to keep yer feet warm. I know it's freezin' cold up there in the loft."

"Rennie, sometimes ye act as if you was my Ma. Ye treat me jest like ye do Sarah Ellen." Rennie couldn't understand why he was so angry.

"Well, Johnnie, I count ye same as my brother. Ye work so hard here and help out so much it pleasures me to do little things fer ye, jest as I would have done fer Little Owen had he lived. I don't see how we could get along without ye."

"I don't do any more than I should. This is my home. Where would I go if I didn't stay here? Back to West Virginia to one of those stinkin' old coal camps and move in with one of my sisters? Most of 'em have more childern than ye could stir with a stick. No, I don't think they'd want me. Oh, I know they'd keep me because we're family, but they really wouldn't want me, and I'm shore they don't need me. I'd jest be a drag on 'em. But here I know that I'm needed."

Rennie reached him the iron, now wrapped up in an old

piece of blanket. Johnnie took it without looking at her and said, "Thanks, Ma."

Rennie went to bed with Sarah Ellen, and Johnnie climbed the stair ladder to the loft. Both lay awake for a long time before going to sleep, thinking back on what had been said.

16

"Johnnie," Rennie said one morning as he was getting up from the breakfast table, "Aunt Nance said fer me to tell ye she wanted to see ye about somethin', when ye had any spare time to come up there fer a while."

"Well, I didn't have anythin' in mind fer today, so I'll go right now." Getting his hat from the peg on the back of the kitchen door, he went whistling up the hill. In a few moments Rennie heard a lot of loud squealing and giggling from Aunt Nance's house, and she knew the kids had been watching and had come to meet him. They all thought the world of Johnnie.

"Everone loves Johnnie that knows him," Rennie said to herself. "Sometimes I think he's too good fer his own good."

Aunt Nance opened the door. Johnnie had to stoop to get in because he had Little Rose on his shoulder and two more of the children holding onto his legs. He went to the back of the room and dumped the squealing baby on one of the three large beds that took up almost all the space. Then he turned toward the fireplace and sat down beside Aunt Nance.

"Rennie said that ye wanted to see me about somethin'. Hope ye hain't heard of some meanness that I've been into," Johnnie laughed.

"Yeah. I've got a commadation that I want to ask of ye,"

Aunt Nance said as she lifted a coal from the grate on the end of a shovel and lit her pipe.

"Ye jest ask it and I'll do it if I can," Johnnie replied.

"Well, it's not such a big job. It's jest somethin' that me ner Susan can do. I have a old, wore out crosscut saw out there in the corn crib, hangin' on the wall. Been there fer years I guess. Ain't got any teeth, they all wore off, but if I had it took over to the old man Bish that lives on Coon Creek and has a blacksmith shop, he could make me several hoe blades out of it." She paused and puffed her pipe to make it burn better. "Everone of these young'ns that's big enough to use a hoe is goin' to have to help tend a crop if we want to make enough to winter 'em."

"Do ye want me to have him put handles in 'em, too?" Johnnie asked.

"No, jest the diggin' part. I can put the handles in myself. Already got some good seasoned sassafras saplin's up in the barn loft all ready. I want to make the hoe handle to fit the child, if ye know what I mean."

"I don't know fer shore if I know where the old man Bish lives. I've never been on Coon Creek, but I guess I can ask along the way and find it."

"Be quicker if ye jest went up to the head of Lonesome Holler and around the ridge to the head of Coon Creek, an it's jest a hop and a jump down to his house. Ye can't get lost. Jest follow the ridge around the top of the hill till ye come to a big rock. The bridle path goes around that rock and right down to his house and shop. Ye can't get lost."

"Ye don't know me, Aunt Nance. I can get lost in the middle of a corn field. And remember, I didn't grow up in Knott County." Johnnie laughed.

"If ye do get lost, jest come and get me and I'll show ye the way home." Aunt Nance could joke, too.

Johnnie went to the crib and found the saw. He wrapped it in an old coffee sack, balanced it across his shoulder, and started for the path that would lead him to the big road that ran up Lonesome Holler. He was going to enjoy this day. There was nothing he liked better than to get out and ramble through the hills. The sky was so blue, and the first few plants were beginning to peep up from their winter sleep.

"Nothin' like this around the coal camps," he thought. Even the picture shows didn't come up to this, and they were the best part he could remember about his home in West Virginia. "I'd like to take Rennie to a pitcher show!" he thought to himself. "The way she takes to readin' books I jest know she'd like a show." Back at the coal camps boys were laughed at and teased if they took their sisters or cousins to the show with them. It was a place to take your girlfriend. It was thought that if you took some of your family it was because you couldn't get a girl.

"But I never think of Rennie as a cousin," he mused. "We didn't grow up together like I did with Uncle Bill's girls. No, I'm afraid that I love her like a man loves the woman he wants to marry, and I hate myself fer feelin' that way. I know I should leave before things gets worse, but I just can't, and they do need my help so much."

Johnnie stopped and looked around on both sides of the road. He felt as if someone had heard his thoughts. "I'll jest have to get these feelin's out of my mind before I let somethin' slip and Rennie and Uncle John learns how I feel. Then I'd have to leave, because Uncle John wouldn't let us marry even if Rennie. . . . Oh heck, what am I doin'. I must think of somethin' else before I go crazy."

Johnnie soon learned that a crosscut saw isn't easy to carry on your shoulder. It just won't balance. He had placed it as near as he could to the middle, but as he walked, when one end wobbled up, the other end wanted to jiggle down. He soon found it was better to match his steps to the saw than to try to make the saw go along with his steps. "Old saw, ye shore have a mind of yer own. I'm glad ye're soon goin' to be hoes. Walkin' with a saw is kind of like dancin'."

When he came to the place where he left the big road and the open fields, Johnnie thought of what he had told Aunt Nance about not growing up in Knott County. All the folks living on Lonesome Holler knew him, but what about the folks on the Coon Creek side of the hill. Would they know who he was? A stranger wasn't welcome going through the hills. "Guess I'd better begin singin' to let anyone know that I'm comin' and that I'm not a revenuer. If I can jest sing in tune with my wobbly saw."

Johnnie knew there could be a look-out man behind any of the large trees or rocks along the bridle path he was following, with a gun pointing straight at him, placed there to protect the stills that were hidden in many of the smaller hollows. As long as he didn't look to either side of the path and kept singing, he was as safe as at home, for that showed that he wasn't interested in their stills and was just passing through. He sang as loud as he could.

> Chickens crowin' in the Sourwood Mountains,
>   Hey hoe diddle to my day.
> Got so many kids that I can't count 'em
> Hey hoe diddle to my day.
>
> I have a girl that lives in Letcher.
> Hey hoe diddle to my day.
> She won't come and I won't fetch her,
> Hey hoe diddle to my day.
>
> I've got a girl that's a humped-backed Daisy.
> Hey hoe diddle to my day.
> Hump on her back would run a man crazy,
> Hey hoe diddle to my day.

Johnnie stopped to catch his breath. The saw was not all that heavy. It was just the strain of having to keep it evenly balanced so the ends wouldn't bounce up and down and singing at the top of his voice at the same time. He leaned his back against a tree. A squirrel ran across the path and up a tree. Johnnie chuckled to himself. "Well, Rennie's allus tellin' me that my singin' would run the varmints out of the woods, and it looks like she was right." He started on again and began another song.

> Hard hard is the fortune of all women kind.
> They are allus controlled, they are allus confined.
> They are bossed by their parents until they are made wives,
> Then slaves fer their husbands the rest of their lives.

Yer parents don't like me because I am poor.
They say that I am not worthy to enter yer door.
I work fer my livin', my money is my own,
And them that don't like me can leave me alone.

As Johnnie walked along, being careful to keep his eyes down, he noticed a small, dark green plant growing near the ground along the sides of the path. "I wonder if that could be Mountain Tea," he thought to himself. He eased the saw from his shoulder and stooped to take a closer look. Picking a few leaves, he rubbed them against his pants leg to remove the dust, filled his mouth full, and began to chew. What a nice, refreshing taste. He gathered a large handful and filled his picket. He would take that to Sarah Ellen and Hank.

Shouldering his saw, he resumed his journey and began another song.

> Me and my wife and my wife's pap
> Walked all the way from the "Cumblin Gap."
> "Cumblin Gap" is a heck of a place.
> Ye can't get water to wash yer face.
>
> Me and my wife and my little dog
> Crossed the creek on a hickory log.
> My foot slipped and I fell in.
> That little dog set there and grinned.

As he finished that song and tried to think what to sing next, Johnnie heard a dog bark. It sounded close, but he knew that sounds could be deceiving this far up on the hill. Without thinking he looked in the direction from which the sound came. Far down on the Lonesome Holler side, he saw smoke rising from among the trees, drifting skyward. He quickly turned his eyes back to the path and, with fast-beating heart, began another song.

> Hey, old man, I want yer daughter,
> Bake my bread and carry my water.
> Hey, young man, ye can't get her.
> She has to stay here and use the gritter.

He couldn't remember the rest of the words to that one, so he started still another.

> There is just one thing to make me happy.
> Two little boys to call me Pappy.
> One named John, the other Davie.
> One like sop and the other gravy.

Johnnie sang on and on. He sang every song he knew and then began singing the same ones over. Finally he said to himself, "I'm gettin' tired of my own voice." He had walked for what seemed like miles before he came to the place where the bridle path led around the big rock and started down the other side of the hill. Going down the hill with the saw on his back was a lot easier than coming up had been, but the thing still jiggled and wobbled and made a slight humming noise. "I guess I can stop singin' now," he said to himself. "I've jest about ran out of breath and songs. If I ever come this way agin I will bring my fiddle."

The first house he came to was a rundown shack, and the fence running around it was no better. Not a chicken or pig in sight. "Don't guess anyone lives here," he thought. "I'll mosey on a piece further and see. Bet I've lost my way. But Aunt Nance said the first house." "Howdy, the house. Anybody home?" he yelled. Then he saw smoke rising just around the next bend in the road. "Well, saw, we're here at last, I hope."

He walked toward the smoke, and sure enough, there was the blacksmith shop—a small, rough log building, no floor and no dobbin between the logs. The roof extended out on one side to make a covered shed. One end of the roof wasn't covered with boards, just an open hole. It was from this hole that black smoke was rising, and it told Johnnie he'd reached the blacksmith shop. Under the shed he saw a beautiful black horse and an old man bent over with one of the horse's feet caught between his knees as he tapped the bottom of the shoe he was fastening on. "Lay that saw down quiet like," he said. "Might scare this horse. He's kind of skiddish, anyway."

"Ye got eyes in the back of yer head? How did ye know that I was totin' a saw?"

"I saw ye a long way off and heard ye singin' before I seed ye," the old man explained. He let the horse's foot down and straightened up with his hand on his back, as if it pained him.

"That's a very fine horse ye have there. Ye don't see many that purty around here. Most folks prefer mules. Who owns that critter?" Johnnie asked.

"Belongs to one of the Gents, yound side of the mountain," the old man said. "They allus have good stock, horses and mules. They must like my work, cause they bring 'em to me to shoe." There was pride in his voice. "What can I do fer ye?"

"Aunt Nance had me to bring this wored-out saw to have ye to make some diggin' hoes fer her."

"Is that Nance Slone from Lonesome Holler?"

"Yeah, that's the one. Do ye know her?"

"I knowed her when we were young, growin' up. Well I know that ye're not her brother John's. He only had girls. So which one of the Slones are ye?"

"I'm John's brother Tate's boy. Named John after Uncle John, but everbody calls me Johnnie. Do ye remember Tate?"

"Shore, shore, knowed him jest like a book. We run around together a lot in our young days. Knowed all about him and Bill gettin' their still smashed up. Me and some more men went and seed them horses. What a sight! Their heads almost cut off. When them revenuers come back they found that someone had cut their saddles and bridles all to pieces. Don't know who could have done such a thing." He grinned slyly at Johnnie. "I jest never could abide revenuers."

"Will ye be able to make the hoes fer me?" Johnnie asked.

"I have some more work ahead that I have to do first, but I'll make 'em jest as soon as I can get to 'em. I've made many a diggin' hoe out of old saws. Never like to see anythin' throwed away if it could be used. A saw makes good fire shevels, too." He came and sat down beside Johnnie on an upturned stump. "I may not get to them diggin' hoes until next week. Send ye word by someone, er I jest might bring 'em myself some Sunday. Would like to see Nance and John. Jest come and have dinner and set a spell and talk about the old days."

"That's what to do. Ye'd be welcome, and John's girl is a right smart cook."

"Is John beginnin' to break in his health?" Bish asked Johnnie.

"He can't get around like he used to. Those years that he spent in the pen did a lot to him. He don't never talk any about them times, but ye can tell when he's thinkin' about the years that he lost. I get so sarry fer him I try to take all the work I can off of him." Johnnie looked up. "I never did see a blacksmith shop. Mind if I go in and take a look-see?"

"Go right on. I better get back to shoein' this horse," Bish said. "This shop has been here fer quite a spell. It was built by my grandfather. They used to be a shed just out here," he pointed to a spot near a large stump, "where we shoed large oxen. Ye know, ye have to tie an ox up with ropes and lift him from the ground before ye can shoe him. Folks don't keep oxen anymore these days. Used to be a lot of 'em around here."

Johnnie went into the shop. Although the fire had died down, it was still hot. One end was built up with rocks like a wall, and on top of it was a shallow dip where the fire was burning. Close by were the big bellows. They were fastened to a pedal so that by stepping on the pedal one man could blow the bellows and still work at the forge. On the wall close by hung Bish's big leather apron. This he wore when he was working close to the fire to protect himself from sparks. On another bench was the anvil and a big hammer. Johnnie promised himself that he would come back later sometime and watch Bish work.

"Must take a very strong man to use one of them things," Johnnie told Bish as he came back outside. "Where do ye sleep at night?"

"Well, if it's not too cold er too hot from the fire, I jest sleep here, and if not I go back to that tumbledown shack ye seed back there. I don't have any family. Never was married, and after Pa and Ma died I jest let the old house kind of run down. Sometimes I cook what little I eat here on the fire in the forge. Can't get time to raise me no vittles, so folks pay me fer my work in beans and stuff like that. I never get lonesome, 'cept at night sometimes. Allus someone comin' er goin'. I make my own horseshoes. Of course, I have to catch someone goin' out and have 'em to pick me up some pig iron. I've allus got a little somethin' to do fer somebody—a little of this and that." Johnnie saw that Bish liked to talk.

"Guess I'd better be gettin' along to the house, but I think I'll go back by goin' down Coon Creek and up Lonesome Holler. I'm plum tired of singin'."

"It's all of five miles if ye go that way," Bish told him. "If ye want to wait I'll fix us up a bite to eat. That is, if ye're willin' to eat my cookin'."

"Thanks jest the same, but I guess I'll mosey along. Maybe some good-hearted person will see me passin' and ask me in fer dinner. If not, I know that Rennie will have some left-overs fer me at the house when I get there."

"Come back sometime," Bish told Johnnie as he picked up his hat and started to leave.

"We'll be lookin' fer ye. Be sure and come and I'll be back. Want to see ye work at that forge."

Johnnie still thought he would rather go the long way around, but he wished he had brought a little snack along with him. "Some of Aunt Nance's gingerbread would shore taste good about now," he said to himself.

17 _____

Every two or three weeks Miss Rose would stop by to see how her namesake was doing. She would always bring her something—a sweater, a pair of soft shoes, or a little toy of some kind. She also brought clothes for the older children. These had been sent to them from Mrs. Lloyd from the Community Center.

"I don't feel jest right to be takin' these things," Susan would say with a smile. "I don't like to be beholden to anyone when I have no way to pay her back."

"They're sent to Mrs. Lloyd from her friends up north to be given to folks like you. They're rich and don't need them, and they're good at heart and it makes them feel good to know they can help someone less fortunate than they are," Miss Rose explained.

"Well, ye put it that way I don't feel so bad and it shore helps us out aplenty."

"I'm almost sure I could get Joan and Jane in school over at the Community Center if you'd let them go," Miss Rose would say each time she came.

"As much as I'd like to, I can't do that. They're all the help I've got to help me make a crop 'er we won't have any grub to eat this winter, and anyhow they didn't get fer in school at the coal camp school. Joan, she had jest got to the third grade and Jane was still in the second. They would be plagued to be in class with them little childern." Susan gathered her apron hem and began making pleats in it with her fingers. She always did this when she was nervous.

"The rest of your little ones are too young for Mrs. Lloyd to keep. She does take a few small ones, but just when they have no one else to live with," Miss Rose explained.

"Law me. I thought everbody here in the hills had some kinfolks that would see to one another's little ones what had been left alone. Maybe they'd have to scrouge up quite a smart, yet they would never be turned away." Susan wiped her eyes with the corner of her apron and sniffed.

Miss Rose wondered how Susan's family "scrouged" into Aunt Nance's two-room house and the loft, where she knew there was just a shakedown shuck bed for the girls and some of the small ones. But there were plenty of quilts and home-woven blankets. The long table almost filled the kitchen, and a wooden bench ran the whole length between the table and the wall. Here the little ones found a place to eat, sitting like crows on a fence. If someone whose place was in the middle wanted to leave the table first, then all on that side had to sidle out one at a time.

Aunt Nance and Susan had made up their mind to have a working. February had been cold, and March had come in with a four-inch snow, so they knew that the last of March would be pretty weather. If March came in like a lamb it went out like a lion, and if it came in like a lion it would go out like a lamb. So they set the day for the working on the twentieth, a Friday.

Johnnie left word at Long Bill's store. "Ye tell everbody ye see to come and bring a hoe, axe, mule, and mattock. We goin' to clean up that big cove jest above Aunt Nance's house. There'll be work fer everone, young er old, and a plenty to eat. I don't know about drinks. I don't know if we can slip a jug of moonshine into the barn loft er not. It's hard to pull anythin' over on Uncle John. We'll have a play party that night fer the young'ns if they ain't too tired to play. No dancin' though. Uncle John's agin that, too."

Preacher John told all the folks that were at church that Sunday about the working. "We all need to help these poor women folks. Ye never lose anythin' by helpin' someone in need. The Good Lord will make it up to ye in the long run."

Rennie awoke at first rooster crow that Friday morning. She heard Johnnie whistling in the barn. She was looking forward to the day. She would get to see a lot of her old friends. Hard work, but it was all in fun. She got up and hurried through breakfast and put away the milk that Johnnie brought in from the barn. She filled a basket with the fried pies she had made the night before— apple, a few from dried peaches, and the rest berry. She put a jar of jelly in the basket and a jar of pickled beets. "I know someone will bring shucky beans, and they're no good without beets to go with 'em," she said to herself.

Pa was not planning on going. He'd stay and mind Sarah

Ellen. "Hank will be here jest as shore as certain, jest as soon as he gets up, ye wait and see. Put them two together and ye got yer hands full. If I was younger I'd druther grub any time than mind young'ns," John grumbled.

"Now, Pa, ye know that ye love both of them childern as much as any of us do. Ye jest like to have somethin' to fret about," Rennie said as she picked up the full basket and started through the door.

"Yeah, I guess I am. I jest can't bear to think that my workin' days are over, that I can't do a day's work like a man and have to stay at the house and mind the kids like a woman."

"I'll send y'all somethin' to eat. I guess dinner will be a little late, but I'll either bring yers early er send it by someone. Ye take care now."

"Bet Old Kate will be there jest as soon as she hears the dinner bell ring. She won't do a lick of work ner bring a thing. Won't even stay to help wash the dishes. She goes so dirty I wouldn't want to eat anythin' she fixed, and I wouldn't want to eat a thing she had, and I wouldn't want to eat from a dish that she washed." Rennie was surprised at her father, for it was seldom that she had heard him say a mean thing about anyone. He really must be upset over something.

Early as it was when Rennie arrived at Aunt Nance's house, the yard was full of women and girls. Two of the older women were doing something around a large black mink kettle sitting on two large rocks over a fire. A pleasant odor came from it. Small boys and girls were running all over the place, getting in everyone's way. A few larger girls were sitting on the porch with babies in their arms. Whole families would come to a working. From the hillside came the sound of men at work— the ring of an axe, the whine of a crosscut saw, the voices shouting, "Whoh, haw and gee, get up" to their mules. More men were coming up the road and going up the hill. Everyone on Lonesome Holler must be here and some from farther away.

"Looks like ye got Cox's army here," Rennie laughed as she gave Hank a big hug. She shook hands with some of the older women as she made her way through the crowd and passed the open door. Aunt Nance said, "Iffen ye got anythin' in that basket that might spile, take it down to the spring house, and if not jest push everthin' back until ye find room fer it there on the table." She wiped the sweat from her face with her apron. The kitchen had already begun to get hot from the fire in the stove, which was covered with pots and kettles, full and bubbling away.

"Shore is a purty day fer a workin'" someone said.

"Yet jest enough nip of cold in the air to keep the men hard at work to keep warm," another one answered.

"And not warm enough to have flies swarmin' around. I shore dread it when there's a lot of food and it takes two er three with switches to keep the flies from dabbin' on the food er gettin' drowned in the coffee er milk. If they is anythin' I can't abide it's flies."

Inside, Rennie found Joan and Jane. "Which does Aunt Nance want us girls to do—help the women cook er help the men? We can pile brush," Rennie said to them as she placed her basket with all the other bowls and platters. The table was covered with a sheet, and some delicious smells rose from it.

"That's why we been waitin' until ye got here," said Jane. "There's aplenty of women here to do all the cookin'. Let's go pile brush. There should be some ready fer us by now. That's why I have on my old clothes and wore out shoes." Rennie could see that both girls were glad to be working outside. She herself really didn't care. She was by herself so much that she was glad just to be with other girls her age once again.

"Grandma said this cove had laid out fer three years and growed up a right smart. By rights it should have been bushwhacked last fall so the brush could have been burned. It may not dry out enough so as to be burned this spring, and we'll jest have to work around the brush piles. That way we lose a lot of ground and it makes fer snakes' dens," Joan told Rennie as they climbed the hill. "But as we ain't got no mule and no one to plow even if we did have one, we'll jest tend a crop where it can be dug in," she added.

Sure enough, when they got to where the men had been

working, many of the largest saplings had been cut down and the smaller twigs and limbs stripped from them, ready for the girls to gather and pile up. They took as many as they could over to the edge of the field near the timber line to be out of the way. If they had been going to burn them that spring they would have piled them in the middle of the field.

A few of the younger boys began to help the girls. Men with mules were hauling the larger saplings to the lower edge of the field. There they could be piled along like a fence row. Later many of them would be used for firewood or a pole fence for a cow lot or a pig pen, and some would be used for pole beans or peas in the neighbors' gardens. There was a lot of joking and teasing going on between the men, but out of respect for the girls they were careful not to curse or use bad language.

It was almost unbelievable how much work was under way. These men had worked together all their lives. No one had to tell the others what to do. They just fell in and worked as a team. By the time the sun had reached the middle of the sky so it no longer cast a shadow, half of the field was cleared of all the small trees and saplings. When the old dinner bell sent its clamor up and down Lonesome Holler, half of the allotted work was finished.

"We'll shore get this ready fer plantin' by quit time," Big Jed remarked to Josh as they made their way down the hill toward the house, where the womenfolks had a huge dinner waiting. "Allus heard it said that there was seven acres in this cove. Best piece of corn growin' ground on Lonesome Holler."

"Yeah," Josh emptied his mouth of a wad of tobacco. "I'd say they is ever' foot of seven acres, maybe more, and layin' on the north side like this it'll be a caution to the beans there will be. Yeah, I'll say this'll make all Susan and her kids can handle and be a plenty fer to winter 'em."

"If they can jest get 'em planted in the right time of the moon and the signs jest right." Big Jed emptied his mouth of his tobacco.

By now they had reached the back yard of Nance's house.

All the men were lined up near the well, taking turns washing their hands and faces in a tin wash pail, then dumping the water over the fence. A piece of an old sheet hanging from the fence served in place of a towel. Water was drawn up from the well in a wooden bucket. Some of the men spit out their tobacco and then washed their mouths out with water from the gourd dipper by the well and spit over the fence.

Aunt Nance's table was large enough to seat twelve if they sat a little scrouged. "Jest so as I have elbow room," Big Jed laughed. Some of the women sat near the table watching to see when anyone needed more coffee, filling their cups as soon as they became half empty and refilling the large bowls and platters from the pots on the stove. There were shucky beans, chicken and dumplings, fried pork, boiled eggs, fried and boiled potatoes, baked and boiled sweet potatoes, fried pies, stack cake made from gingerbread and apple butter sweetened with molasses, and more and more—so many things that it would have been impossible for anyone to taste of every dish. These mountain folks sure knew how to cook for a working.

"I like my coffee like I do my women—hot, strong, and dark," said Big Jed, and everyone laughed as if they hadn't heard him say that many times before. As soon as one man got up from the table, his plate, cup, and silverware were washed in a pan of water on the stove, and someone else was called from the yard to fill the empty space. When all the men had eaten, then the women ate. Some fed their little ones from their own plates. The younger ones ate later, but everyone had all they wanted.

Just as John had predicted, Old Kate arrived just a little after the big dinner bell rang. She not only ate but she brought a big empty lard bucket and asked for some of the scraps, "to take to my dog."

"Bet she eats them scraps herself," Joan whispered to Rennie.

"I wouldn't put it past her," Rennie whispered back.

While the menfolks were eating, Rennie prepared some food to take to her father, Hank, and Sarah Ellen. When she picked up her basket to go, Joan asked her mother, "Is it all right if I walk along with her?"

"Run along. There's a plenty of others that can help wash the dishes." Her mother gave her a pat on the back and a knowing look.

As they strolled down the narrow path that ran between the fence and the bank of Lonesome Holler, Joan said, "Let's rest a while. There's somethin' that I want to ask ye. That's why I wanted to get ye by yerself."

"Shore," Rennie answered as she looked for a rock to set her basket on. "Fire away. I'm all ears."

"Rennie, don't get mad. Promise me that ye won't get mad." Joan was so upset.

"Well, how can I promise if I don't know what it is? I can't think of anythin' that ye could say to me that would make me mad at ye." Rennie was really puzzled by now.

Joan dropped her eyes and began kicking at a small root that stuck out from the side of the path. Then raising her eyes, she looked back toward the house and sighed.

"Well, out with it. Nothin' can be that bad," Rennie begged.

"Do ye like Joe Smith?" Poor Joan. Her face was as red as fire.

"Do I like Joe Smith? Do I like Joe Smith?" Rennie repeated, too surprised to think straight. "Well, I guess I like him well enough. I jest never asked myself if I did er not. At least, I don't hate him," Joan really had Rennie guessing now. "Why do ye ask?"

"I mean . . . are ye struck on him?" Now she was beginning to make sense.

"Oh, my Lord God, no! Whatever put that into yer head?" Rennie wanted to know.

"Well, Johnnie said that he bought yer box at the pie supper, and I . . . I kind of think he's cute, and I believe he may be struck on me, maybe, but I didn't want to go with him if he was yer feller and all." For the first time Joan looked Rennie in the face.

"Well, ye can rest easy about that. I don't want no feller, now er ever. I ain't never goin' to marry. I'm goin' to see that Sarah Ellen grows up and gets a good education. Sarah Ellen is all the family I will ever want in this world. I'll never spark any boy," Rennie finished.

"Rennie, I'm past sixteen and ye're very near that old. Many of our friends are already married and all the rest have begun settin' up with boys fer a long time," Joan said. "If Joe asks me I'm goin' to let him come and see me. Now that I know that ye don't like him."

"You live yer life and I'll live mine. I think I was born to be an old maid."

18

It was true that the brush piles in Susan's field didn't get dry enough to burn before it was time to plant her corn. She knew that when the oak leaves got to be the size of a squirrel's ear, it was time to plant her corn. It was about the middle of April. All her children who were big enough to handle a hoe she took to the field. Beginning at the bottom, they shaved the weeds, cutting them as close to the ground as they could, and removing as little of the topsoil as possible. Each child shaved a switch as far as their hoes would reach. Susan was in the first row, Joan next, and then Jane, each raking the weeds down onto the row below. The smaller kids were above the girls, some two in a row, but always the first row would be finished before the next one was done, so they were lined up the hill, one just above the other and a little behind the one below, all strung out like a chain gang.

Working from early morning to late, in a week they had about half of the field finished, "shaved and drugged." Then they began to plant this first half. They didn't want to plant it all at once so it would all come in at the same time. This way the weeds wouldn't take over before they had time to hoe it. Susan showed them how to dig holes about three feet apart in rows around the hill and drop five grains of corn into each hill, then cover them over and pat the top of the hill with the flat part of their hoe.

> One fer the ground squirrel,
> One fer the crow,
> One to rot,
> And two to grow.

After they had finished planting the first half, they did the upper half the same way.

"This should have been grubbed, but we didn't have time, and we can jest do so much. By it not bein' grubbed it will make hard hoein'. We'll have to swap work with some family," Susan told her children, "but if we don't have too wet a summer we can keep the grubs fit down."

"What do ye mean swap work?" one of the children wanted to know.

"Oh, I ferget that you kids don't know much about tendin' a crop, growin' up around the coal camps like ye did. We jest go and help some other family work one day when our corn is not needin' to be worked and theirs is, and then they come back and work with us a day to pay us back," she explained.

"That sounds like fun," Joan said. "We could swap work with Uncle John."

"I don't think John is goin' to be able to do much work. He ain't doin' much good these days," Susan answered. "Course, we could swap with Rennie, and Johnnie will help, I'm shore."

"Guess Joan would like to swap work with Joe Smith's family," teased Jane.

Johnnie used up some of the brush from Susan's field. He took the fodder sled and the mule to the edge of the field and loaded the sled with a lot of the green saplings and larger twigs and hauled them to John's garden where John wanted to burn off a tobacco bed. He trimmed up the larger saplings and placed them up against the fence to be used later to stake the pole beans and peas. The smaller ones he piled up and burned on a spot about the size of a bed. As they burned he kept adding more and more. Then taking a hoe he huck

117

off all the unburned stuff and dug up the ground till it was loose, and burned some more on top of this. This would get rid of all the weed seed and any worms or bugs that might have made this place their winter home.

About the middle of March, John said he thought the moon was in the right place and that all the signs were right to sow his tobacco bed. He mixed the seed with an equal amount of cornmeal. Tobacco seeds are so small it's hard to scatter them evenly. They are also of a dark color; the meal lets you see if you're getting them evenly sown. Some folks use a salt shaker.

As John scattered the seeds over the nice soft bed Johnnie had prepared, he said, "These plants will be ready to set out by the middle of May. They won't be any frost after the eighth of May this year because that's the last time it thundered in February." He then covered the bed with burlap coffee sacks and placed rocks on the ends of them to hold them in place. "I'll sow enough to give Nance some plants."

"And of course Old Kate will come abeggin' fer some. Jest as well sow some fer her, too," Johnnie laughed.

"Better to give her the plants and let her raise her own than have her comin' abeggin' tobacco all winter," Rennie added.

"Y'all shouldn't talk about yer neighbors that way," John said. "The Good Book says to love yer neighbors like yerself."

"Nobody could like that old witch," Johnnie threw back at him.

"Judge not er so shall ye be judged." John never missed a chance to preach at Rennie or Johnnie. "All in all, y'all are purty good people. But ye can't make grown folks out of childern."

"If we're not grown up now, I wonder when we will be?" Johnnie asked.

"When ye begin to act like grown-ups," John smiled. It was seldom that he joked with Johnnie and Rennie. They were glad to see him in such a good humor.

19 _____

Now that warm weather had set in, Johnnie was sleeping in the barn loft. It really wasn't so bad up there—an old quilt thrown over a large pile of shucks. An old mother cat and her family of five had their home in the opposite corner to keep him company and to frighten away the rats and mice that might want to visit him.

Johnnie stayed awake long after he climbed into his makeshift bed, thinking about his feelings for Rennie. He had never had a girlfriend. He had never sparked any girl. He didn't know how a boy should feel about a girl he wanted to marry. He just knew that the feeling he had for Rennie was different from the way he felt about his cousins, the daughters of his Uncle Bill. He had no one to talk with about it, and he couldn't explain it to himself. He knew that he enjoyed being in the room with her and that he loved to make her laugh. He loved to bring her things that would please her, like the first violets he found along the creek banks, fresh wild strawberries, or a bright colored ribbon when he had a little cash to spend. But when he tried to imagine how it would feel to put his arms around her and kiss her on the mouth, it made him feel dirty. He even felt he was making Rennie dirty, too, just thinking about her that way.

He knew how his Uncle John felt about cousins getting married, for not long before, a couple had come to the house asking him to marry them, and he had told them in no uncertain terms that in no way would he "join in holy matrimony" the children of blood brothers.

Johnnie told himself that it would be better for all if he left and went far away, but he was happy here and he knew they needed him. It felt good to be needed, and he didn't see how Rennie could take care of her father and Sarah Ellen on her own. Maybe it would help if he started seeing some other girl, but would that be fair to the other girl? Fer when a boy began settin' up with a girl, that meant he wanted to get married. If only he could get a job and make some cash money. But would Uncle John accept cash money? Receiving work from someone in the family was all right, but taking money was different. For that you had to be under obligation to them.

Johnnie slept late the next morning. He had awakened at first rooster crow, but on remembering that it was Sunday he just turned over and went back to sleep. No work today.

When he came into the kitchen he saw that breakfast was over. Uncle John had already gone to church. He knew this because the mule was gone from the stable. Hank and Sarah Ellen were playing some game out in the yard. He opened the stove door and saw that Rennie had put his breakfast back in the oven where it would keep warm for him. He let the oven door down, pulled the plate out onto the door, pulled a chair up, and began eating.

"Where have ye been, lazy bones?" Rennie asked as she came into the kitchen. She got a cup from the shelf, filled it with coffee from a pot on the stove, and set it down on the stove beside Johnnie's plate.

"Jest tryin' to make the day shorter," Johnnie said as he took his first sip of the coffee, "knowin' it was Sunday and there wouldn't be anythin' to do to make the time pass. Is someone sick up at Aunt Nance's? I saw a light on away after midnight."

"No, I expect that it's Joan and Joe Smith a settin' up with each other. They been sparkin' ever since Susan had the workin' to clean up her crop field," Rennie laughed.

"Well, that's a new one on me. I thought Joe Smith was struck on you. He bought yer box at the pie supper."

"Don't ever tell Joan, but he did ask me to be his girl, but I told him I didn't want no feller. What fer do I want to go with a boy? I made up my mind a long time ago that I would never marry. I guess I was jest borned to be an old maid. Ever' community has to have one. Ye know, I read somewhere the reason old maids are called spinsters is because women that didn't marry went from house to house helpin' with the spinnin' to pay fer their board and keep. All families need someone to be ready to help out when needed. But the real reason I made up my mind to never marry was because of Sarah Ellen. She means the whole world to me, and I mean to do all I can to see that she gets the education Ma wanted so badly fer me. I don't want her to have to slave her life away on these old worn-out hills adiggin' to keep herself alive like I have. No siree!"

Johnnie almost choked on his bite of bread. He got up and refilled his cup from the pot. His hands shook as he poured the coffee. "Ye don't know if Sarah Ellen will want to go to school." Johnnie's voice sounded funny to Rennie. "Rennie, don't ye ever think of yerself? What about yer own life?"

"Sarah Ellen *is* my life, don't ye understand?" There was a threat of anger in her voice. "She means the whole world to me."

"No, I don't understand. But it answers a lot of my ponderin's." Rennie was left to puzzle on what Johnnie had meant. It was to come back to her again and again, but it would be years before she would know.

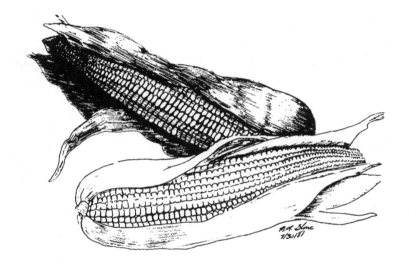

20 _____

Rennie came out on the porch and looked up and down Lonesome Holler. What a warm day to be the first of November. A smoky haze hid the usually bright blue sky. A soft warm breeze was bringing down the last of the leaves from the almost bare trees and flipping Rennie's hair across her face. "This is the settin' in of Indian Summer, a good time to get the rest of the fodder and corn into the barn. We have all the potatoes dug. We'll need some paper to wrap all our sweet potatoes in. I think I'll see if Joan and Jane will go with me to the Community Center and get us a load of newspapers and magazines."

"Talkin' to yerself agin?" Johnnie had slipped up behind her.

"Yeah. I like to talk to a smart person ever' now and then," she answered with a laugh. "Why do we call this time of the year Indian Summer?" she asked.

"I thought you were the smart one," Johnnie smiled. "Why ask me? Grandpa allus told us," he went on, "that it was when the Indians were burnin' off the prairie grasslands so the green grass would come up next spring, and the haze in the air is from the smoke," Johnnie explained.

"I can believe the smoke could drift this far, but I don't believe it could make the air this warm," Rennie replied.

"Maybe the Good Lord sends us these few warm days before winter sets in to get us ready fer the cold times ahead," John spoke up from where he was sitting with his chair leaned back against the wall of the house. The sun had already begun its crawl across that end of the porch.

"I love this time of year, but it gives me a lonesome feelin', like I'm sayin' goodbye to a friend that I know I'll never see agin. You watch Sarah Ellen and I'll go up and see if one of Susan's girls will go over to the Community Center with me to'mar and get us some papers fer our late apples and sweet potatoes. If they want some too, we may have to take one of the mules."

Rennie started for the gate. Both girls were more than willing to go. Neither had ever been to the school, and both wanted to see it.

"How much does these papers cost?" Susan asked anxiously.

"Ye get a big, oh, stack fer a quarter. Ye can pay 'em in anythin' that ye have to eat. I'm goin' to get one stack of newspaper and catalogues to wrap my apples and sweet potatoes in and some magazines to paper the wall of my kitchen. The old ones are smoked up somethin' awful," Rennie told her.

"Well, we don't have any apples, but we do need some paper fer our sweet potatoes, and I think I'd jest as well get some to paper my house, although I'm goin' to let it go 'til spring. I don't think we have anythin' we can rightly spare unless it's a cushaw er pumpkins. We have a right smart of 'em."

"They'll do jest fine. I'm almost shore they'd like to have a pumpkin er two fer pies this near Thanksgivin'. I'm goin' to take some sweet potatoes. Ours turned out jest fine this year."

So, bright and early the very next morning found Jane on Johnnie's mule riding on top of two bags stuffed with sweet potatoes and pumpkins, and Rennie and Joan walking along beside, going down Lonesome Holler.

Rennie had been to the Community Center several times with her mother. This was the first time for the other girls, and they were looking forward to it. They had heard so much about the school from Rennie and Miss Rose. "I hope Miss Rose will be there today and we can get to see her," Jane said from her high perch on the mule. They all agreed.

As they went down Lonesome Holler, folks were all busy digging potatoes, pulling fodder from their late corn patches, hauling in their corn, and putting it into their corn cribs. From the hillside came the ring of axes and the whine of saws. Folks getting in wood for the cold days soon to come. But as the girls passed, everyone quit their work and took time to say, "Howdy. Why don't y'all come in and talk a spell. How's yer folks? Stop on yer way back." Rennie answered each one but told them they were in a hurry, but if they needed anything from the Community Center they'd bring it for them.

At the mouth of Lonesome Holler they turned down Caney Creek road. "It's jest a mile er two now, girls," Rennie told them.

When they got to the school, Rennie tied the mule to the hitching post in front of the post office. She told Joan and Jane to remain there while she went on up to the "If" office, where the papers were stacked. She said some boys would be sent to get the sacks of food and then return with the papers in their sacks and load them on the mule. Rennie had warned the girls not to get insulted if the boys didn't speak to them, that it was a strict rule of the school that boys and girls didn't talk with each other at any time. Miss Rose had told her this.

Joan and Jane sat there on a rock wall that enclosed the school. It had been built to protect the school from the spring washout after a large portion of the school had been destroyed when the creek overflowed one spring. It made a good seat if you didn't mind letting your legs hang over the side. They sat there and looked around at the little plank houses up and down beside the road and some way up on the hill, their fronts reaching way out over the ground while the backs sat on the ground. Across the creek was the sawmill where large logs were being sawed into planks. Huge piles of sawdust almost filled the creek banks. The whine of the saw was so loud the girls almost had to shout to be heard.

"I bet that's the printin' office that Miss Rose told us about in that long buildin' jest back of us. I shore would like to watch how they print," Jane told Joan. "I'd like to go all over the whole school. If Miss Rose was here she might takes us, but we don't have time today. Maybe some other time."

"A stove as big as a hog pen and pots as big as washin' tubs. It's hard to believe. Twelve tables in the eatin' room. Boys eat at one end and girls at the other." Miss Rose had told the girls a lot about the school, but hearing isn't like seeing.

They hushed talking when some boys came to get the sacks of food. The girls couldn't keep from staring at them. They were dressed in coats and wore ties. Rennie returned with the news that Miss Rose was out on a case. It wasn't long until the boys returned and loaded the mule with two sacks of papers. The load was so big now that Jane thought it would be better for her to walk than to try sticking up on top of that bundle and letting Rennie lead the mule.

"I hope Johnnie's at the house so he can help us unload," Rennie said. As luck would have it, he came to meet them as they left the big road. He'd been watching for them. "Does it matter which sack goes where?" he asked.

"No, they're both the same. Jest dump one on our porch and take the other one up to Susan's house," Rennie instructed him.

"We'll not get a word out of ye fer the next six weeks. Ye'll even do the cookin' and churnin' with one of those magazines in yer hand," Johnnie teased.

"Shore, I love to read. Why don't ye try it sometime? Ye might learn somethin' that way," Rennie returned.

"I swear," Joan said to Jane. "To hear them two talk to each other ye'd think they hated each other, yet they don't mean a thing they say."

"Joan," Johnnie asked, "when are we goin' to have them chicken and dumplin's?" Joan blushed but didn't answer.

"Any time now," Jane answered for her. "Joe has already asked Ma, and she said it was all right with her."

"What's the hold-up then?" Johnnie wanted to know. Again Joan wouldn't answer, and Jane spoke up for her. "She said she hated to leave Ma as long as she was needed, but now that the crops is in and all the stuff put away fer winter, that's no excuse. I think she jest don't like the idea of livin' in the house with Joe's folks and that's what they'd have to do now fer a while."

"There's a little one-room shack of a place that Joe's father said we could use," Joan finally began to explain. "Joe's been workin' on it, but he can't get it finished before winter. After it gets so cold he can't work on it at all. I don't know but we might get married sometime about Christmas. If he could only get a job so's we could buy us a little house plunder to set up housekeepin'. He knows of a piece of land that he could rent next year by jest givin' the man that owns it a third

126

of the corn." Now that Joan had begun talking she seemed not to want to quit.

"There's a lot of us that would like to have a job so's we could make a little cash money," Johnnie said.

"We better be gettin' along to the house and help Ma with supper," Jane said.

"Which reminds me," Rennie said. "We've all done without dinner, and I'm as hungry as can be, but I'm too tired to cook. If we have any cold bread I'll make 'em eat milk and bread fer supper."

"I doubt if ye'll find any. Ye must remember we ain't had any dinner, either," Johnnie said. "Why not make us some mush?"

"Like Old Kate said, 'I'd make me some mush if I had any meal if I had any milk.'"

It had been such a beautiful day, and Rennie had enjoyed it so much. It did one good to get away from the house every now and then. "But it's good to get back," she told herself.

That evening, after they had finished their bowls of crumble-in and Rennie had washed the bowls and spoons, she came into the big room, where John had built a little fire. "Jest to take the chill out of the air," he explained. Johnnie had stacked the papers and magazines in the corner. Rennie was pleased because she couldn't wait to get at them. She tore a few pages from one of the little sales catalogues, hunted a pair of scissors, and showed Sarah Ellen how to cut out the pictures. Johnnie was thumbing through the newspapers.

"I don't put a lot of trust of what they say in any of them papers," John said as he spit toward the grate. "Not since they wrote all them lies about Nance's rockin' chair."

"I don't believe I ever heard that," Johnnie said. "Ye mean Aunt Nance got her pitcher in the newspaper?"

"Yeah. It's a long story, but if ye want to hear it I'll tell ye."

"I'm all ears," Johnnie nodded.

"They were some folks, two women, come around. Ye know, some people from off yonder, stayed a while with Aunt Nance. Stayed about two weeks. Went around takin' pictures of birds and flowers and, ye know, stuff like that. When they got ready to leave they tried to pay Aunt Nance

127

fer lettin' 'em stay with her, but she told 'em that in no way would she accept money fer someone visitin' with her. Ye know that's jest not our way of doin' things. They told her they'd send her a present if that would be all right, and she said yeah, if they wanted to do that, that would be jest fine with her.

"A few weeks after they left, Aunt Nance got this card from the depot at Garrett and it said they was a box over there fer her to come and pick up. Well, Big Jed took his mules and wagon and got this box, and when they opened it, it was a rockin' chair. It was right purty but put together with glue, shackley as could be. Aunt Nance couldn't leave it out on the porch overnight, the glue would've come loose, and she couldn't let the sun shine on it because the glue would melt. She got so tired of draggin' it in and out of the house that she took it upstairs and used it to stack her spare quilts on."

"But when does the newspaper part come in?" Johnnie wanted to know.

"Well, I'm gettin' to that. It seems that these women got someone from the Community Center to take Aunt Nance's pitcher settin' in this chair on her porch and send it to 'em, and I jest happened to get the paper that had Aunt Nance's pitcher in it. Almost shocked me to death when I opened that paper and saw Nance, but it was the readin' below the pitcher that made us all so mad. It said this was the first rockin' chair that anyone on Lonesome Holler had ever seed, and the first time Aunt Nance had ever got time to set down and relax and rest. Yer Aunt Nance has still got her Grandma's rockin' chair, and it's as good now as the day it was made, although it's rocked three generation of young'ns to sleep many of a time." John spit again toward the grate as if he'd tasted something bitter. "And I almost know that ever' woman on Lonesome Holler, er even as fer that part, all of Knott County, has a rockin' chair, a good strong homemade one that will last fer a long time."

For a while everything was quiet. Just the rustling of the papers, the clicking of Sarah Ellen's scissors, and the crackling of the fire. Then all of a sudden Rennie cried out, "Oh, no!" so

128

loud that John dropped his Bible, Sarah Ellen dropped her papers, and Johnnie came to the back of her chair.

"What in the world's wrong? Did the fire pop out and burn ye?" John asked.

"No! Jest look at this pitcher." She held the magazine up for Johnnie to see. "That's the old man that used to live in yer house. James Spradlow. And he's dead!"

Johnnie gave one look. "That's him, all right. Read what it says about him, Rennie."

Rennie read a page or two and stopped to tell the others. "It tells a lot about the books he's written, but not much about him. It seems they don't know much about him. That he has no family as fer as they know. Came to Kentucky ever summer between teachin'. He was an English perfessor at a college. No one knew much about his private life. When he missed comin' to his classroom two mornin's, the police went to his room in a cheap boardin' house and found him in his bed dead. They thought he'd been dead fer a few days. Apparently of a heart attack." Rennie wiped tears from her eyes.

"I'll not know what to do with his things that are still over in my house." There was a squeak in Johnnie's voice. "It really can shake ye up when ye read in a paper about the death of someone ye've had dealin's with, even if ye don't know 'em that well and never been close."

"My advice would be to jest let 'em set there and take as good a care of 'em as ye can until someone comes with papers statin' they have a right to 'em, and if not I'd jest keep 'em," John told him.

"I think I'll go over there to'mar and see how everthin' looks. I might decide to stay over there this winter. If I can fix a place fer my mule. That old barn ain't worth anythin' but firewood. I been thinkin' about sellin' my mule if I can't get some work fer him and me. It jest don't pay to winter a mule if ye can't work him. Ye work all summer to make corn and then feed half of it to the mule that helped ye to grow it," Johnnie said.

Rennie and John were surprised that Johnnie might consider moving out. "Ye know ye're welcome here jest as long as ye want to stay. I think of you as my own son." John reached out and patted him on the back. John was never one to show his feelings.

"I know that, and I'll be back whenever ye need me and to get a good home-cooked meal ever' now and then."

They didn't know it then, but feelings between Johnnie and Rennie would never be the same again. Johnnie had made his decision and meant to stick to it.

21

Back then little boy children didn't begin to wear pants until they were three or four years old. Till that age they wore dresses just like the ones worn by little girls of the same age. The only difference was that boys' dresses had a row of buttons all up and down the back, while the girls' buttons were in front, and sometimes the boys' dresses had a half belt reaching from side to side in the back. In winter their underwear was the same—long legs, long sleeves, a three-button drop seat in the back made from cotton "out-in'" flannel. Boys as old as seven or more didn't wear pants in the summertime, just a knee-length shirt, which they also slept in.

Clothes were handed down, made over, and patched, and sometimes the patches were patched. The day a boy received his first pair of long-legged pants was a very important day in his life, one to remember for a long time. That put him in the ledge with the big boys, one step nearer to being a man.

When the days began to get chilly that fall, Hank's grandmother decided to make him a pair of pants from an old skirt of hers. He was so excited he just kept running around and around. He helped her tug the old sewing machine from against the wall, where it had been gathering dust for a long time, and pull it in front of the open door, where she could see to sew. He was getting in the way so much that she had to call Jane to come and hold him still so she could measure him.

"Ye'll have to hold still. I ain't made a pair of britches in quite a spell. I'll make these jest a little bit too large so ye can grow into 'em. That way they'll last a long time. Don't know when ye'll get another pair."

"Can ye get 'em done agin dark so as I can go down and show 'em to Sarah Ellen?" Hank asked, his voice pleading.

"Ye can't be in too much of a hurry when ye're makin' a feller his first pair of britches, but I promise that if nothin' unexpected happens I'll have 'em ready so's ye can go and show 'em to Sarah Ellen to'mar." Aunt Nance was almost as excited as Hank.

Next morning about noon, Hank went strutting around the little path that ran between the two houses, his pants held up with strings, as he didn't have a belt yet, and the bottom of the legs turned up about two inches so he wouldn't get them muddy. His little heart was beating as fast as the wings of a humming bird. Long before he got to the house he began to yell, "Oh, Sarah Ellen, come look. Bet ye can't guess what I got."

Rennie opened the door just as Hank came through the gate. Sarah Ellen came running out with a big smile on her face. But after one look at Hank, she fell against Rennie's side and began crying like a stuck pig. She turned and threw herself on the bed, beating the pillow with both fists, kicking and screaming to the tops of the hills. John and Johnnie came running from the barn. "What's the matter? What's the matter?" both said at once.

"Did ye hit her?" John asked Hank when he saw him standing by the bed.

"No, I never hit Sarah Ellen. I jest asked her to come look at my new britches. I don't know why she's so mad at me. I never done a thing." Poor Hank! His happiness had turned to hurt surprise.

"Sarah Ellen, please calm down and tell what's wrong," Rennie begged, gathering her into her arms. "Did somethin' sting ye?" Hank stood there too amazed to know what to do. "Sarah Ellen, ye're scarin' Hank to death."

"I don't like Hank any more. Her's not a girl any more. Her is a boy."

"Hank has allus been a boy!" All the grown-ups wanted to laugh, but when they saw the tears gathering in Hank's eyes, they realized that to the two little ones this was a very serious matter.

It was a long time before Sarah Ellen quit crying. Every time she looked at Hank she would burst out again louder than ever.

"Guess ye'd better take him home," Rennie whispered to Johnnie.

"Come on, Hank. Let's go ride Old Barney. Us boys'll show these girls what's what. And I'll give ye a nice haircut to go with them britches." Johnnie left with the puzzled and disappointed boy, while Rennie tried to get Sarah Ellen interested in something else.

It was over a week before Sarah Ellen would even look at Hank, and over a month before she forgave him enough to play with him.

"I noticed that she allus said 'Hank she' or 'Hank her,' but I never dreamed that she thought he was a girl. I jest thought it was because she was jest beginnin' to learn to talk." Rennie felt sorry for them both. She wanted to cry and laugh at the same time. It *was* funny. She hoped they'd soon be just as good friends as they had been.

"Childern outgrow hurts like that," John told her. But Rennie sometimes wondered if they really did.

22 _____

Rennie didn't get to line the walls of her kitchen with the pages from the magazines as she had planned. For the next two weeks she was busy helping her father get the last of the apples, cushaws, pumpkins, and sweet and Irish potatoes stored away for winter use. John took up some of the boards from the floor of the front room close to the hearth, exposing two now empty holes in the earth. They had been there for many years and had been used every winter for the same purpose. Into one hole he poured the Irish potatoes they had dried; into the other went the late apples, Black Twigs, a very small but tasty apple, Winesaps, and Johnson Winter Keepers. A layer of straw came next and a few boards on top.

John and Rennie removed the cushaws and pumpkins from the fodder shocks where they had been kept safe from early frost and rolled them back under the beds in the front room. Later many of them would be dried for late winter and early spring use. When it was time to begin having fires in the grate, a long slim hickory pole would be hung by strings from two nails just above the fire and under the fireboard. The cushaws and pumpkins would be cut into two-inch rings and hung along this pole. When they were dry they would be removed and put away in a safe place in the loft, and the pole would be filled again.

The sweet potatoes they stored in a wooden barrel, each wrapped in a piece of newspaper or a page from a catalog. The Roman Beauty apples were saved for later use in a barrel or wooden box the same way. They would be eaten raw as a snack. They were too good to be fried or used for pies. Rennie also dried a lot of the Rusty Sweets and a few peaches on the kiln in the back yard that had been built by her grandfather from slate rocks and clay many years before.

Then winter set in with a vengeance. Early in December the Slone family woke up to see a six-inch snow that "layed on" for over two weeks. Old Mother Nature had sure been shaking her feather bed. Rennie put on her father's big boots and bundled up as well as she could, wearing the beloved tam and scarf that she'd now had for three years. She made her way to the barn to feed the stock, milk the cow, scatter corn for the chickens, and fill the water trough. Then she stomped a path to the outhouse and woodshed.

Johnnie was now staying in his own home. He would come over now and then about suppertime and share a meal with them. Rennie always had enough cooked, for mountain women always cooked "more'n a plenty" just in case someone chanced to stop by. The leftovers could always be fed to the dogs and cats and pigs. With the pigs the food found its way back to the table in the long run in the form of bacon, sausage, or side meat to cook with the shucky beans, dried apples, cushaws, and pumpkins.

Johnnie too had been preparing for winter. He laid up coal and wood for his fire and cookstove. By taking down the old barn, a very large one, he found enough good logs and planks to build a small shed for his mule. The rest of the wood from the demolished barn he stacked for firewood. He also cut down a large beech tree that stood just back of the barn. The next time he had supper with Rennie and her father he had an interesting story to tell. He waited until they were finished eating. When Uncle John pushed his chair back from the table, Johnnie said, "Wait jest a while. I want to tell ye somethin' that's hard to believe. Ye know that big beech tree that grew just back of the old barn?"

"I shore do. Yer mother would never have it cut down. She said her hens ate the beech nuts and got fat. I remember I used to pick up beech nuts and eat 'em, but they were such little bitty things I could never get a mouthful." John smiled at the recollection.

Rennie arose from the table and said, "Pa used to take us young'ns over there to rake away the leaves in the spring and hunt fer the nuts jest after they had sprouted. The sprouts'd be thick and real good, jest before the little leaves began to form. They're real tasty and fillin'."

"Well, this tree had got so old and rotten I was afraid the next big windstorm would blow it down on my mule stall. I had to cut it high up, leavin' a tall stump, because it was kind of on sidlin' ground. I notched it on the side so it would fall the way I wanted it to, away from my barn. Ye know, jest like ye showed me to cut a tree. But when I looked down into that hollow stump, ye'll never guess what I found. A half-gallon fruit jar full of moonshine! It had been put in the tree when it was small and the tree had grown around it. I took my knife and worked around it real careful like and got it out without breakin' the jar. It was still sealed, but the lead was so rusty it crumbled up in my hand. But I tasted of it. It was good moonshine." Johnnie was so excited that he was red in the face.

"That's shore strange," Uncle John said. "I say yer father put it there a long time ago, when the tree was younger and had jest a very small holler in it, and then he went away and no one found it."

"What did ye do with it?" Rennie asked.

"Give it to Big Jed fer his rheumatism," Johnnie laughed. Everyone on Lonesome Holler knew about Big Jed's love for moonshine and his excuse for using it.

Rennie picked up the water bucket and took a dishpan from a nail on the wall. Placing the pan on the back of the stove, she filled it with water from the bucket. Then with the empty bucket she started for the kitchen door. Johnnie arose from the table, stepped in front of her, and took the bucket out of her hand. "Let me go get that water. Let me feel like I'm payin' fer my supper. Where's the other bucket? As well get enough fer the night while I'm at it."

"Shore, and ye can wash the dishes, too, if ye have a mind to when ye come back," Rennie laughed.

"Thank ye, but no thanks. I don't care about that job. Might ruin my lily white hands. Ye should see the pile of dishes that have piled up over to my house. I keep on till I use up all the plates and then I start turnin' 'em over and eatin' on the bottom side." Johnnie's eyes belied his words.

"What do ye do about the platters and bowls?" Rennie went along with the joke.

"What platters and bowls? I jest rake my vittles from the pot onto my plate and sometimes I jest eat from the pot, and if I can't eat it all I set the pot on the floor and let the dog have the rest. He licks it clean and then I don't have to wash the pot." Johnnie's laugh was so loud that Sarah Ellen joined in.

"I know that ye're sayin' that fer a joke but I bet ye're tellin' the truth. Go on with those buckets before it gets dark."

Uncle John picked up his chair and went into the front room and sat down before the brightly burning fire. He took out his pipe and filled it with tobacco from a pouch in his pocket. Reaching up on the fireboard he got a squib, a twisted piece of newspaper about as long as a pencil, and lit his pipe with it.

Sarah Ellen soon followed him. She got her dolls from a box under one of the beds in the back of the room and began undressing them, getting them ready for bed. She slept with so many dolls that Rennie told her she didn't leave room for her sister. Sometimes after Sarah Ellen was asleep Rennie would remove some of the dolls, but she tried to replace them before the child awoke.

Soon Johnnie returned with the two buckets of water. After setting them on the side table, he gave Rennie's apron a friendly tug and untied her apron strings. She struck at him with her wet dishcloth, but he dodged her. Then he got a chair from the table and carried it to the front room, where Uncle John and Sarah Ellen were enjoying the fire. They needed no light, for the fire lighted up the whole room.

Rennie emptied the table scraps and the dishwater into the slop bucket that hung from a nail just outside the kitchen door. Next day she would feed this to the pig. If it was frozen she'd have to thaw it out in front of the fire or on the back of the stove after breakfast had been cooked.

Then she brought another chair from the kitchen into the front room. She sat down close to Johnnie and took out a small square of paper she'd cut from a newspaper. "Here's somethin' that I want to ask yer advice about. I found this in one of the newspapers I got the other day. It tells about a company that buys dried roots and hides. We've always sold ours to Long Bill. I know he can't give us as much fer 'em as he gets, he has to make a profit. But if we could ship these our own selves we'd get a lot more. But the thing about it is, they have to be shipped. We can't send them by mail, and we'd have to take 'em to a depot station."

There was too much of a question in Rennie's voice for

Johnnie to miss her meaning. She wanted him to take them for her. He knew that she and Joan and Jane had been digging roots all summer. Every chance they could take time off from the work in the cornfields and gardens, they had gone root hunting. They had taken their sang hoes and their dog (in case of meeting a snake) and climbed up one hill and then another hunting for may apple roots, snake root, yellow root, and others. They brought them home and washed them, then spread them on an old sheet or blanket to dry in the sun. Some were strung on twine with a needle, like beads, and hung from a nail on the wall of the house. Sassafras roots were larger and more plentiful but took a lot more work. The outside bark had to be removed and the inner bark shaved off, for this was the part that was used. Rennie always kept the woody parts of the roots to burn with the firewood. "It smells so nice." She never sold all she had. She kept some to make tea for the family or to flavor her homemade candy. Some folks even put it in their homemade soap to give it a nice smell. Ginseng brought much more money but was hard to find. They always left it to Johnnie to dig that.

"How many dried roots do ye have?" Johnnie asked with interest.

"We each have enough to fill a large sack, I'd say." Rennie knew that she had what she wanted. Johnnie would help them get their roots to the depot station.

"I'll make a trade with you three girls. If ye'll come over to my house and clean it all spick and span, I'll take yer roots and see that they're shipped to the address ye have there." Johnnie smiled at Rennie. "Will I have to make three different shipments, one fer each of ye?"

"No, I don't think so. I know it'll be all right with me. We all have about the same amount, more or less. If it's all right with Joan and Jane, ye can jest ship it in your name. Be easier that way, and when ye get the check we can divide it."

"And what if I should decide to keep it all?" Johnnie asked with a laugh.

"Well, we'd jest go over to yer house and gomm it all up agin," Rennie said. "Er better still, maybe we should wait till we get the check before we clean yer house for ye."

"If ye don't go clean it soon it'll be so 'gommed' up that ye won't be able to stand the smell."

John had been listening to their bantering talk. "If ye're done with yer trading, I'd like to ask ye a question, Johnnie. As part of the family I don't think that I'll be steppin' over my boundary. What are ye doin' about buyin' groceries fer yerself? Ye know that ye're due any of the sass that we've put away and feed fer yer mule, fer ye helped to grow it as much if not more than any of us. But yer salt, coffee, sugar, and things like that—I worry about that."

"I made a deal with Long Bill at his grocery store. He's lettin' me have a charge account. I gave him a lien on my mule. I jest get what I can get by with. If I don't get any work soon, I believe I can catch enough varmints this winter to sell the hides to him to pay him off in full by spring."

"Payin' the taxes is what worries me so much," said Rennie as she gazed into the fire.

"The Lord'll provide," John answered. Rennie thought to herself how many times she'd heard him say that. She wished she had his faith. She remembered the times they had had to sell laying hens they needed themselves, and once it had been a young heifer that her mother had wanted to keep for a milk cow. Her mother had cried, but she had said nothing.

"I went over to the courthouse to make sure that James Spradlow had paid up my taxes," Johnnie said, "and found that he'd paid two years ahead of time. So I won't have to worry about that fer a while."

23 _____

Everywhere up and down Lonesome Holler, Joan and Jane were known as "The Girls" or "Susan's Girls." There never were two sisters as different in personality or looks. Joan was short and heavy set, with black hair and brown eyes. She never ran out of something to talk about. Jane, on the other hand, although the younger, was taller by an inch or two, slim as a fence rail, and had blue eyes and curly yellow hair with almost a tint of red. She hardly ever spoke a word. Yet you never saw one without the other. It sure was going to be hard on Jane when Joan married and left the house.

The girls were pleased to learn that Johnnie was going to help them sell their dried roots, and as far as helping to clean his house, they were standing on their heads to get to see the inside of his house and all the things that Rennie had told them about.

"I've allus wanted to see inside that house," Joan told Rennie, and Jane whispered, "Me too." They planned to go the next Friday. Rennie asked Johnnie to come over and mind Sarah Ellen. "We have to get him out of the house that day. No woman can clean house with a man around, and we all three can move any of the heavy stuff that needs be."

Johnnie loaded the three sacks of dried roots on his mule, two tied together and laid across the saddle, the other across his lap. It looked like a large load, but the roots weren't all that heavy. He came back late that night, and it was next morning before he came over to let Rennie know that everything had gone well. He had seen the roots all packed into a large paper box he had bummed from a clerk at the coal company commissary, addressed, put on the train, and headed north. The station master had told him to be looking for the check in the mail in about two weeks. Rennie and the girls began counting off the days.

Johnnie came over early Friday morning and gave Rennie the keys to his front door. No one on Lonesome Holler ever fastened their doors when they were away from the house. Some neighbor might need to borrow something or someone might pass by who was hungry and wanted to stop for something to eat. Only at night were the doors fastened. But Mr. Spradlow had given Johnnie the keys and had asked him to take care of his things, and Johnnie had promised him he would. Johnnie wasn't the kind to break a solemn promise.

Just as soon as Joan and Jane saw Johnnie's mule hitched up in front of John's house, they came down, all bundled up and ready to go, loaded with old rags for cleaning cloths, brooms, buckets, and scrub brushes made from corn shucks. Rennie was just finishing the breakfast dishes. She asked Johnnie would he mind feeding the stock and milking the cow for her. She told him to strain the milk into the churn and tie a clean cloth over the top and set it by the fire.

"If I'd known I'd have to do all yer work, I'd not have asked ye to do mine." But Johnnie was smiling.

Rennie gathered up her share of the housecleaning needs, bundled up against the cold outside, and they were on their way. They laughed, talked, and giggled as they tramped along in the snow, except when they were passing some-one's house. Then they were very quiet. If they saw someone outside the house they would give them a "Howdy." The other person would ask them to come in and set a spell. When told they couldn't, they'd be invited to stop on their way back. Mountain people were always friendly.

Before they got to Johnnie's house they saw blue smoke rising from the chimney and the kitchen flue. Johnnie had left a good fire so the house would be warm when they got there. They found when they went in that he had also set a washtub of water on the stove to heat and had a large pile of stovewood near the stove and plenty more near the grate. "That Johnnie," Rennie said when she saw this. "He thinks of everthin'."

After they had removed their coats and wraps, Rennie took Joan and Jane from room to room. Unlike most houses on Lonesome Holler, this one had two bedrooms and a kitch-en. Mr. Spradlow had furnished it well. There were many things the girls had never seen before. The walls weren't lined with newspapers but with heavy brown paper fastened up with tacks called buttons, each about the size of a quarter.

They went up the ladder stairs to the room in the loft. It

was a mess. Mr. Spradlow hadn't used it for an extra bedroom, for there was only him, and as far as anyone knew he had never had any visitors. The loft was full of junk and leftovers from an earlier time. They took one look and decided to wait until later to do anything with it. It was too cold up there, anyway. If Johnnie wanted them to they would come back in the spring, go through the stored junk, and burn what was of no use or was too worn-out and old to be of any use to anyone.

They began dusting what needed dusting, and scrubbing what needed scrubbing, and washing what needed washing. They tried to wash the windows, but the water would freeze, so they just dusted them. Rennie took down the pretty, lacy white curtains to take home and wash. One whole side of the room where the grate was had been covered with shelves filled with books—more books than Rennie had ever seen before. She took one quick look and told the girls they had better be the ones to dust those books. "Fer if I took one of those books down and opened it, I'd start readin' it and I couldn't put it down." Then with a sigh she added, "I'll read 'em all, one at a time later, except the ones that are too hard fer me." Rennie had quit school before finishing the eighth grade, but Miss Rose had told her she read at a high school level. All she knew was that she loved to read and couldn't understand why anyone didn't like to. She didn't read to improve herself or for the information, she just read for the pleasure.

By the middle of the day they were hungry. "Why didn't we think to bring us some vittles from the house?" Joan asked. They looked around and couldn't find anything that wouldn't take too long to fix. "I know!" Jane said. "I'll go to the barn and get an ear of the mule's corn and we'll parch it." No quicker said than done. The corn was shelled and poured into a hot skillet in which a small amount of lard had been melted. Rennie added a little salt and stirred the corn continuously until the kernels began to swell up and turn brown. Oh, how good the smell was to the starving girls! They could hardly wait until it was cool enough to eat. Rennie had poured it into a large platter and scattered it out. They began filling their hands and then their mouths. It was so crunchy, brickley, and tasty. Such an appetizing odor. For those poor people who've never had any, parched corn is to be eaten with the hands.

"This is the first parched corn I've had this year. Glad ye thought of it," Rennie told Joan.

Rennie took a few grains in her hand, shut her fingers over them, and stuck out her hand toward Joan. "Hully Gully," she said to Joan.

"Hand fully," Joan answered with a laugh.

"How many," asked Rennie. "Nine er tennie?"

"I guess eight," Joan said.

Rennie opened her hand. There were nine grains. "I owe ye one. If ye'd guessed more than what I had, ye'd have had to give me the difference. Remember how we used to play that?"

"I shore do. We didn't know we were learnin' to count. And we'd end up eatin' the corn after it had passed from hand to hand over and over agin. We must parch some corn fer Hank and Sarah Ellen sometime and teach 'em how to play Hully Gully. Little Rose might get choked."

The girls were soon finished with their work, and after locking the door they went home tired but satisfied with a job well done.

"Shore glad I'll have time to rest a little while before I have to get supper and do up the rest of the work. I can get a look at the two books I sneaked into this bundle of winder curtains."

In two weeks' time Johnnie came home from the post office with the check from the dried root company, almost twenty-seven dollars. Rennie couldn't believe her eyes. "Why, that's almost nine dollars each. Jest wait till I tell Jane and Joan."

"I'll go to town to'mar and get it cashed," Johnnie told her.

When Rennie got her money she took out enough to buy herself and Sarah Ellen some winter shoes. The rest she stashed in the old leather trunk under the bed in the loft. Every nickel or dime that she just did not have to spend she would add to the pile so as to have something with which she could buy Sarah Ellen some pretty clothes for school.

Johnnie had said something that had bothered Rennie ever since. The thought kept buzzing around in her head like a new bee. "What if Sarah Ellen doesn't want to go to school?" he had asked. That had never entered Rennie's mind. She was so wrapped up in her own dream that she had never considered that her little sister might not have the same dream. "Am I just so disappointed that I had to quit school myself that I'm jest tryin' to live my dream in Sarah Ellen?" she asked herself. "My dream," she pondered. "Sarah Ellen may not want to go to school. How blind have I been?" Rennie sat for a long time, her mind going over and over the problem. Each time she came around to the same thought. "I can't give up my dream. I've gone too fer now. But I'll do all I can to see that she has the choice, and if she has other ideas, then I won't push her." She knew that Sarah Ellen would be able to learn. Even now as a toddler she showed signs of being intelligent. "She's smart," Johnnie had said. "But stubborn as a mule."

When Johnnie got back from buying the winter shoes for the girls, he had some exciting news. He had just by chance run into a man in town who was looking for someone willing to furnish him with mining props, or timbers, the small poles used to hold up the roofs of the coalmines. Johnnie came back to Lonesome Holler with a signed contract to furnish the man with all he needed for the next three years. What a break!

Johnnie was so excited he could hardly talk as he tried to tell his Uncle John the good news. "Jest think, Uncle John, he's givin' me six cents each fer hard wood and five fer soft wood, to cut and haul 'em near the big road where he can have 'em loaded on his log wagon. I figger I can give you and Aunt Nance a penny each fer 'em on the stump. I can pay ye a quarter a day fer the use of yer mule, and with what timber I have on my land, guess I'll send my sisters some of that, after I get started. I haven't mentioned it to him, but I'm shore Joe Smith will help me as a gin hand, now that he's wantin' to get married."

Johnnie was out of breath. He had gone on and on about the job. It was something to be tickled about. It meant cash money to spend for all of them for the next three years.

"That don't sound like much when ye talk about it in pennies, but when ye think that ye can cut and haul over a hundred a day, it soon mounts up to quite a lot."

John was as pleased as Johnnie. "I knowed the Lord would make a way."

Just as soon as the weather faired up, Johnnie and Joe got busy chopping, sawing, splitting, and hauling. Rennie loved to stand on her porch and listen to the whine of the crosscut saw, the crack of the axe, the thump of the falling tree after the yell "Timber!!"

Johnnie seemed like a different person. His laugh could be heard ringing out over the hillsides as the props kept piling up along the sides of the big road. He now had a job that he loved, and soon he would have money to spend. Rennie wouldn't have to worry about the tax money. Joe was as happy, but he was a quieter person and didn't express his feelings like Johnnie in laughter and in song.

Joan was the happiest of all. "Johnnie," she said, "I could jest love ye to death."

"Better save all that love fer Joe," Johnnie answered. "He's goin' to have to work purty hard to keep up with me." Joan knew that now she and Joe could get married. She spent some of her part of the root money on a wedding dress, not just a dress for that one day but a pretty one that could later be used for a Sunday-go-to-meetin' dress. With the rest she bought yards and yards of muslin, "factory" (so called because it came from the factory unbleached) that she would sew into sheets and pillow slips.

Jane had bought shoes for all her little sisters and Hank and herself. She thought nothing about spending her money for her family. That was the custom of the hills. Everyone in a family shared and shared alike. Life was so hard and love was so plentiful, that was all the way families could survive. But Jane didn't think anything about the fact that Joan had spent her money on herself, for soon she would be starting a new family. Yet she would always be a part of this one.

Johnnie took a day off now and then to do the plowing for Uncle John and himself. They had to grow their gardens and corn, because no matter what, you had to raise something to eat or you didn't eat. If for some reason, sickness or death, a family couldn't grow their own food, then the neighbors would come and help out. But no one had any to sell, or very little.

Rennie always cooked dinner for Johnnie and Joe when they were working in the woods nearby, on the hillsides above her home. They had dinner at noon and in the evening just as big a supper. When Rennie got the food on the table she rang the dinner bell and the men came to the house, washed their hands and faces in a pan of water outside the back door, and sat down at the loaded table.

Sometimes when the men were working too far away in the woods to hear the dinner bell, Rennie, Sarah Ellen, and Hank would take the warm, freshly cooked food to them in baskets. Rennie knew she had to take enough for the children, too, for they so loved to eat in the woods. Johnnie warned them to be sure and "holler" big and loud just as soon as they could hear the axes or saw, and wait until they heard him or Joe answer.

One day that spring Rennie decided it was time to line the walls of her house with the pages from the magazines she had bought last fall. She had read them from cover to cover and even borrowed Susan's.

John had gone to the Association meeting and would be gone for four or five days, and while he was gone would be a good time to get that paper on the walls. First she took all the magazines apart and separated the different size pages. Then she made her paste. She filled the largest pot she had with water and placed it on the stove to heat, then in a smaller pot she mixed flour and cold water and stirred it into a thin paste, pouring this into the boiling water and stirring it until there were no more lumps. Going up the stair ladder to the loft, she removed three or four red hot peppers from a string hanging from the ceiling and returned to the kitchen. She crumbled the pods into the paste and pushed the pot to the back of the stove to cool.

Then she went out to the front porch to check on Hank

and Sarah Ellen. She heard the back door open and heard Johnnie yell, "What's fer supper?" Just as she came into the kitchen, she saw him lift a large spoon of the paste to his mouth. "Don't!" yelled Rennie. But Johnnie just smiled and swallowed the spoonful with a big smile. Instantly he covered his mouth with both hands, and tears began running down his face. He grabbed the gourd and dipped it full and filled his mouth, then ran for the back door.

"What have ye done? Ye tryin' to poison us to death? What is that stuff?"

"Did ye not hear me yell at ye to not do that?"

"Yeah, I heard ye, but I jest thought ye were tryin' to be my mother agin, like ye're allus doin', and didn't want me to eat from the kittle."

"That's paste that I jest made to stick up my paper onto the walls. I filled it with red hot peppers so the mice wouldn't try to eat it."

"Eat it! No mouse with a lick of sense would come in a mile of that stuff."

Rennie was laughing her head off. It wasn't often that she got such a chance to rib Johnnie. "Here," she said. She reached inside the oven and gave him a large baked sweet potato. "This will take the sting out. Eat this." Rennie was still doubled over and holding her sides with laughter.

"Well, it's not so funny to me. That stuff burned all the hair from my tongue. I won't be able to eat fer a month."

"I see ye can still talk."

24 _____

Rennie grew up in a place and at a time when how a person looked didn't matter all that much. Girls weren't encouraged to try to make themselves appealing to the opposite sex. "Pretty is as pretty does" was not just said, it was taught and observed by the young folks of that day. Even had they known about make-up they wouldn't have been allowed to use it, nor would they have had the money to buy it. Every woman and girl wore her hair long. To bob your hair was a sin and was thought of as the sign of a "woman with a bad name." Just as soon as a woman married (and they sometimes married at fourteen) she must begin dressing like her older women relatives—long dresses with long sleeves, high-necked collars.

Once one of Rennie's cousins stopped and spent the night with them on her way from her father's farm to one of the coal camps. After she left, Sarah Ellen remarked how pretty her clothes were and how soft and nice her hands were. "Not rough and chapped like Rennie's."

John heard what she had said and scolded her. "Yer sister's hands are the way they are because she works hard fer you and me. The hard places are jewels in the sight of the Lord. Yer cousin needs to look nice fer the job she's chosen, but it's the devil's work." Sarah Ellen wasn't old enough to understand, but Rennie could guess at what he meant, and she blushed, not because he had praised her but because he had hinted at what her cousin did at the mining camp.

Rennie had never paid any never mind to how she looked. The only place she could see her face was in the cracked looking glass tacked up over the wash bench, above the wash pan and comb case in the kitchen. She had never seen her whole reflection until she and Jane and Joan were cleaning the house for Johnnie. In one of the bedrooms was a large mirror on a dresser, and by standing far back in the room they could see all of themselves in the mirror. It had been a lot of fun for them, but there had been no pride.

Some stranger would have seen Rennie as plain if it hadn't been for her beautiful chestnut brown hair, verging on red, and her sparkling bright green eyes. Her sharp nose was just a little long to match her strong chin. It was a face that spoke of strength of character more than beauty, but a face that you were not likely to forget once seen.

Sarah Ellen was just the opposite. Even at the age of three she showed signs of being a beautiful person. A lovely child, full of love and strong feelings, she had curly, light yellow hair that would turn to a bright yellow as she grew into womanhood. It was so curly that it seemed to be growing on her head at both ends, and it didn't grow long as Rennie's had. Once Hank threw a handful of cuckleburs into her hair, and it took Rennie hours to get them out. Sarah Ellen had done the same to Hank's hair, but his hair was so short and straight it wasn't such a job, although he yelled just as loud.

Sarah Ellen had large, round, light blue eyes and a heart-shaped mouth that could spread into a bright smile or droop into a pout, depending on her mood—which could change in a second without warning. "Ye better get married before Sarah Ellen gets grown," Rennie's friends would tease her. "She's so purty she'll get all the boys."

Rennie didn't mind. To her Sarah Ellen was her "heart and joy." Where Rennie, even as a child, had been quiet and thoughtful, Sarah Ellen was never still from the time she got out of bed until she returned at night so tired that she fell asleep the moment her head touched the pillow. She never walked if she had room to run, she never whispered, and she never spoke in a quiet voice if she could yell. "Can't ye keep that child quiet so as I can read? A man can't hear himself think around here anymore," John would complain to Rennie.

You couldn't say that John was mean to his children. He just never gave them much attention. If they didn't interfere with him he seldom seemed to see them. Just so he had clean clothes when he needed them to wear to church, so there were three hot meals on the table on time, quiet when he wanted to read, and his bed ready when he wanted to go to sleep, he was content.

Rennie knew that the fathers of many of her friends on Lonesome Holler "took a limb to their children and made 'em mind." She had learned more about God from her mother's kindness than from all the preaching she'd heard from her father. She didn't miss a father's love because she'd never seen her father until she was ten years old. She no longer hated him, as she had at first when she had blamed him for making her mother cry. And she obeyed him as a matter of course and taught Sarah Ellen to do the same. But he was gone from home so much of the time. She never went to him for advice and seldom asked him for help.

It was just a little after Sarah Ellen's fourth birthday that Rennie noticed a change in her father. He no longer went to church each Sunday. He didn't get up early and ate very little of the breakfast that Rennie had kept warm for him in the oven. Then he just kept getting weaker and weaker until he finally didn't get out of bed at all. Rennie went to see what Aunt Nance thought about his sickness. She made him some sassafras tea, but he refused to drink it. "No," he said, "my time has come. I'll never walk agin in this world." He never did, but he lived almost two more years.

Rennie took care of him just as if he were a baby, never complaining, never questioning why. It was just her duty. She respected and honored her father because he was her father. She would have helped anyone that needed help the same way.

She didn't have to ask for the neighbors' help. They just came and gave what they could of their time and their food, bringing what they had, trying to tempt John to eat, though he barely ate enough to keep body and soul together. Sometimes his preacher friends would come and pray and sing some of the beautiful Baptist songs. "I am a poor wayfaring stranger, traveling in this world of woe," or "Jesus left His home in Glory, came to die for you and me," and many others—sad but uplifting.

It wasn't long before John began to lose his mind. He would sometimes think Rennie was his mother and that he was a child again. Other times he would call her Mary. But the times that hurt Rennie most were when he thought he was back in prison. Then he'd yell and scream and beg. Rennie didn't like to have Sarah Ellen exposed to this, to so much sadness. A child had only one childhood and it should be a happy one. Rennie kept Sarah Ellen out of the house as much as she could, letting her stay more and more with Hank at Susan's house. Many times Johnnie took the two little ones with him when he was working in the fields.

In the spring, just before Sarah Ellen was to start school, John died. Just passed away one evening at nightfall. Rennie went outside and rang the dinner bell. Soon folks from all up and down Lonesome Holler began to gather around the house, on the porch and inside. Some of the men bathed the body and laid it out, dressing John in his best pants and a white shirt that Miss Rose had sent him for a Christmas present and he'd never worn. Next day they made the coffin from some dry oak boards that John had put in the barn loft a long time before for just this purpose. They lined the outside of the coffin with black cambric and the inside with white. Rennie gave them one of her mother's beautiful hand-stitched quilts for the body to lie on.

All this while other men were digging a grave by the side of Mary's. Next day, a little after the sun had passed the halfway mark, they put John away with a song and a prayer. While the burial was going on and everyone was out of the house, some of the neighbor women cleaned the house and put away anything that would remind the two girls of their father. All his clothes were put in a chest and his Bible and pipe went in the little leather trunk under the bed in the loft. Then everyone returned home, leaving Rennie and Sarah Ellen alone.

Johnnie asked Rennie if she wanted him to spend the first night with her, but she told him, "No, I must get used to bein' alone. And I still have Sarah Ellen."

25

The long months that Rennie had spent caring for her father had taken a lot from her both physically and emotionally. It had kept her housebound. She had been thankful for the large supply of books that Mr. Spradlow had left in the tall bookshelves in Johnnie's house. She had sat by her father's bed many hours reading. Sometimes John had asked her to read the Bible aloud to him, but he would soon drift off to sleep. Susan and Aunt Nance had spelled her many times, giving her a chance to catch up with her other work. But John would rather that Rennie be there. When he awoke from one of his many naps he would turn his eyes and look all around the room to see if his daughter was there.

Now Rennie was free to plant her garden. Being out in the fresh mountain air was wonderful. She had the help or hindrance, whichever way you looked at it, of Sarah Ellen and Hank. Hank had a sled that Johnnie had made for him by putting runners on an old worn-out washtub. The children would fill it with rocks gathered from the garden and dump them along the creek bank. They also cleaned out the chicken house and spread the manure over the garden, having as much fun working as if it were play. Every day that wasn't needed for the garden found Rennie and Jane rambling the hillsides hunting roots to dig and dry. Joan was now married to Joe and expecting her first child. Johnnie had finished his contract with the coal company and was looking for another job. He had cut all the timber on the three farms that was of the size needed to make props.

The summer passed too quickly for Rennie. She was of a double mind. She wanted Sarah Ellen to begin school, and yet she dreaded to see her start. She just couldn't make herself willing to see Sarah Ellen go, she looked so small. But Rennie just bit her tongue and gritted her teeth and held onto her dream. She began imagining all the things that could happen to her little sister. Maybe the schoolhouse would catch fire, or there might come a fresh flood and she would drown. Then she began to imagine impossible things.

She had planned on teaching Sarah Ellen her alphabet and

numbers before school started, but she hadn't gotten around to it, what with the care of her father. Rennie liked to remember how her mother had taught her, showing her the letters on the newspapers that lined the inside wall of their house.

One day when it had rained, keeping Rennie from her work in the field or garden and Sarah Ellen inside from her play, Rennie thought this would be a good time to help Sarah Ellen start learning her letters. Calling her over to the wall she showed her the letter A and asked her to show her another one. To her astonishment, Sarah Ellen told her the correct name for all the letters and numbers.

"But how did ye know all of this? I can't believe it." Rennie was so impressed.

"Hank learned me," Sarah Ellen said with a child's voice full of pride. "He learned me to count. I can count to one hundred by ones and fives and tens, and I can count to twenty by two's." She stopped to catch her breath. "And he says that I can have his primer book when we go to school. He was savin' it fer Little Rose, but she won't be goin' to school till next year, and Hank is in the first grade this year. Me and Hank used little sticks to count with, and I can add a little and do some take aways, but not much."

"Well, I never," was all Rennie could say. She was glad to learn that all the time she had sent Sarah Ellen to play with Hank had been put to some good use and that she wouldn't have to buy a book for her this year. Rennie had felt so guilty because she hadn't had the time to spend with Sarah Ellen that she would have liked to.

"It seems as if you and Hank has got it all worked out and I won't have anythin' to do." Rennie gave her a big hug.

"Oh yeah, ye've got my dresses and bloomers to make, and ye must buy me a tablet and a pencil. And please, Rennie, don't get me one of them penny pencils, them little old ugly brown things. I hate 'em. Get me a purty nickel one, the ones that's blue er yellow er red er green er all sorts of colors. I jest must have one."

"Yeah, I think that I can do that all right."

The talk had put Rennie to thinking. The money Johnnie had been paying them for timber and for the use of the mule had come in handy at a time when they needed it most, but it had been spent. Rennie had added a little from time to time to the stash in the old leather trunk under the bed in the loft. Now she took eight dollars from it and bought a pair of shoes for Sarah Ellen. There wasn't much choice in what kind to buy, for all the shoes in Long Bill's store were made just alike. The right size was all Rennie had to see about. She measured Sarah Ellen's foot with a stick, allowing some length "fer her to grow into."

But choosing the cloth for her dresses was a different matter. One whole side of the store was filled with bolts of cloth— "factory," calico, percale, gingham, oilcloth, Indianhead. So many beautiful colors that Rennie knew not to take Sarah Ellen with her when she went to get the cloth for her school dresses. She got two yards of three different pieces, five yards of the factory for bloomers and underskirts, three yards of elastic, and two cards of buttons. She also bought four spools of white thread. There were only four kinds of thread to choose from—black and white in either hand sewing thread or machine thread.

Rennie had never learned to use a sewing machine. Her mother didn't have one and had taught her to sew well with her hands. But she had so much to sew now. She went to Aunt Nance's for help. She asked if the older woman would help her cut the dresses out and let her use her sewing machine. No one bought a paper pattern then. They cut their own patterns from newspapers or from another dress, or by just looking at one. Aunt Nance said that she'd have loved to make Sarah Ellen's clothes for her but she wasn't feeling very pert and her eyes were failing her. Susan said that if Rennie would help Jane hoe out the corn, she'd do the sewing in exchange. Rennie was more than pleased. To work outside and to be with Jane would be more fun than work. So they made the swap.

By the end of the week the corn was hoed and the sewing was finished. Rennie said that she could do the buttons and button holes and put in the elastic. Now all that was left was to wait until school began. To Sarah Ellen it was a time of anticipation, and to Rennie a time of dread.

The first day of school came. Sarah Ellen was up early. Rennie had to call her just one time. She dressed herself in one of her new dresses, over the white underskirt and long-legged bloomers. She would rather have left off the stockings and shoes, but Rennie told her that everyone else would be wearing their new shoes on the first day of school; maybe later she might go barefooted. Hank and Sarah Ellen hadn't had on shoes since the first day of May. Rennie too liked to kick off her shoes now and then and feel the fresh earth on her bare toes.

After breakfast, of which Sarah Ellen ate very little, Rennie took an empty four-pound lard bucket and filled it about half full of warm, fresh, sweet milk, crumbled a large piece of cornbread into the milk, and shut the lid. She wrapped a teaspoon in a piece of brown paper poke that had once held brown sugar bought at Long Bill's store. "Put this spoon in yer pocket, and don't lose it. After eatin' yer dinner be shore and remember to wash the spoon and bucket under the pump. We don't want 'em to turn sour er rust. And be shore and set yer bucket with all the others at the spring of water near the creek under that big tree. Hank will show ye where. I've scratched yer name here on the side of the bucket so ye'll know which is yers."

Sarah Ellen heard a yell from the gate and ran out to see Hank waiting for her. His bucket and book were under his arms.

"Take good care of her, Hank," Rennie called.

"Course," Hank answered, as if the request had been an insult.

This was going to be a long day for Rennie. She began watching the sun creep across the porch. Long before noon she had tried washing the windows, scrubbing the floors. It was too cloudy to take all the quilts out to sun. Would the day never end?

Sarah Ellen and Hank were among the first to arrive. They went and sat on the schoolhouse steps. Soon the schoolyard began to fill up. The schoolhouse was a large one-room build-ing that sat far back from the road, enclosed with a paling fence to keep out the roaming stock that was allowed to graze loose. The fence kept the animals from leaving a nasty mess that the schoolchildren would be sure to step in. Steps led up to the front door. There were three windows along each side of the building. Out back were two outhouses, one marked Boys, the other, Girls. The letters had been burned into the wood with a red hot fire poker.

Inside, a pot-belly stove sat in the center of the room in a low box of sand. A blackboard covered the middle of the back wall facing the front door. A wooden bench ran along the wall from the blackboard to one corner of the room, where a bucket of water sat on a stool with a gourd hanging above it on a nail.

On each side of the stove were two rows of wooden seats, so made that the front was a seat for two students while the back was a desk and shelf for the students behind. The boys sat on one side of the room, the girls on the other. The teacher had a small desk and chair just in front of the blackboard.

Outside, beside the steps, stood a tall flagpole. Each morning before school, the students lined up in two rows in front of the flagpole, boys on one side, girls on the other, and gave the flag salute. Then they marched inside and stood by their desks and repeated the Lord's Prayer, sang one or two songs, either religious or patriotic, and sat down in their seats while the teacher read a passage from the Bible. Then the teacher "took up books"—began classes.

This year they had a new teacher. A stranger to all the students, he was from an adjoining county who had gotten his education at the Caney Creek Community Center.

Sarah Ellen was one of seven beginners this year. All the others had come with a bigger brother or sister and had taken a seat with them. Sarah Ellen followed Hank to his seat, but the teacher made her move. "Boys on one side, girls on the other," he said. He tried to be kind when he saw how frightened she was. "I'll be in the seat jest across from you," Hank said. He asked if the boy sitting opposite Sarah Ellen would mind moving back. The teacher would soon rearrange them, yet Hank watched out so he could be as close as possible to Sarah Ellen.

"My name," said the teacher, "is Richard Tate. You all call me Mr. Tate." He took out from his desk a large record book. "The first thing I have to do is register you all in this book. I want to know your name, your age, your birthday, and your parents' names, and if this isn't your first year I'll need to know what grade you were in last year. I want the eighth graders in the back rows and the seventh next and so on. I want the beginners in the front row. Everyone keep the same seat and that way I'll soon learn your names and who you are. For this first day I'll allow the little ones to sit with their big brothers or sisters, but only today. After that they must sit in the first row where I can keep an eye on them."

When he got to Sarah Ellen and asked her name, age, and birthday, she spoke right up nice and answered all the questions. When the teacher asked her what her father's name was, she said, "John Slone, Preacher John Slone. He's dead," she added.

"What's your mother's name?"

"Rennie."

Hank raised his hand for permission to speak, and the teacher nodded to him. "Rennie isn't her mother, Rennie's her sister."

"Rennie is too my mother. She raised me and she takes care of me. We sleep together and she calls me her own little baby child." Sarah Ellen's eyes were begging to fill with tears. Some of the other students began to giggle, but a stern look from the teacher stopped that in a hurry.

"Her real mother is dead. Ma said that her name was Mary. Rennie took care of her," Hank explained.

"Is that what you want me to put down?" the teacher asked Sarah Ellen.

"Write down whatever ye want. It won't change things, because Rennie is the best Mommie in the whole wide world."

Teacher made up his mind then and there that he was going to make it a point to meet this Rennie. She must be worth knowing to have earned such love, loyalty, and devotion from such a small child. But now he had work to do.

Because Mr. Tate lived a long way from the school, he boarded out with the students' parents, first one family, then another. This came as a matter of course with his small salary. But he wouldn't stay at Hank's or Sarah Ellen's because neither had "a man of the house."

Sarah Ellen and Hank ran all the way home that first day. "Rennie will be so lonesome by herself," they agreed. Rennie was watching from the front porch.

26

It wasn't long before Mr. Tate got his chance to meet Rennie. It had begun raining just a little after school began one day—not a heavy rain, just a steady fall that kept up all day. He didn't let the children out for recess, only the brave ones that had a call from nature and had to go to the outhouse. He tried to keep the children amused by letting them sing songs. Noon came and still the rain kept coming down. They ate their dinner inside. It was so dark there was no thought of trying to have regular classes. Some of the boys built a fire in the stove, "jest to take the chill out of the air."

By afternoon Mr. Tate was at his wits' end. He didn't know what to do. He couldn't send the students home because by now he could hear the roar of water in the creek, and he knew it was rising higher and higher. As the day wore on the larger children became hard to control and the smaller ones were beginning to get frightened. He tried to have a spelling bee, but there was such a difference in their ability to spell that it didn't hold their interest for long. He was almost ready to cry, but he mustn't let the small ones know that he was as frightened as they were.

He went over to one of the windows to see if the rain had lightened up any. That's when he saw someone coming around the hillside far above the road, even above the fence that ran along the pasture fields. He couldn't tell if it was a woman or a man. The person was bundled up and using a long stick but kept sliding and slipping, getting up and coming on toward the schoolhouse. Mr. Tate stood there and watched until the person turned in at the school yard. Then he went to open the door.

At the same moment he opened the door from the inside, the person opened it from the outside and tumbled in, almost falling. She had on a man's overcoat and a man's floppy hat, and under her arms she carried a large bundle. A yell of "Rennie," and Sarah Ellen came running. "I knowed ye'd come. I jest knowed that ye would."

Rennie dropped the bundle and clasped Sarah Ellen to one side and Hank to the other. "Stand back and let me get out of this coat and hat so's I can see what I'm doin'." Rennie looked up and a blush gathered on her face as she met the eyes of the teacher. "I hated to disturb yer classes," she said, "but the road is washed in some places. I jest had to get the childern to the house as soon as I could."

"My name is Richard Tate," he said as he offered her his hand, "and you must be Rennie. I've heard so much about you."

"All good, I hope." She smiled, and that smile changed her whole face. Her fright was now gone. She took his hand. Mr. Tate got a shock of surprise when he took her hand, it was so hard and rough. It didn't match the gentleness of her eyes as she stooped down and put one arm around Sarah Ellen and the other around Hank and gave them each a tight hug and placed a kiss on the cheek of her little sister. "She's been real frightened," he thought. "What a woman. I must get to know her better."

"I'll take 'em to the house now, if ye don't mind." And then to the children she said, "I brought ye some coats to bundle up in."

"Mind? I'm so glad. I don't know what to do with the rest of them. I wish someone would come get the others." He spoke in a low voice, not wanting to frighten the children.

"I'll take all that are goin' my way, but I say there'll be other parents along soon. Please promise me ye'll not let a one of 'em start to the house by themselves. Stay here all night if need be. I know ye'll get hungry, but better that than run the risk of bein' drowned." As Rennie finished speaking there was another knock on the door, another yell from one of the children as he recognized his mother. Soon the schoolhouse was full of men and women. The smell of wet clothes filled the warm room. Some had ridden mules. Soon all the children were on their way to their own homes.

Rennie had her group ready. She bundled them up the best she could and they started up the hill. They had to crawl under fences, over fences, around large rocks going through corn fields and over gardens, and once through a man's yard. But they did get home safely.

The waters hadn't gone down enough the next day to have school, so school stayed closed until the beginning of the following week. All the men on Lonesome Holler spent their time trying to repair the road, though it wasn't much of a road, anyway, just a bridle path along the side of the hill. Wagons and sleds went along the creek bed when it wasn't full of water. Otherwise they just didn't go anywhere.

Richard Tate kept thinking more and more about Rennie. He had made up his mind to call on her some time, until he learned that she lived alone with just Sarah Ellen. It would show disrespect for him to go to her house and no menfolks around. He had made no friends since coming to Lonesome Holler. Everyone was friendly enough, but he needed a close friend, someone near his own age.

The following Sunday he went to church to see if Rennie might be there, but she wasn't. Outside, after church broke, all the folks gathered to exchange news and friendly greetings. He was asked to have dinner with many of them, but he just returned to the house where he was boarding that week. He tried to read, grade some papers, and write some overdue letters back home, but he couldn't get settled down, so he decided to take a walk and maybe pass Rennie's house. There could be no harm in that, he told himself.

His mind just kept going back to her. Why was he so intrigued with her after spending such a short time with her and exchanging only a few words, and in the presence of a schoolhouse full of children. "I couldn't be falling in love, could I?" he asked himself. There had been a girl back home that had meant a lot to him once. They had even talked a little of marriage, but she hadn't been willing to wait until he finished school, and she married someone else. It had hurt at the time, but now, looking back on it, it had been his pride more than his heart that had been hurt.

He wondered if Rennie had a sweetheart already. Most girls at her age were already married and had started a family. He knew that she must be about nineteen, for someone had told him that she had quit school at the age of twelve to care for her sister when her mother died, and he knew that Sarah Ellen was almost seven. Here in Eastern Kentucky a girl was called an old maid at the age of twenty, and if she married after that it was usually to an older man, a widower with a house full of children that needed a new mother. Rennie was too nice a person for that.

Richard started on his Sunday walk. He thought he would go the long way around and no one would guess what he was doing. At every house he passed, folks were sitting out on their front porches, enjoying the warm afternoon. The children all came to the gate to say "Howdy" to teacher, and the older folks invited him to "come in and set a spell." When he came to Johnnie's house he got the surprise of his life. He hadn't expected to see a house and yard like that here on Lonesome Holler. Mr. Spradlow had done a wonderful job in improving the place, and Johnnie had tried his best to keep it up. The yard was large and beautiful. A rock walkway led up to the front door, and the back porch was screened in. The window frames were painted, and Richard could see that white lace curtains hung over them inside. Johnnie had tried to keep everything just as Mr. Spradlow had left it, to the amusement of his neighbors. "Better plant vegetables in that yard. Nobody ever ate a mess of flowers," he'd been told more than once.

As Richard paused in the road, trying to take in the beauty of the place, Johnnie came through the door dragging a wooden chair with him. "Come in, teacher," he invited.

"Don't care if I do," was Richard's reply. "Just been admiring your place."

"Here, take this chair while I go get me another." Johnnie let the screen door slam as Richard sat down. He soon returned and sat down beside him.

"Such a pretty yard, and this house," Richard said with a question in his voice. Johnnie told him the story of Mr. Spradlow.

"After ye rest a while I'll take ye inside. He left a lot of things that ye don't usually find on Lonesome Holler," Johnnie told him. "I don't know what else to do with 'em except take care of 'em until someone comes and asks fer 'em and can prove they have more right to 'em than I do."

"I don't blame you. What else can you do? And believe me, I'd love to have had a gift like this dropped into my lap."

Richard thought he had seen a lot, but when he saw the shelves full of books he was flabbergasted. "Wow," he gasped. "Have you read all these books?"

"No," Johnnie answered, "but my cousin Rennie has, er she's workin' on it. She has three er four over to her house all the time. When she finishes with a bunch, she brings 'em back and gets more. That girl would rather read than eat any old time."

Richard was glad to hear that about Rennie. He too would rather read than do anything else. "Would you care to loan me some of these?" he asked.

"No. Go ahead, take all ye want," replied Johnnie, "jest so's ye bring 'em back. I can't rightly call 'em mine, but I don't care who reads 'em."

Richard was hoping Johnnie would say something more about Rennie, but Johnnie began talking about growing up in the coal camps and how much better he liked living here on Lonesome Holler. Richard had grown up close to a coal camp and knew a little about the life there.

"Don't any of the young folks around here have get-togethers where boys and girls meet?" Richard finally tried to get the talk turned his way.

"Yeah, we have bean stringin's, log rollin's, corn huskin's, and so on. We have fun getting together to work. We make fun at our play and play at our work. Ever' now and then we have play parties and candy pullin's, but as ye know most all folks around here are Old Regular Baptists and they don't allow us to have dances. If ye want somethin' like that ye'll have to go to a town somewheres."

"I know, I grew up in a hollow just like this. Does Rennie go to any of these shindigs?" Richard could feel himself blushing.

"She ain't been goin' out much fer the last two years. Ye see, her father has been bedfast, and she took care of him."

So that's the way the wind is blowin', Johnnie thought to himself. He was amazed that he felt no anger or jealousy. He had told himself over and over again that the love he had for Rennie was just friendship and kinship because they were of the same family. In his mind he wanted to believe it, but in his heart he knew better. He had learned to live with it. Like learning to live with the toothache, he told himself. Johnnie was so carried away in his own thoughts that Richard was afraid he had said something to offend him.

"Her father is dead now, is he not?" Richard asked.

"What?" Johnnie said. He was jerked back from his own thoughts. He had been far away. "Yeah," he said before Richard could repeat the question. "I thought a lot of Uncle John." He was trying to cover up his absentmindedness. "He was a good man. We really give him up two years ago. His body was jest a shell, no life in it. It was a blessin' when God finally released his soul from that tortured body."

"Rennie is a very strong person. You can see it in her face and eyes." Richard seemed as lost in thought as Johnnie.

"Yeah, God broke the mold when He made Rennie. There'll never be another jest like her. But she's not all work, sacrifice fer the welfare of others. She also has her lighter side. She can have a smart answer to match yers anytime. All that keeps her goin' is that dream that she has of sendin' Sarah Ellen to college. I think she's tryin' to make up to herself because her dream was so shattered when she had to stop school. I try to help her all that she'll let me, but she doesn't realize how much cash money it takes to send a kid to college. She's havin' a hard time jest feedin' the two of 'em."

Richard began looking over the books. "This is heavy stuff," he remarked. "How far did you say Rennie went in school?"

"She quit before she finished grade school. The seventh, I think, er maybe she started the eighth."

"But this is college material!" Richard mused.

"Rennie's taught herself by readin' ever' and anythin' she can get her hands on. She says that she gets more pleasure from learnin' about other times, other people, and other places than anythin' else she can do. She says she doesn't read fer information er improvement, but fer pleasure only. Yet she'd rather live on Lonesome Holler than anywhere she's ever heard about in all the books that have come her way."

"You seem to understand a lot about Rennie, don't you?" Richard asked.

"Yeah, I guess I do. She's my cousin and I once lived over there with her and Uncle John."

Richard saw a dark look come on Johnnie's face and wondered what caused it. He thought, "There must have been a fight with some of them." He wouldn't have guessed the truth in a hundred years, and it was better for all that he didn't. This secret belonged to Johnnie, and it was too deep ever to share with anyone but his Lord.

"The next get-together that we have around here," Johnnie said "is the pie supper that we have each year at the schoolhouse to raise money fer Christmas presents fer the kids."

"Yes, I've been told about that, and we always had them at home, where I grew up." Richard was glad to get back to the present, although he had at first wanted to hear more about Rennie.

"If Rennie brings a box I promise to not run the biddin' too high fer ye." Johnnie smiled, and Richard saw that he hadn't fooled Johnnie.

"It's time I learned more about your cousin. She seems to be a very interesting person." Johnnie laughed and Richard smiled.

After they shared a cup of coffee and a slice of the apple pie Rennie had sent over that morning, Richard said, "What, even a good cook, too? I'm beginning to believe she's just too good to be true." With two of the books under his arms he left with a promise to come again soon.

Johnnie sat on the porch a long time and thought. Richard would make a good catch for Rennie, but he didn't know how Rennie would feel about that. He knew he'd have to get used to the idea that Rennie might marry someone sometime, and that he wasn't going to live his whole life without a wife and family. But somehow he believed Rennie had meant it when she said, "I was borned to be an old maid. Ever' community needs and has one. I'll never marry. Sarah Ellen is all the family I'll ever need." Rennie had had to grow up too fast. She had taken on the responsibility of a grown woman at an age when most girls had just begun to think about boys.

27 _____

The next three years were long years for Rennie. It was hard to adjust to being alone. Her father and Sarah Ellen had taken up so much of her time, there had never been enough hours in the day to get all done that needed to be. Now she found herself hunting up jobs to do just to pass the time.

Winter was the worst. She got out a quilt that her mother had started and never finished before she died. Rennie thought she would try to finish it. Looking at the tiny stitches and even design almost discouraged her. And all the memories it brought back—sitting on the floor beneath the quilting frame, playing with her dolls, sometimes forgetting and raising up and bumping the quilt. A gentle tap on the top of her head from her mother's thimble had reminded her, and she would sit back down.

Susan, Aunt Nance, and even Johnnie admired her work on the quilt and tried to tell her it was as good as her mother's work, but she could tell the difference. Yet she kept on, determined to finish it. The only way to learn was by doing the job over and over, and she wanted to make quilts, not just for their use but for their beauty.

Johnnie was now working at a sawmill in another county, somewhere on down below where Caney ran into Beaver Creek, too far away to come home at night. He was "shantin'" with other men in a small shedlike house made from leftover slabs from the log sawing. It had a pot-bellied stove for heat and army cots for beds. One of the men did the cooking with the help of the daughter of the mill owner. Johnnie only came home some on weekends. He had asked Rennie to look out for his house and things. There wasn't much for her to do; he had taken his mule and of course his fiddle with him. Every now and then she went over and aired the rooms by opening the windows and doors and sunned the bedclothes by hanging them outside.

Sarah Ellen was now in fourth grade. The teacher had let her pass two grades in one year. She was catching up with Hank. She and Hank weren't together as much as when they were younger. They still walked to and from school together, but now they had their own group of friends, Hank's with the boys and Sarah Ellen's with the girls. Hank and his friends played Round Town, a game something like baseball. Their bat was whittled from a hickory stick and the ball was made from yarn and leather. They played in a lot just back of the schoolhouse.

They also played with marbles they made themselves. They used small pebbles of the only hard stone in Eastern Kentucky, called marble or soapstone. When they'd find a really large stone close by the creek bank, they'd chip a small hole in the top, place the piece of marble in the hole, and use rocks and clay to maneuver a small part of the creek so it would fall gently on top of the stone, causing it to turn over and over. In a week or two the stone would begin to be smoothed round. It took almost all summer to make a set of marbles, and sometimes there might come a washout and the marbles would be lost and they'd have to start all over again. You could only make one at a time. But once made they lasted forever and were passed down from one generation to another. The boys would carry them in a leather drawstring pouch.

Sarah Ellen and her girlfriends spent their free time down near the creek. A large sycamore tree gave them plenty of shade, and the exposed roots were used for seats. A few flat slate rocks made chairs, beds, and tables, moss served as pillows and quilts, broken pieces of plates and empty tin cans made dishes and pots and pans. Forked sticks made good spoons and forks. Acorns from a nearby oak tree furnished cups and saucers. One flat slate rock lain across two others with a hole dug under it made a stove in which a real fire could be built. They'd cook greens over it in an empty lard bucket.

The girls played other games, too, games their ancestors had brought from England when they settled in these hills. "London Bridge is Falling Down," "Ring around the Rosey," "Skip to My Lou," "Drop the Handkerchief," "Froggie in the Meadow," and many others.

One day when Rennie went to the springhouse to get some milk for Sarah Ellen's school dinner, she was surprised to find that one of the jars she had left full there the night before was almost empty. She couldn't understand how this had happened. She looked the jar over carefully to see if it had a crack, but no, and the lid was on tight. Who or what had emptied the jar? She puzzled about it all day. Next morning it was the same. She mentioned it to Johnnie when he came over that evening, and he told her she wasn't the only one that had been missing food—not much, just a little here and there. Some had missed a few eggs from their hen's nest, others a few hills of potatoes and a ear or two of fresh corn. Johnnie worried about Rennie and Sarah Ellen. He didn't like them to stay by themselves. Folks at the store thought it might be someone dodging from the law, maybe from a long way off. Others said it could be revenuers. Those less frightened said it was someone just looking over the stands of timber to see what it was worth, planning to come back later and buy it.

The next day Johnnie went back in the woods. He took his gun, saying he was going to see if he could find a squirrel.

When he came back he told Rennie that someone had been camping out under the old cave were Granny Alice had first lived when she came to Caney. There was a long-handled tin skillet and a blackened lard bucket and remains of a fire.

Next night when Rennie took her jars of milk to the spring-house she wrapped up a large piece of cornbread in a news-paper and laid it on top of the jars. Next morning they were both gone, and the word "thanks" was scratched in the dirt near where the milk sat. They never did find out who the stranger was, but he was never heard from again. Johnnie said that Rennie had done a foolish thing but that it might have been the very thing that scared the man away. He may have figured it was a trap to catch him. The mystery was never solved. Rennie said, "It's only in story books that the mystery is solved and that the boy gets the girl and they live happy ever after. This is real life. In real life everthin' don't turn out the way we want it to."

Johnnie didn't like for Rennie and Sarah Ellen to be alone. Rennie just smiled and said, "Who's bein' the Ma now? It was jest some bum that don't like to work."

"I'd quit my job and come back home," said Johnnie, "but right now so much depends on me bein' there. The boss is gone. Be shore and keep yer door shut, and please don't feed him anymore. Promise me! The boss has left me in charge while he works at his other sawmill farther down the river. I'd not have got to come home this time but we ran out of timber."

No one ever learned who the stranger had been.

Every year Rennie had worried about the cash money for shoes and taxes, and each time something always came along just at the right time. "The Lord will make a way," her father had always said, and just when Rennie had worried and wor-ried and almost given up to despair, something would hap-pen and she would have the money.

Every year a drover came to the area to buy up all the stock that folks had for sale. Most people just kept the cows and mules they needed to help them live. They hardly ever raised any just to sell. So most of what the drover bought was stock that had gotten too old to be of any more use. Some folks said he bought them to sell to the glue factories. Johnnie advised Rennie to sell her father's mule to the drover, so that year she had the money in time for the taxes and winter shoes for her and Sarah Ellen.

The next year, when she had almost worried herself into a fit, a tree buyer came around looking for walnut timbers. There were six large walnut trees just above Rennie's corn field. She said it was like selling the goose that laid the golden eggs, for they had gathered walnuts and hulled them and dried them for winter use for years. They'd crack them before the fire and throw the shells into the fire on winter evenings, and she also used them in her cakes and candy. It wouldn't seem like Christmas without walnut candy. She sold the man four, saving two for the nuts. Once again the shoes were bought and the taxes paid. What would it be next year, she asked herself. If only she had her father's faith.

Rennie and Mr. Tate had become friends. He had bought her box at the yearly pie supper and had walked her to and from church, but she had always left him at the gate, never inviting him to sit on the porch and talk a spell. With a woman's instinct, she knew that with a little encouragement from her he would ask her to marry him. She liked him as a friend. They had so much in common—they liked to read the same books. And to marry him would solve all her money problems. His $58.00 a year for teaching seemed like a fortune to her. School only lasted for six months.

But Rennie wasn't the kind of person that would marry just to help herself. She wouldn't do that even to help Sarah Ellen. Rennie liked her life just the way it was. Why was everyone trying to get her married? She liked being her own boss. Why was it so hard for people to believe that she liked being alone, just her and Sarah Ellen? It was only in story books that men and women fell in love. She had seen too many of her friends living from day to day, each year another child to take care of. True, when Joan brought her new babies to show her, she felt a twinge of regret, but she soon forgot it in a new book to read or something to do that would please Sarah Ellen.

One day she noticed a strange horse hitched up in front of Susan's house. She wondered who it could be but thought little more about it until she saw the same horse there the next weekend and the next. She asked Hank who it was.

"I don't know his name," he took time to say as he ran through the house after Sarah Ellen. "Some old widower from Coon Creek."

Rennie knew that to Hank anyone over thirty was old. Could Susan be seeing someone after all these years?

Next time she saw Jane she asked her about the stranger. Jane began to stutter and blush. "No, it ain't Ma that he's comin' to see, it's me. He's already asked Ma fer my hand in marriage, and she said that she'd let him know. She told me that she wanted to find out more about him. She was goin' to ask Johnnie to do some checkin' up on him without lettin' him know. He works over there at the sawmill where Johnnie works. He said that his wife died six months ago when her second child was born. His baby girl and a two-year-old boy is stayin' with his mother now, but he says he'd like to have 'em back at his house."

A few weeks later Jane married and moved away from Lonesome Holler. Rennie now had no close girlfriends of her age. She would have no one to go root hunting with, and she just had to have that root money. She had promised Johnnie not to go into the hills alone, so that year she took Hank and Sarah Ellen. They didn't dig many roots but were plenty of company and "kept the buggers scared away," as Hank said.

28 _____

The years slipped away one at a time, winter following summer. Johnnie was still working at the sawmill. Sarah Ellen was now in the eighth grade. One evening when Johnnie was having supper with them he said, just as casually as if he were telling her about buying a mule, "I'm gettin' married this next weekend." Rennie was too stunned to speak. She knocked over a glass of milk, and in the fuss of cleaning up the mess, she had time to get control of herself.

"Ye're what?" She spoke at last and hoped that her voice sounded normal.

"The old bachelor's finally let himself get caught. Betsy is her name. She's the daughter of the man I've been workin' fer. She's been helpin' cook fer the men at the shanty."

"Well, I'm glad there'll be someone livin' in yer house. Ye *will* be livin' there, won't ye?" Rennie asked.

"Yeah, we're goin' to marry and move right in. She'll be there and I'll still be workin' at the mill. I'm goin' to try and buy me an old truck so that I can stay at home and drive in to work. I was goin' to ask ye if ye'd help her until she learns the ropes of light housekeepin'. Cookin' fer two will be a lot different from cookin' fer several."

"Shore, I'll do all I can. Shore will be good havin' another girl about my age to talk to again, another woman to buddy with."

"Well, she's not much younger than you. Let's see, ye're twenty-four now and she's twenty-three, and me, I'm twenty-nine. This is her second time around. She was married five years ago and her husband got killed when a log rolled off the skids, less than a year after they were married."

"How sad," Rennie said. "Were there any childern?"

"No," Johnnie said, "and she loves childern, so we hope to have a houseful fer ye to help take care of."

"Countin' yer chickens before they're hatched, aren't ye?" Rennie laughed.

"No, countin' my childern before they hatch."

That night Rennie lay awake a long time thinking. Would Johnnie still be the same? Would she still be his best friend?

There were many questions that didn't have answers. "This isn't a story book," she told herself. "This is real life and we must live it as it's meted out to us."

Two weeks later Johnnie came by with Betsy, and Rennie saw at first glance that they were going to be friends. She was so small it was hard to think of her as being a grown woman, only coming to Johnnie's ears, and he was only five ten. "She's not much larger than Sarah Ellen," thought Rennie, "and her only twelve." But strength of character seemed to flow from Betsy like a living stream. She was a person it would be well to have on your side, but threatening if against you.

"I'm an only child," she told Rennie. "I've never had a family except father. I've followed him from place to place as he set up sawmills. When he gets all the trees cut from one holler, he moves on to another locality. I think that Johnnie jest married me to get the sawmill where he's been workin'."

Her laugh told Rennie that she was joking, but it was true that her father had given them the sawmill. "It's better that ye have it now. Ye'd get it when I die," he had told them, and Johnnie had accepted, although it went against his pride.

It wasn't long until Johnnie bought his truck. It was far from new, but it was the first truck that had ever been up Lonesome Holler. All the folks came to their doors to see this new marvel. There was no road, and Johnnie had to follow the creek over the bumps and rocks, but he got there somehow.

29

Rennie never knew for sure what happened between Sarah Ellen and Hank that broke up their friendship. It must have been something very upsetting to both, for they didn't try to make it up. Hank quit coming home on the weekends, and when he did he never stopped at Rennie's house, and if Sarah Ellen saw him passing, she went inside. He stayed at the shanty with the other men that worked for Johnnie. Just as soon as he finished the eighth grade, Johnnie gave him a job as gin hand around the sawmill and to help with the cooking, now that Betsy no longer worked there. Rennie and Susan had tried to talk him into going to high school, but no deal. Most of the boys on Lonesome Holler never finished the eighth grade, most quitting school at the fifth or sixth grade. Hank said he wanted to be making some money. He could have ridden home with Johnnie in his rattletrap truck. Johnnie even offered to teach him how to drive. But he told Johnnie that he would rather wear out his feet walking than have his head bounced off riding.

At first Hank worked hard. He helped his mother, giving her some from each paycheck and giving the rest to Johnnie to save for him, just spending a few nickels and dimes every now and then for himself. But after his trouble with Sarah Ellen, everything changed.

Rennie tried to talk to Sarah Ellen about it, but she would just burst out crying and say, "I don't want to talk about it." She tried to talk to Hank, but he told her to mind her own business. When Rennie asked Johnnie what had come over Hank to make him change so, Johnnie was as puzzled as she was but promised to try and find out. When she asked him where Hank spent his weekends, Johnnie was embarrassed to talk.

"Well, him and some more boys go to this, it's a . . . well it's a kind of place where, well . . . . Rennie, ye don't know what kind of a house it is. Nice women like you don't know about places like those."

Rennie blushed. "Well, I don't guess me and my friends talk about places like that in our everday talk, but, Johnnie, I've read a lot of books in my lifetime. I know what ye're tryin' to tell me."

"Well, this house, it's on the other side of the county line. They sell moonshine there, and there are these girls," again Johnnie blushed, "and they dance and so on. Hank is wastin' all his money and has been barrowin' from me. Misses a lot of work, comes in Sunday night drunk and I can't get him up in the mornin' Monday. If he wasn't in the family I'd fire him jest like that." Johnnie's voice told how hurt he was. "I've tried to talk to him but he jest cusses me out. "

"His mother is worried sick because he don't come home and don't give her any more money. I try to make her believe that ye need him to stay over to watch the mill. I hope she never learns the truth." Rennie wiped her eyes. "She knows there's somethin' wrong and she blames Sarah Ellen some-how, but Sarah Ellen won't talk about it, either. Poor kids, and they used to be such friends. I didn't think that anythin' could ever come between 'em. Why, they're a part of each other. I know that Hank don't want Sarah Ellen to go on to school, but surely that couldn't cause so much hurt."

Sarah Ellen was thirteen that October, and she would finish grade school at the end of the school year and be ready for high school next year. At the end of the year, Rennie still didn't know where she was going to come up with the money she'd need for Sarah Ellen to start school. She hadn't yet asked the school if they would take her in or not, but some-how that didn't worry her as much as where the cash money was going to come from. She kept praying that there would be a way made for her.

It wouldn't really take too much money. Mrs. Lloyd allowed the students to work their way through school. Many of the parents brought what food they had to spare and donated it for the kitchen. It wasn't required but was gladly accepted. And a "gift offering" of five dollars was asked for each semes-ter—asked for but not required. If a student didn't have the five dollars, he or she wasn't asked to pay.

When Rennie got worried and couldn't see any way out of her troubles, she would visit her father's and mother's graves. There she would busy herself by cleaning away the weeds and briars. It was so peaceful and quiet there. She would talk out all her unanswered questions. She wasn't going to give up her dream. It had been a part of her very soul for so long that she would rather die than give up trying to get Sarah Ellen an education. She couldn't think of her sister having to live the life that she herself had. She would find the money somehow. "The Lord will find a way." She almost thought she had heard her father speak those words as they came to her mind. She went back to the house more in heart that a way would be found.

She talked to Johnnie about trying to sell part of the farm, but he told her that since it belonged partly to Sarah Ellen, she couldn't make a good deed because Sarah Ellen wasn't old enough to sign it. If she borrowed money from the bank and took out a mortgage on the farm, she would have to pay the interest each year, and that and the taxes would be more than she could manage.

Then the unexpected happened. Later Rennie would say, "God works in mysterious ways His wonders to perform."

One nice, sunshiny day after school was out, Rennie and Sarah Ellen were sitting on the front porch taking a rest. They had just finished eating dinner and washing the dishes and were resting a while and letting their dinner settle before going back to the corn field to hoe corn, when a stranger rode up to their front gate and stopped. His fine horse, squeaky saddle, and fine clothes "smelled" money. He looked to the girls like a brought-on person, but when he spoke, they knew he was a mountain man.

"Is this where John and Mary Slone live?" he asked.

"This is their house, but they're both dead. We're their childern. Get down and rest a while and talk a spell." Rennie couldn't for the life of her think who nor what this meant. The man hitched his horse to the gate post and, taking some papers from his saddle bags, came in. Sarah Ellen gave him her chair and went back into the house and brought out another for herself.

"I'm a lawyer. I was sent here by your mother's family. Your grandfather died just a few weeks ago," he told them.

"I hate to hear that," Rennie said, "but I can't say that it grieves me any, as I never even knew that I had a grand-father, other than Grandpa Jim."

"Did your mother ever talk to you about her folks?" The lawyer had now found his glasses and was looking over the papers.

"No, all that I know is that their last name was Gent. They none of 'em ever come about us. She said she wrote her mother a few times, but when she didn't get an answer back she jest tried to forget 'em. She said that if they didn't want to have any truck with her, she didn't want any with them. But I caught her cryin' many times, and sometimes I'd wake up and she'd be cryin' and when I asked her what was wrong, she would say, 'Jest rememberin' things.'"

"Well, your grandfather died without making a will. He wasn't a real rich man, but he had plenty. A large farm, a few hundred dollars in the bank, and some very fine horses and cattle. He had eight children besides your mother, and his wife died years ago. Your Uncle Bob came to me to have the court settle the estate, and your mother is heir to a child's part, one-ninth of all your grandfather owned. As her chil-dern, it will go to you and your sister."

"I don't know if I want anythin' of his, if he didn't care enough to even come and see Ma when she was alive ner even when she died." Rennie's eyes were filled with tears.

"I can understand how you feel, but if you don't accept it, it will just lie there for so many years and then go to the state," he tried to explain.

Rennie was torn apart. Here was the answer to her pray-ers, and yet on the other side was her stubborn pride. What would her mother want her to do? She thought, "Jest a little while ago I said that I'd do anythin' to have the money fer Sarah Ellen's education, but I never thought it would be any-thin' this hard."

"Of course, you'll have to prove that you're Mary's chil-dern. You do have your birth records?"

"Yeah, do ye want 'em now?" She rose and started to the door.

"No," he said. "You'll have to come to the county courthouse and bring them. I'll write and let you know just when. You'll also get a child's part of the farm, and as I don't think you'd want the land, your Uncle Bob is willing to buy your part. He said that he would have to pay you just a small amount each year, maybe fifty dollars a year until it's paid. But the court will fix it up all neat and legal and safe. You're over twenty-one?" At Rennie's nod, he continued, "As your sister is too young to sign the deed, it will be put in a trust fund for her until she's old enough."

Things were going too fast for Rennie to grasp. This couldn't be happening to her. Things like this happened only in story books, not in real life. "A small sum," he had said. Fifty dollars a small sum! To Rennie that meant a small fortune.

Rennie remembered her manners and asked him if he had had dinner, and would he come in the house and eat a bite. They had just finished eating and there was plenty left. The lawyer thanked them but said, "No," but he would like a nice cold drink of water. Sarah Ellen got a bucket from the kitchen and brought the water from the springhouse.

The lawyer thanked them and left, telling them again that he'd let them know when to meet him and her uncle at the courthouse.

The girls were too excited to go back to work. They had to tell someone. They decided to clean up and be ready to walk over to Johnnie's house by the time he came home from work so they could share with him the news of their good fortune. But before they went, Rennie went to her parents' graves. She still didn't know if she had done the right thing. What would her father and mother have done? She would have to swallow a lot of mountain pride. "I wish I knew what the trouble was between mother and her family. Was it Pa that they didn't like? But I guess that will jest be another mystery with no answer. Well, my prayer has been answered, but not the way I would have liked fer it to have been. But who am I to grumble? I had jest said that I'd even be willin' to die if that was what it took to get Sarah Ellen a better life, and here I am not willin' to eat a little dirt."

Johnnie was so pleased for them. He got out his fiddle and

played while the women washed up the dishes, for Betsy would have them eat supper. They planned to go to town and buy all Sarah Ellen needed for school just as soon as she got the money. "And that will be a good chance fer y'all to take a ride in my rattletrap of a truck."

30 _____

Rennie decided that it would be best for them to go to the school and see if Sarah Ellen would be accepted before they bought her clothes. There were always more wanting to go than the school had room for.

Sarah Ellen had been helping Rennie with the garden work and hoeing corn. They now had the corn laid by, and there wasn't much to do in the garden except wait until canning time. That morning the sun came up bright and promised a nice day for traveling, so they put on their prettiest dresses and cleaned and shined their shoes. They would carry the shoes and go barefooted until they were out of the hollow and came to the big road.

Rennie had never liked meeting and talking to the brought-on folks that worked at the school. It was hard to understand them and harder to get them to understand her. She had met Mrs. Lloyd once years before, and she had gone again and again to get magazines and newspapers. She had liked Mrs. Lloyd.

They started as early as they could after doing up the morning chores. It was a long walk and hot. Just outside the school, they stopped under a sycamore tree that stood near the road to rest and eat the lunch they'd brought with them and drink from a nearby spring. Rennie didn't know just where to go at the school nor whom to see. She knew where

Mrs. Lloyd's office was, so she decided to go there and ask her. If she wasn't the one to ask, then she would tell her who was.

They climbed the long flight of steps that led up to the office, and with trembling hands Rennie knocked on the door. A soft voice said, "Come in." She pushed the door open and stepped in, with Sarah Ellen at her heels. She blinked her eyes, the room was so dark. Heavy curtains covered the windows. It was a while before her eyes could adjust to the darkness after the bright sunlight outside. Why would anyone want to keep out the light? she wondered.

"Come on in and sit down," the gentle voice spoke up from the back corner of the room. By now Rennie was able to see the small woman sitting behind a desk and almost hidden from view by an old-fashioned typewriter. Rennie slowly made her way across the room, leaving Sarah Ellen still standing at the door. "My name is Mrs. Lloyd. What's yours?"

"My name is Rennie Slone and this is my sister, Sarah Ellen. I came to see if I could get a place fer her in yer school. I want her to go to high school."

"And what does *she* want?" Mrs. Lloyd asked. Sarah Ellen answered. "I want to go to school more than anythin' else in the world, but I don't think it would do me any good if I didn't want to, anyway, because that's all I've heard as fer back as I can remember. It's been Rennie's whole life, this dream that I would some day get an education. She has done everthin' in her power with that as her life's only goal." Rennie had never heard Sarah Ellen have so much to say to a stranger.

"Why didn't your parents bring you?" Mrs. Lloyd asked.

"Our parents are both dead. My mother died when I was born and Rennie was jest twelve years old. She's taken care of me ever since."

"Oh, I seem to remember. Are you the little girl that brought her baby sister here to get some medicine from our nurse?" Mrs. Lloyd smiled.

"Yeah, and ye gave me your tam and scarf. I still have 'em and still wear 'em."

"I don't know just how many students have registered for

next term," said Mrs. Lloyd. "We never have room for all who apply. I take it that you want to stay at the school. You don't live close enough to walk from home?" she asked.

"No, it's quite a walk. It took us over two hours to walk this mornin'," Rennie told her.

"Well, I'll get someone to show you the way to the registrar's office. Ruth," she called, and a girl came in from the back room. She was about Sarah Ellen's age. "Will you take these girls to the registrar's office, please?"

"Yes, Mam. Come this way if ye will, please." The girl led Rennie and Sarah Ellen out the door, across the porch, and along a bannistered walkway across to another office. Over the door was the word "If." Sarah Ellen would later learn that all the offices and buildings had names taken from famous books or famous people. Inside Ruth introduced them to Mr. Summerfield and explained to him what they were here for.

"You're very lucky. We have room for only one more student. Did you bring your report card with you? We only accept students with a B average or above." Sarah Ellen showed him the papers she had with her. He looked them over and said, "Yes, these look O.K. We've never had a student from Lonesome Hollow before."

He pulled some papers from a drawer. "You'll be staying in room 5 downstairs in the Girls' Old Dorm. There will be three other girls in the room with you. Here's a list of the rules and regulations and what kind of clothes you'll need. The bed linens and towels are furnished, except blankets and quilts. You'll have to see to your own personal laundry, but the school takes care of laundering the linens.

"We also furnish the books, but they're only loaned. When you finish with them they're to be returned to this office. We expect you to take as good care of them as you can so they can be used again and again. You'll be told later what your job will be. Your room will be inspected once a week and you'll be graded on how clean you keep it. Are there any questions?" he asked.

"How often do they get to come home fer a visit," Rennie wanted to know.

"Once a month for a weekend if they're not needed for work and if they're not being punished for something."

"How often does their family get to visit them?"

"Only female members of the family can visit the girls in their rooms, and only on Sunday afternoon. The same goes for the boys. You'll find all this in the papers I've given you. Hope to see you when school begins," he smiled.

"I'll be here, all right. I've waited and looked forward to this fer so long. It's too late to turn back now," Sarah Ellen said.

"You don't know how many give up when they learn how strict Mrs. Lloyd is, and how many get homesick and go home after a few weeks. We have a waiting list that we take from to fill these vacancies if they occur the first four weeks of school. We think it would be too hard for a student to catch up with the rest of the classes if they enter later."

"We'll be in the same dorm," Ruth told Sarah Ellen as she walked back across the walkway. "I'll be watchin' for ye and show ye around when ye return."

"Thanks," Sarah Ellen said. "That will shore be a big help." I've already made a friend, she thought.

"I know how hard it was fer me last year when I first came," Ruth told her.

Rennie thought, "This is goin' to be harder than I thought. Sarah Ellen is so shy."

A week later Rennie received the letter from the lawyer telling her to meet him at the county courthouse the following Monday. Johnnie offered to take them in his rattletrap truck. Rennie told him, "I hate fer ye to lose a day's work, but I shore don't like to meet all those strange people by myself."

"Well, now that y'all have become rich folks," Johnnie joked, "I'll be honored to take ye, and while ye're in town ye can get the things that Sarah Ellen needs fer school. You can find a lot more in the stores there than what Long Bill has."

The next weeks were busy ones for Rennie and Sarah Ellen—the trip to town, getting the papers signed, being handed a check for a hundred dollars and a promise of fifty dollars a year for the next eight years, until Sarah Ellen would be old enough to make her deed. It all seemed like a dream to Rennie, a pleasant dream from which she didn't want to awaken. But the business with the Gents she wanted to get done and over with. Her Uncle Bob was the only one she had to meet face to face, and he made it plain that he didn't want to meet his dead sister's children.

The list Mr. Summerfield had given Rennie for Sarah Ellen's clothes called for black skirts for weekdays, white ones for Sundays, white middy sailor-type blouses, one pair each of black and white low-heeled oxfords, long stockings of black and white, black and white long-legged bloomers, and a red tie. Rennie gasped when she saw how much they cost. What would she have done if she hadn't gotten the money from her despised kinfolks. Maybe it was worth swallowing her mountain pride.

The clothes had to be sewed, as there were none in the stores that fitted the description. Rennie bought yards and yards of white Indianhead, yards of black woolen flannel for the skirts, black percale for the bloomers, and a nice soft poplin for nightgowns. She didn't know how she was going to get them made. She didn't want to ask Susan to help her or let her use her sewing machine. Aunt Nance was dead now—and how Rennie missed the kind old woman. Susan hadn't been friendly with Sarah Ellen since she and Hank broke up their friendship. She blamed Sarah Ellen for Hank's turning bad. Rennie couldn't see why she thought Sarah Ellen had anything to do with Hank's mean ways, but then she thought, "It's hard fer a mother to accept the wrongs of her own child. It's easier to lay the blame on someone else. It makes it easier to accept."

Rennie didn't know what to do until Betsy told her she thought there was an old sewing machine in all that junk up in their loft. She didn't know if it would sew or not. "It's been there since before the Flood. But we'll try it and see." The next day Johnnie had off from work, he and Rennie, after much tugging and moving stuff around, got the sewing machine out where they could see it.

But now the problem was how on earth they were going to get it down the ladder stairway from the loft to the front room. At last, when they had all but given up, Johnnie came up with a plan that might just work. In all these old houses there was a small opening in the loft with a doorlike covering hung on hinges. If he could tie ropes around the sewing machine and push it through the opening, then let it down to the ground, it just might make it. Then they could carry it into the front room. They all held their breath and hoped for the best, and sure enough they got the sewing machine into the front room safe and sound.

After an hour or two of dusting and scrubbing, the sewing machine emerged from all the rust and dirt. But then they found that the leather belt that turned the wheel was dry rotted. A trip to the store to buy another and to get a bottle of three-in-one oil, and "Glory be!" it worked. Rennie had gone back to the school and borrowed a skirt and middy from Ruth to use as patterns, and before long the yards of cloth were turned into skirts, middies, and bloomers. With the white percale she made two pretty nightgowns trimmed with lace, ribbons, and ruffles, and with hand stitching in bright colored threads. They were beautiful. "Fit fer a queen," Betsy said.

The days flew by. Soon the day came for Sarah Ellen to leave for school. It was a Sunday, and Johnnie was home from work, so he came in his truck and loaded the old battered leather suitcase and several boxes in the back. Sarah Ellen got in the seat with him while Rennie stood on the porch and tried to hold back the tears. Sarah Ellen looked so pretty wearing her school uniform for the first time.

Rennie watched them almost out of sight, then turned and went inside to have her cry. She didn't believe in the old superstition that if you watched someone out of sight they would never return, but she wasn't taking any chances.

31

When Johnnie drove up to the school, sure enough, Ruth was at the big gate in front of the post office. The gate was the only break in the rock wall that enclosed the school.

"Well, I see ye really mean business," was her greeting to Sarah Ellen.

Johnnie began unloading the truck and placing the boxes on top of the rock wall. "Where does this stuff go?" he asked Ruth.

"Oh, ye're not allowed to go to the girls' dorm." Ruth didn't even look toward him as she spoke.

"Oh, shorely they wouldn't care fer me. I'm an old married man and her cousin to boot." Johnnie was laughing, but you could tell he was mad.

"If ye were her father ye wouldn't be allowed in the girls' dorm. If I was caught talkin' to ye I'd be punished. I'll help Sarah Ellen carry her things. Jest set 'em there. We'll take what we can now and be back fer the rest later," Ruth said as she picked up one of the boxes. "What in the world do ye have so much of, anyway?" she asked Sarah Ellen.

"Besides my clothes, there's a quilt er two, a box of apples, another with gingerbread. I don't know what all my sister packed. I think she thought she was sendin' me off to starve to death," Sarah Ellen smiled.

"If ye have food of any kind ye'll be the most popular girl in the dorm."

Johnnie sat there until all the boxes had been removed from the rock wall. Then he turned and started back to home. He didn't know which would be best. Should he go by Rennie's house, or would she rather be alone? He knew she was crying her heart out.

Sarah Ellen spent the rest of the afternoon unpacking and trying to put away her things. There just wasn't much space in the tiny room. She saw that she had much more than the other three girls who shared the room. Two double-deck bunk beds, handmade from rough two-by-fours, filled one end. A three-cornered shelf occupied one corner, with a cloth curtain in place of a door. It had four shelves, one for each girl. Sarah

Ellen had more than enough to fill the whole thing. There were nails along all the walls from which clothes hangers could be hung. A larger curtain hanging from the ceiling took up the other corner. Behind this curtain was a small wash-bench, a washpan, and two pails, one for clean water and the other for slop water. Four towels and washcloths hung on nails. The girls could take a washpan bath here and have privacy to dress.

Five other rooms built and furnished just like this one surrounded a square hallway containing a pot-belly stove, a table, and several handmade chairs. Here the girls from all the rooms could meet to study. The stove was all the heat they would have during the winter. There was no heat in the bedrooms. All the windows in the dorm were partially covered with narrow planks, about three inches apart.

After storing away all her things as best she could, Sarah Ellen filled her arms with apples and went into the hallway, where several girls were gathered. "Have some fruit," she offered. The girls smiled and thanked her and took an apple from her arms.

One of the older girls said, "My name's Sally. This is my second year here and I thought I should fill you newcomers in on some of the ways and means around here. Did y'all notice that big bell on the porch at the office? Well, that's the boss. It tells us when to get up, when to go to bed, when to eat, when to go to class. When ye hear that bell, ye jump! A woman that works in the office there has a clock, and when it gets to a certain time she goes out and gives that big bell a kick er two.

"Now about meals. On Sunday we have a late breakfast, sometimes salmon patties and flour gravy and homemade biscuits, then dinner at two. We all meet, boys on one side and girls on the other, late in the evening on the large porch and steps that lead up to 'Hungry Din,' the dining room, and have tea and sandwiches, and sing songs."

Just as she finished, the bell began to ring. All the girls scrambled up the stairs, where they were joined by the upstairs girls, and with their housemother in the lead they marched single-file to the porch, where all the rest of the school was gathering. After a light snack they returned to the dorms. It was now time to go to bed. Each room had an oil lamp, and one of the girls lit it. One at a time the girls went behind the corner curtain to wash and change for bed. Sarah Ellen waited until last. When the other girls came out they were all wearing pajamas. This was the first time Sarah Ellen had ever seen anyone in pajamas. She knew what they were because she'd seen pictures in catalogues, but in her father's church women were forbidden to wear anything that resembled pants. Poor Sarah Ellen! She thought of her pretty nightgown. What would the other girls say? Would they laugh and make fun of her?

She waited and stood around, putting off getting ready for bed just as long as she could. Finally Sally reminded her that the get-in-bed bell would soon sound, the signal for lights out. The fifteen-minute bell had already rung. Sarah Ellen took her gown and went behind the curtain, washed in the pan, poured the water in the slop pail, braided her hair, and, trembling all over, stepped out. There was a gasp from all the girls.

"How beautiful!"

"Ye look like a princess."

"Where on earth did ye get such a beautiful thing?"

Sarah Ellen's heart dropped back down in its normal place. "My sister made it fer me," she said with pride.

"That's almost too purty to sleep in," Sally whispered as the last bell rang. Sarah Ellen climbed into bed just as Sally blew out the lamp. As she went to sleep she thought, "I'm goin' to like it here."

Back home, Rennie lay awake far into the night. She didn't know a person could hurt so much and still live. Such a heavy lump of lonesomeness in her insides. It was almost a physical pain. How could she go on alone? Why had she sent Sarah Ellen away? She got up and went outside. The moon was shining on the white tombstones in the family graveyard. "Please help me, Lord," she cried.

32

Sarah Ellen loved school, but there were a few things she didn't like. For one thing, the beds were so hard—no springs, just a thin flat pad on the hard rough boards. She often thought of the big goose feather bed that she had shared with Rennie.

Not being allowed to talk with the boys didn't bother her the way it did some of the other girls. Many broke the iron-clad segregation rule. They had several ways. One was by passing love notes to each other, nicknamed "three corners" because they would be folded up into small, three-cornered parcels that could be passed from hand to hand as one person passed the other going through a door or along a narrow path. Another way was called "wahawing." There were wahoo trees growing all over the campus, many near the girls' dorms. The mountain people called them cucumber trees because the seed pods were the size and shape of cucumbers. The boys would climb up into the branches of these trees at night and talk to the girls through the windows. There was no way they could get inside because of the wooden slats over all the windows.

Some of the braver girls would steal the outside door key from the house mother's room after she went to sleep and sneak out of the dorm. Another way was for the girl to tie bedsheets together and let them down through the windows. The boy would climb up the sheets and talk to the girl through the windows. Once one of the men teachers thought he would try to catch the girls and learn who was breaking the rule. He climbed up the sheet rope. But when the girls saw who it was they were so frightened they let loose of the sheets and the poor teacher hit the ground with a thump.

When boys and girls were caught talking, the girl would be dismissed from the school for good and the boy would be punished. It was looked upon as a bigger crime for the girl than for the boy because "boys will be boys" but girls are supposed to be ladies. But there's no rule in the world, and no precaution, that will keep a young boy and girl apart when they think they're in love. And puppy love is stronger than real love.

Only a few broke the rules. Mrs. Lloyd set high standards for her students and expected them to live up to them, and most did. It wasn't easy for these mountain boys and girls to leave home. It took someone that was really interested to go through the hardships imposed, and it was hard on the parents to give up their children's labor just as they got old enough to help with the farm work. It took a lot of doing for a family to dig out a living on these poor-soiled mountainsides. But everyone who saw what an advantage an education was would do whatever they could to see that their loved ones got it.

On the outside wall of Mrs. Lloyd's office there was a big bulletin board. Here the students learned what their jobs were for the day and read all other important announcements. Sarah Ellen's first job was in the dining room, Hungry Din, washing dishes. The dining room was just behind Mrs. Lloyd's office and connected with the kitchen and other buildings by a long, wide porch. Opposite the large front door was a small table where some of the most important faculty members and all visitors ate, and sometimes a really good student would be invited to eat there. Up and down each wall ran a row of long, homemade wooden tables, with a handmade bark-woven bench on each side and at each end a handmade chair. These chairs were made in a chair shop on campus where some of the boys worked; many of them were sold to folks up North. Eight students could eat at each table. As usual, the boys and girls were separated. They were expected to leave the tables in good order— tableware on the plates, napkins in their holders, benches and chairs pushed back against the table. Each day after meals, each table was inspected and graded, and the grades were read in front of everybody at the next meal.

In the classrooms, the boys and girls were again separated, boys on one side of the room, girls on the other.

Sarah Ellen loved to learn, unlike Rennie, who only read for pleasure. She wanted to learn the answers to so many questions. Even as a young child she had always been wanting to know—Why the sky didn't fall? What held the moon in place? Where did the rain come from? Her father would just give her a Bible answer. "God made 'em and He controls 'em." That didn't satisfy Sarah Ellen; she wanted more. Now she had a chance to learn.

She did well in all her classes, but science was what she liked best. Once in biology they had to dissect a frog. Most of the girls were "squermish," and even the woman teacher was pale and looked as if she was going to lose her dinner. They were all amazed at how Sarah Ellen went about the job as if she enjoyed it. She told them, "When ye've helped slaughter as many hogs, cut up as many chickens, skinned and gutted as many squirrels and rabbits as I have, a little dead frog ain't nothin'."

Mrs. Lloyd had her own sawmill and her own lumber to build her houses. Every other Friday the mill was used to grind corn. The folks from all the hollows and creeks from far and near brought their corn to be ground into meal. The school received a portion, or "toll," for each bushel ground. In this way Mrs. Lloyd had meal for the school kitchen. It would be turned into cornbread, or cooked in water to which a little sugar and milk had been added for breakfast cereal. Cornbread and pinto bean soup were the standard diet. It was said to be brain food.

Every time Rennie came to pick up Sarah Ellen's laundry or bring it back, she would always bring a box of food from home. Many of the girls received food packages from home, and they always shared with each other. It was against the rule, but after the lights were out, and with only the light that filtered through the slatted windows, the girls would meet in the hall and have a feast. They had an empty lard bucket in which they made coffee by setting it on top of the pot-belly stove. Each dorm had a house mother. Sarah Ellen's house mother was Miss Young. One night when the girls were having a feast, thinking they were being quiet and safe, not realizing that the odor of their coffee was going all through the dorm, they heard someone coming down the stairs. Quickly they pushed their bucket of coffee under a bed and dived under the covers, pretending to be asleep. Miss Young looked around and went back upstairs. The girls got back out of bed. But just as they were enjoying their coffee, there in the door stood Miss Young with a cup in her hand and a big grin on her face. "I'll have a cup of that coffee if you girls don't mind."

> Miss Young came down
> And we could see by her frown
> That the coffee had gone to her head.
> She left the room
> To return very soon.
> I'll take a cup, if you girls don't mind.

Sarah Ellen was always making up little rhymes and jingles to amuse the girls about things that happened at the school. Every boy had to wear a tie even at work, so she made this one:

> Now, this is the rule
> Of the Caney School.
> I wonder if we were to die,
> Would St. Peter say, "Go,
> You belong down below,
> Because, boy, you don't have a tie"?

She also liked to play practical jokes on the other girls.

There was a great need for more classrooms. Up until then, Mrs. Lloyd had built her houses from wood. It was cheap, there was plenty of timber on the hill around the school, and she owned her own sawmill. But so many of the buildings had been destroyed by fire that she decided to build one from stone. There were plenty of rocks close by and some very good stone masons who lived nearby. They had built the rock wall that surrounded the school and all the chimneys and flues. Now they were to build a large building with many rooms and a new, much-needed lab.

Mrs. Lloyd got most of her money from friends and organizations up North. She had started the new building hoping to get it finished before the next school term, but something happened. It may be that the money didn't come through in time, or perhaps the workmen just didn't get as much done as they had hoped to. Anyway, school began and classes were started inside the new building while it was only partly finished. The walls were all up but the roof was not on. The students sat in class with their coats on while the snow drifted in on them through the cracks. The teacher had to shout over the noise of hammers and saws.

About this time a woman doctor, a friend of Mrs. Lloyd's, died and left all her office equipment to the school. Among it was a skeleton in a glass case. Now, back then skeletons were real—the bones of a real person who had lived and breathed and died, now wired together so that the joints could be moved. This skeleton was placed in one corner of the new lab. One of Sarah Ellen's jobs was to clean the lab after classes were over for the day. Because the building was still being worked on, there was only a subfloor down in the lab, and some of the planks weren't nailed down solid. While sweeping the floor, Sarah Ellen discovered that by stepping on one end of a plank it would cause the other end, on which the skeleton case was sitting, to move in such a way that the bones would jiggle and move as if the skeleton were alive.

One day she asked Ruth to help her clean up the lab, making some kind of excuse. Ruth stayed. Sarah Ellen got to talking about the skeleton, how it had been part of a real human being. How it had once lived, maybe loved, breathed, just like one of them. Then she dared Ruth to touch it. Ruth drew back. It was scary. "I'll put my finger in its mouth if you will," Sarah Ellen dared. Ruth still held back. "Fraidy cat," Sarah Ellen teased.

Finally Ruth said, "I will if you will first." That was just what Sarah Ellen wanted. Acting as if she was really scared, she stuck her finger in the skeleton's mouth and quickly drew it out. "Now you."

With trembling hand, Ruth followed Sarah Ellen's example. At that moment, Sarah Ellen stepped back on the plank and the skeleton's teeth closed on Ruth's fingers. Poor Ruth! She gave a scream and sank to the floor in a dead faint. Later in life, Ruth became a nurse, and she would tell folks that she was the only nurse that was ever bitten by a skeleton.

That winter, when Sarah Ellen got out the quilts she had brought from home, Miss Young was so impressed with the beautiful handwork that she asked who had made them and whether she would sell them. Sarah Ellen explained that they had been made by her mother, who was dead. No, she wouldn't sell them, and most mountain folks felt the same way. Quilts were a family thing that was passed down from generation to generation. They belonged to a family and held it together. They were something like a family crest, a chain that must not be broken. A quilt held the family's history—a scrap from the first baby dress, the wedding gown, the burial shroud, the dress of your best friend. Sarah Ellen promised to see if she could find someone to make one for Miss Young, but she doubted that she could. She told how her mother had made some for a lady from the school before she was born.

The school had a basketball team for the boys and a small outdoor ball ground. The girls were allowed to attend these games, but they had to stand, as there were no seats. The "Creek" folks were invited, but they too had to observe the usual rule—boys on one side, girls on the other. The girls could shout but couldn't name any of the players, and there was to be no jumping around or other undignified movements. Sometimes the whole school would walk the eight miles to the nearest high school to play against their team. The boys had to start an hour before the girls. House mothers and teachers went with each group. But they borrowed a truck from one of the families that lived near the school for the coach and team.

They had other get-togethers on the ball ground to which the Creek people were invited. One that Sarah Ellen really enjoyed was the corn roast. The corn would be gathered and brought in by some of the farmers living near the school while it was still young, in the roasting stage. Some folks called it in the milking stage because when you stuck your fingernail into one of the grains of corn, a milklike substance would run out. It took bushels of corn for all the school and guests.

First, two large fires were built, one on one end of the field for the boys, one at the other for the girls. When the fire became a bed of glowing coals, it was ready for the corn. Meanwhile, the girls were busy. First, they would open the shucks and turn them back, remove the silks and cut out any bad places, and remove any worms. Then they'd turn back the shucks and tie over the ends, dip them into a bucket of water, and throw them into the bed of hot coals. When the corn was cooked and ready to eat, all you did was rake it from the coals, remove what little of the shuck hadn't burned away, add a little salt butter, and gnaw the sweet, juicy kernels right off the cob—some of the best eating you ever had. Never mind if you got yourself covered with corn and butter. It was nothing that soap and water wouldn't take care of.

There were serious get-togethers, too, such as Student Council or Senate meetings, where each student was allowed to air his or her views about the school—anything going on, good or bad. They had secret voting, but Mrs. Lloyd had the final say. She could accept or veto anything that concerned the school.

The Sabbath was observed with a church service in Cushing Hall each and every Sunday. Again the Creek people were invited. Some Sundays it would be the Old Regular Baptists, other times it was the a pastor from the Baptist church from a neighboring town. When the Old Regulars were in charge, there was no Sunday School, but with the other churches there would be an evening service and Sunday School. No student was allowed to miss church. "No excuse but death," was the saying.

33 _____

Hank went to the school drunk more than once and caused a lot of trouble. One time he got himself arrested and put in jail. Johnnie went and paid his fine, bailed him out, and gave him a good tongue lashing. Rennie was afraid he would get Sarah Ellen expelled from school.

Then there came that awful night! Rennie had gone to bed early, very tired. A noise woke her up. She listened and thought she heard a horse or mule coming up the hollow. Then everything was quiet again. Then, just as she was dropping off to sleep, someone stumbled up the steps and pounded on her door. She ran to the door and asked, "Who's there?" No one answered, but she could hear someone breathing loud and moaning as if in terrible pain. There was so much weight on the door that when she lifted the latch, the door flew open and Hank fell across the opening.

He fell on his face, and Rennie could see that the back of his shirt was covered with blood. She stooped and turned him face upward. His eyes were shut, but he was trying to mumble something. Running to the edge of the porch, she grasped the dinner bell rope with tug after tug, sending the sound all up and down Lonesome Holler. Men from all the houses jumped from their beds and into their shoes and pants, stopping on the porch only long enough to discover where the sound was coming from, for they knew it was a call for help and meant someone had trouble. In a short time the yard was full of men. When they saw Hank they didn't have to ask what the trouble was.

"Has anyone gone after Susan?" someone asked, and when Rennie shook her head, one man went up the hill to Susan's house.

"Johnnie lives so far away he can't hear the bell," said Rennie. "Will someone go after him? He'll know what to do." One of the men jumped on his mule and started at a run.

Some of the men carried Hank into the house and lay him on Uncle John's bed. He screamed when they moved him. He asked for water, but Rennie didn't know if she should give him any or not. She had heard that if someone was shot through the lungs it was best not to let them drink. But she did wet his lips and wash his face in cold water fresh from the spring. He was trying to say something. Rennie thought he was calling for Sarah Ellen.

When Susan came, Rennie got up from beside Hank's bed and gave her a chair. Neither spoke. Their hearts were too full for words. They just compressed their lips and mourned. Mountain women learn early to carry heavy loads.

After a time Johnnie's truck could be heard rattling up the hollow. Until he arrived no one examined Hank to see how he was hurt. Johnnie removed Hank's shirt. There were two bullet holes in his chest.

"Should we send fer a doctor?" Rennie whispered tò Johnnie as he left the room. "No, there's no need. I don't see how he's lived this long. He's tryin' to tell us somethin'. I asked him who shot him, but he only shook his head and kept mumblin' somethin' that sounded like he was callin' fer Sarah Ellen. I'm goin' after her."

Johnnie drove as fast as he could to the school, parked his truck in front of the post office, and ran up the hill to the girls' dorm. He pounded on the door until the house mother came to ask him what was wrong. It had taken some time to light the oil lamp and cover her nightclothes with a wrapper.

"I've come fer Sarah Ellen," he said as soon as the door was open. "Her cousin is dyin' and askin' fer her."

"I can't let her go without permission from Mrs. Lloyd," the house mother told him.

"We don't have time fer that," Johnnie said. "She must come now."

"But I may lose my job if I let her go. It's against the rules," she protested.

"Oh, to heck with the rules. Tell 'em that I took her by force. If ye don't go and get her at once, I'll go through ever' room until I find her."

"I'll go," she said, but she met Sarah Ellen on the stairs, already dressed. She had recognized Johnnie's voice.

The ride back to Lonesome Holler was one that neither would ever forget. They knew they had arrived too late even before they reached the house because they could hear Rennie's and Susan's screams over the noise of the truck. When Sarah Ellen entered the house she ran to the side of the bed where Hank lay and fell down on her knees. "Oh, Hank, why did ye do it? Oh, why?" She thought Hank had shot himself, but Johnnie assured her that the way the bullets had entered the body that couldn't be true. "But I'll find out who it was, if it takes me the rest of my life, and see that he pays fer it."

Later Rennie told Sarah Ellen that just before Hank drew his last breath he had whispered to her, "Tell Sarah Ellen that I love her."

One of the neighbors asked Susan if she wanted them to move the body up to her house. "No," she answered, "jest leave him here. He spent more time here than he ever did at my house, anyway."

"Ye know that we'll have to bury him today. There's no way that we can keep him over until to'mar. A shot victim has lost so much blood that they have to be buried as soon as possible." Johnnie's voice shook.

"Yeah, I understand," Susan replied. "It won't be any easier to see him put down into the ground to'mar than it will be today."

Some of the men were already making the coffin while others were digging the grave. This was Friday, so Sarah Ellen stayed over until Sunday afternoon. Before going back to school she went for another visit to the grave. She ran her fingers over the letters that had been burned with a hot poker into the slab of wood that would serve as a marker until a tombstone could be made. James Henry, it read. He had been named for his two grandfathers. "I wish they had put Hank. No one ever used his real name. He'll always be Hank to me."

Sarah Ellen went back to school, but she was never the same. No longer did she play practical jokes, no longer did she join in midnight parties. She spent her time studying. She was working toward that scholarship. She didn't like to go home anymore but kept giving one excuse after another— she had to work, she had to get her notes in order, she had to study for a test. Every other weekend Rennie came after her laundry on Friday and brought it back on Sunday afternoon. She always stopped at the school library.

Rennie thought that for sure Sarah Ellen would be home for the summer vacation, and she was looking forward to it. She not only needed her sister's company but she needed her to help with the work that's necessary when folks have to grow everything they eat, but Sarah Ellen decided she would work at the school during her vacation. The few times she did come home, she always used the back door, never crossing the front porch. Johnnie had removed the blood-stained boards and replaced them with new ones, but the new ones were so different from the rest that it still reminded them of Hank. Rennie had taken the blood-stained bedclothes to the graveyard and buried them in a deep hole between the graves of Hank's grandparents and laid a large flat stone on top.

It was the next year that Johnnie and Betsy lost their first-born child. They had been so happy as they waited the summer out, looking forward to winter, when the baby was due.

"We're in our late twenties. Most friends our age have three er four childern already, and some have childern goin' to school," Johnnie said. He teased Betsy, told her that she looked like a ball. She was so short she was almost round. "If ye ever fall down don't try to get up. If ye do, ye'll start rollin' and never stop." Rennie had made a beautiful quilt for the baby.

It was a difficult birth. The midwife said it was because Betsy was so small and was too old to be having her first child. It lived just one day. Rennie asked them to line the little coffin with the quilt she had made. The edge of the coffin was trimmed with white lace. "When ye have another child I'll make another little quilt." Just then neither Johnnie nor Betsy wanted to think about having another baby, but before the year was out Betsy was pregnant again.

One evening Johnnie and Betsy were over at Rennie's house, sitting on the porch listening to the whip-poor-wills call to each other. "There's nothin' more lonesome than a whip-poor-will," Rennie said. "Yet there's nothin' that I like better to listen to." She looked up and down Lonesome Holler. "I know now why they named this place Lonesome Holler." Her voice was full of unshed tears. "We've had more trouble. Were we ever as happy as I remember?"

"Yes," Betsy answered, "and we'll be happy again."

Johnnie had said that he was going to learn who had shot Hank. He and the sheriff had checked on every lead that came up, but so far nothing. The last one to see Hank had been Johnnie himself, when Hank quit work at the sawmill and started walking toward town. The two boys he usually ran around with were at home that night—all their families verified this. Rennie said she thought she'd heard a horse or mule coming up the hollow that night, then she'd dozed back off. She had no way of knowing how long she'd been asleep when Hank stumbled against her door. Maybe the rider had nothing to do with Hank, but Johnnie believed that whoever shot him had brought him to Rennie's house and left him. No one up or down Lonesome Holler was ever out riding in the night unless it was an emergency. Everyone they asked said they were at home that night. "I guess it's like you always say," Johnnie told Rennie. "It's only in story books that the mysteries are solved, and this is real life."

That year Sarah Ellen didn't come home for the five-day Christmas vacation. Rennie couldn't believe it. They had never been apart at Christmas. Sarah Ellen was all the family she had, and she was all the family Sarah Ellen had. Sally had invited Sarah Ellen to go home with her. Sally lived in a coal mining camp. Sarah Ellen had never seen one. Although Rennie was very disappointed, she didn't forbid her going. It was hard to let go, but she knew that Sarah Ellen was now grown and it would only make matters worse if she tried to boss her any longer. She had known for a long time that someday she would have to let her go her own way, but it hurt.

Sarah Ellen was amazed at some of the things she saw and disgusted with others. Sally took her to her first picture show. "Rennie would enjoy this," Sarah Ellen thought. It was a love story. Sarah Ellen thought it was "mushy." Sally called it "thrilling." Next, they went to the company store. Sarah Ellen walked up and down between the tables and racks and shelves. She couldn't believe what she was seeing. And the prices! So high—double what they were in the smaller, privately owned stores. The sleazy silk dresses and the high heel slippers, the stockings, or, as Sally called them, hose, so thin they didn't hide your legs at all. She had never seen bread in a loaf before, nor bacon sliced and in a package. "Ye could buy a full-grown shote back home for what ye'd pay here fer a few pounds of meat," she thought.

When Sally went to pay for what she had collected, she didn't give the store money but something called scrip. When Sarah Ellen asked what it was, Sally explained. A miner like her father could draw scrip against his next payday and the amount would be deducted from his paycheck.

Sally's family lived in a two-family, two-story company house. Each family had half of it. The porch was divided with a low wooden gate. There were two rooms downstairs, one the living room, the other the kitchen and dining room combined. Upstairs were three bedrooms. Sarah Ellen didn't think she would like living in the same house with another family, but what really upset her was that the outhouses were also built together. Each house had a number, and the outhouse had the same number. There were several rows of houses with roads running between. The houses faced each other and turned their backs to the row of houses behind. There was a water pump at the end of every three rows. All water had to be carried from this community pump in a bucket except the water for Sally's father's bath. The miners used a company bathhouse when they came out of the mines.

Sarah Ellen really enjoyed the Christmas celebration. On Christmas Eve, from almost every house came the noise of firecrackers, Roman candles, cherry bombs, and sky rockets. Sarah Ellen and Sally stood on their porch and watched. It was beautiful and deafening. The smell of burned powder filled the air. Only children took part in this fun; the older ones just watched. There were no small children in Sally's family, she being the youngest. The others were married and had moved out. So there was no one at their house to shoot fireworks.

As Sally's father went back into the house he smiled and said, "Silent Night, Holy Night."

Another thing that was new to Sarah Ellen was the telephone. Sally called up several of her friends and talked to them. Sarah Ellen would have loved to use the phone, but none of the folks she knew had one.

The next weekend she did go home. She had lots to tell Rennie. That evening when Johnnie came over, he gave Sarah Ellen a really good dressing down. "You ungrateful pup, ye no-good so and so," he began, in a voice that Sarah Ellen had never heard before. "Can't ye see what ye're doing to Rennie? Ye're breakin' her heart by not comin' home to see her. Families need to be together at Christmas time." Johnnie stopped when he saw the tears spring to Sarah Ellen's eyes.

"Rennie understands why I don't like to come back here." Sarah Ellen was sobbing.

"Well, ye ought to be willin' to face yer hurt in order to make hers less. This way she's lost you and Hank both." Johnnie's voice was now softer. "Don't ye know how much Rennie has done fer ye. Don't ye know how much of her life she's wasted fer ye?"

"Yes, of course I know, and I'm grateful. But ye don't know how torn apart I am."

"Ye're not the only one that has troubles. We jest have to pick ourselves up and go on. What can't be cured must be endured." Johnnie gave her a hug and a pat on the back. "Promise me that ye'll come back more often, fer Rennie's sake." And Sarah Ellen nodded her head for "Yes." Her heart was too full of tears to try to speak.

Sarah Ellen did try to come home more often, but each summer she worked at the school. She didn't get very much for her work, but she was saving what she could, and she was working on toward that scholarship.

The years passed, summer came and winter followed. Soon the day came when Sarah Ellen was through with high school. Next year she would be going to Cleveland, Ohio, living among people she didn't know, a way of life that would be so strange. Sometimes she almost backed out, but she couldn't let Rennie down. Mrs. Lloyd was sending one of the teachers, Miss Sparks, with her. They would be going by train. Sarah Ellen had never ridden a train before. "Can this be a girl from Lonesome Holler? Can this really be happenin' to me?" Miss Sparks would get her settled in before leaving her at the college. Sarah Ellen would be staying with some friends of Miss Sparks, doing housework for her board and keep. She would be too busy to get homesick, she hoped.

Sarah Ellen went home and spent a week with Rennie just before going away. It was a happy time and a sorrowful time. Rennie tried to hide her fears from Sarah Ellen. This was what she had looked forward to for so long. But what do you do when a dream comes to an end and you can't wake up? she asked herself.

Rennie had been saving some money, a little at a time. The night before Sarah Ellen had to go back to the Community Center to get ready for her trip, she brought out the little brown leather pouch from its hiding place in the trunk and gave it to her. Sarah Ellen began to cry. "Oh, Rennie, ye're too good fer yer own good. Ye need this more than I will. What if ye became sick? Who would take care of ye?"

"I have Betsy and Johnnie," Rennie said. She was holding back her tears. "Time enough to cry when I'm all alone," she thought.

"Ye do more fer them than they do fer you," Sarah Ellen reminded her.

"That's what families are fer," Rennie answered. "But we're more family to each other than anyone else. Ye're mine. Ma gave ye to me." Then Rennie began telling Sarah Ellen about when she was a small baby. They talked until it was way past bedtime, sometimes crying over something remembered, sometimes laughing. When Rennie told about the time Old Kate milked the cow and stole the milk and described how the old woman looked running through the rain, Sarah Ellen almost burst into tears laughing. "Pa would kill us if he knew that we were talkin' about a dead person this way," Rennie said as she wiped away the tears of laughter.

Next day Johnnie took Sarah Ellen back to the Community Center. This time Rennie did watch the truck out of sight. Then she turned and went to the graveyard and told the folks buried there what had happened.

34 _____

It would be four more years before the sisters saw each other again. Sarah Ellen had promised Rennie she'd write every week. She kept her promise. What Johnnie had said to her had sunk in. She told Rennie all about her classes, the folks she lived with, her friends. "Wish you could see these libraries," she would say. She sounded happy, but Rennie worried that Sarah Ellen was just making it sound too good. She must be having some troubles and making some mistakes, but if so she didn't share them with Rennie.

Rennie wrote to Sarah Ellen every week, keeping her informed of everything that happened on Lonesome Holler— who got married, who had a new baby, who joined the church, when the potato bugs destroyed her patch of potatoes, how many cans of berries she had canned, how much the price of sugar had gone up. When Sarah Ellen read the letters she thought, "Rennie should write a book. A letter from her is just like settin' on the porch and talking. I can't get homesick. All I have to do is read her letters and I feel like I'm back home." She kept every one of the letters in a shoe box and read and read them again and again.

Once she let one of her English teachers read one. "Your sister should try her hand at writing a book."

"But she only has an eighth-grade education."

"Your sister is a born storyteller," he answered her.

The truth is that it was hard for Sarah Ellen to adjust to a life so different from what she had been used to. She didn't like being called a hillbilly, not the way they made it sound. But she was proud of her heritage. She would show them that a girl from Eastern Kentucky had what it takes.

Sarah Ellen wrote to Rennie that she had decided not to come home for summer vacation. It would cost too much for her train ride there and back. She and a friend were going to Canada with a group of young Girl Scouts as counselors. She would get a small salary and get to see a lot of the world. "Did you ever dream that a girl from Lonesome Holler would be in Canada?" she asked Rennie.

The three following summers were the same. Rennie knew it was for the best, but she did so want to see her baby sister.

"I want her to grow up, yet I'd like to keep her a baby forever," she thought.

Now at last the long wait was over. Sarah Ellen was coming back to the hills, this time traveling alone. She had written Rennie what day she and Johnnie should meet her at the depot. When Sarah Ellen first got off the train Rennie didn't know her, she looked so different. Like a brought-on person, she thought. But when Sarah Ellen saw Rennie, she dropped her suitcase and started running and pushing her way through the crowd. She lifted Rennie off the ground and swung her around and around. "Set me down, ye goose," her sister tried to say, but she had no breath. When she could speak, Rennie sobbed, "Sarah Ellen, ye talk like a brought-on person."

"So I do. You pick it up after staying around them for so long, but it will soon wear off now that I'm back with my real folks."

"I jest hope it's not catchin'," said Johnnie teasingly.

"Same old Johnnie," Sarah Ellen said. "And is this the same old truck?"

"Well, in a way it is. I've had to replace a few things, like the motor, the bed, the wheels," Johnnie laughed.

"It don't use gas," Rennie kept up the banter. "It runs on will power—Johnnie's will power."

"Me and this old truck have been together fer a long time. We're the same as married. We've promised to stick together until death do us part."

They were soon on their way. It was amazing how quickly Sarah Ellen slipped back into her hillbilly speech. She didn't notice it herself, but Johnnie and Rennie exchanged smiling glances over her shoulder as she talked on and on and on.

35 _____

Rennie had awakened that morning at the first rooster crow, but she had lain in bed until she heard the birds twittering in the apple tree outside her window. "No use wasting lamp oil by gettin' up before it's daylight," she told herself. Yet out of force of habit she hurried through breakfast. She didn't mind staying alone, but it was so hard to cook for just one person.

Breakfast over and the few dishes washed and put away, she went out to the edge of the porch and looked up the holler and then down, noticing each house, checking to see if there was smoke coming from every flue.

The twenty-two years since her mother's death had brought very little change to Lonesome Holler. Some had grown old and died. New babies had been born, had grown up and married, and now had babies of their own. But the holler looked much the same. There were a few small changes—one or two new log houses, an extra room on Aunt Nance's old place, a new board roof on Rennie's own house.

Of course, Old Kate's house was gone. Good riddance, Rennie thought. One day—Sarah Ellen must have been about five, maybe six—Rennie had noticed that there was no smoke coming from Old Kate's flue. At first she just thought the old woman was oversleeping, but when four o'clock came and there was still no smoke, she told Johnnie. He and his uncle went to investigate and found the old woman dead. She had just gone to sleep and never awakened. They buried her in the Slone graveyard. No one had ever come to claim anything she owned, and there was nothing worth claiming. The few chickens had gone wild and been caught by foxes. The old dog had followed the coffin to the grave and refused to leave. Rennie had taken food and left it, but the dog refused to eat or even drink water. A week later he too was dead, the only friend Old Kate had had. Her land, what little there was, was sold for taxes. One stormy night lightning struck her house and it burned to the ground, adding more fuel to the ghost stories connected with the place.

There were more new graves in the Slone graveyard. Aunt Nance had outlived Rennie's father by only a year. John had now been dead six years. And there was a little white stone just below her father's that read, "The unnamed son of Johnnie and Betsy Slone, aged one day." Rennie could still feel the softly falling snow as she and Johnnie had stood there watching the little casket being lowered into the ground. She felt the trembling of Johnnie's hand as he clung to hers. Later he had stopped for a cup of coffee with her before going home through the snow to comfort Betsy. They had had three girls since then and Betsy was heavy with child again. The last girl was named Rena Lee. "I added the 'Lee' onto yer name, Rennie, so they would not be sayin' 'Big Rennie' and 'Little Rennie,'" Betsy explained.

Betsy and Rennie were still good friends. Betsy was always coming to Rennie for advice, and Rennie went over to help out—when they killed a hog, made soap, canned beans, or anything else that came up. She always went over and kept house for a week or so after each new baby was born. But then, Johnnie always helped her too—dug her coal, plowed her garden. She no longer tried to raise corn, as she now had no cow or mule to feed, just a few chickens.

The years had brought less change to Rennie, though, than they had to Lonesome Holler. She was taller, yet the years of hard work had not stooped her shoulders. Her hair was now more brown than reddish. She wore it in two long braids wound around her head like a kind of crown. The only lines in her face were the laugh lines around her eyes. It was a face that showed strength of character, the marks of sorrows conquered and overcome.

Today was a day she had looked forward to for a long time, yet now she wished it was just over and done with. She had never gotten used to talking to the brought-on people of the Community Center, except for Miss Rose. Miss Rose had been such a good friend. Rennie wondered what had happened to her. For years after she left Lonesome Holler they had written to each other, but then the letters became only Christmas cards. The last time Rennie had written, her letter had been returned. Miss Rose had not wanted to leave Caney but there had been some trouble at the Community Center. Some said that the school didn't like Miss Rose's giving so much of her time to the Creek people. Mrs. Sizemore, the nurse that replaced Miss Rose, sure did nothing for them except come once each year to give the schoolchildren their shots, and the county health program paid for that.

The day Miss Rose left Caney, she came to say good-bye. Johnnie and his uncle were hoeing corn in the upper flat. Miss Rose climbed the hill to talk to them. Rennie stood in the door and cried.

"Well, I must not stand here all day thinkin' about old times," Rennie spoke aloud. Johnnie would soon arrive in his truck. How proud he was of it! He spent more time working on it than he did driving it. Betsy told him she believed he was pleased when something broke because then he could fix it. "It's jest held together with hay wire and 'backer cans," she told Rennie.

When Rennie heard Johnnie coming, she hurried to get ready. "I could have walked down to the big road," she told him as she climbed into the truck.

"And gotten yer new shoes dirty," he teased.

"We used to think nothin' of walkin' clear to the Community Center."

"Yeah, but that was before we got old," Johnnie laughed.

"You won't ever get grown-up, let alone old. Why, when Gabriel blows his trumpet someone will have to knock ye in the head. Ye'll be too mean to die."

"Don't see why I fool with ye if that's the way ye feel about me." The smiles on their faces belied the words they spoke.

"Now that Sarah Ellen's all through school, ye'll be lookin' around fer some old good-lookin' man to marry."

"No, I don't want no man to have to wait on. Those that I would have don't want me, and those that want me I wouldn't have." It was an old mountain saying. Johnnie doubted there had been any that Rennie "would have."

Johnnie parked the old Ford truck behind a green Jeep along the roadside near the post office.

"I won't be goin' in," he told Rennie. "I'll find someone to swap lies with and wait fer ye."

"Wish ye were comin' in. Don't see many people here I know."

"It's still early. They'll be along soon."

Rennie had been to Cushing Hall before, when Sarah Ellen had graduated from high school. As she approached the building, she stopped to admire it. "It's almost as big as my garden patch at home," she thought. It was built in the shape of an H. The lower floor of the left wing was the printing office, and the second floors on both wings were girls' dorms. The cross-bar was the great hall, with its two-story-high ceiling.

The small plank house sitting close to the road, just to the right of the Cushing Hall, caught Rennie's eye. She knew that Mrs. Lloyd had lived in it when she first came to Caney Creek. Between the shack and the hall were some large boulders. Rennie remembered the story about them that her father had told—about an old woman who had lived in the shack and had dried roots on the rocks and burned her cornstalks there to keep snakes away. She wondered what the old woman would think if she could see the place now.

Rennie walked up the stone steps under the shade of the cucumber trees and through the wide open doors of Cushing Hall. The size of the room always awed her, yet Sarah Ellen had told her it was very small compared with some buildings she had seen in the cities she had visited. On her right was the stage, with the curtain pulled back and chairs set up for the graduating students and speakers. The girls were in their white dress uniforms, and the boys wore their black pants, white shirts, and black ties. There were at least twenty of them. In front of the stage ran a curving wall built from creek rock. A large open fireplace covered almost the whole of the wall opposite the stage, with stairs going up on each side. Looking up, she saw the balconies that ran around three sides. They reminded her of porches. On them sat the students who weren't graduating. Rennie always laughed to herself whenever she saw this strange room. It seemed so funny to see a rock wall and porches inside a building. The main floor held rows and rows of handmade chairs set in a slight curve to follow the form of the rock wall. These were for the visitors, and about half were already filled.

Rennie entered and sat down in the first seat of a row near

the back. She put her handbag in the next seat, not wanting any stranger to sit next to her. Then she looked up at the stage, where Sarah Ellen was sitting. She looked so beautiful in her white uniform. Seeing Rennie, she blew a kiss and raised her hand in a small wave.

"I would love to go to her," Sarah Ellen thought, "and introduce her to all my friends, but that would only embarrass her more. I love my sister so much, and I understand her so well."

Sarah Ellen noticed the empty seat next to Rennie, and her eyes filled with tears. Hank should be sitting there. Poor, dear, sweet Hank. The bittersweet memories kept returning, though time had erased all the anger. Sarah Ellen couldn't remember a time before Hank had been a part of her life. He had always been there to help her up when she fell down, to wipe away her tears when she cried, to be pleased when she shared her joys. He had given her the choice of his puppies and gone with her to bury the dog many years later when it died of old age. Only Hank had understood how frightened she was that first day she went to school, holding her hand, eating his lunch with her, although the other boys had laughed at him. A few weeks later, when she had made friends with some of the girls, only then would he go with the boys. And there had been so many other times. Showing her the bird's nest he had found, holding her hand while she peeped into the nest. Sitting at the kitchen table helping her with homework. Popping corn around the fire. Always giving, never asking questions in return.

She was finishing her last year of grade school when she noticed the change in Hank. He had finished the eighth grade two years before and was now working as a gin hand at Johnnie's saw mill. One night he said, "Sarah Ellen, I have some money saved. Let's get married this fall."

"Married! Why Hank, I don't love ye, not that way. Ye seem like my brother. Anyway, we're cousins."

"Jest second cousins. That don't count. Not like first cousins."

"Well, it does to me. Anyway, we're too young to get married. Besides, I thought ye knew, I'm goin' to the Caney Community Center to high school, and then maybe on somewhere to college."

"And who's goin' to pay fer all that?"

"Well, the high school will be free. I can work my way through that at the Communtiy Center, and I hope to win a scholarship fer college."

"Yeah, and that's takin' charity."

"No, it ain't. I'll have to work hard to get that scholarship."

"Ye'll be so stuck-up ye won't speak to me."

"No, ye'll be married and have a whole swarm of young'ns and I'll be a teacher."

Things had never been the same. Hank no longer saved his money but began to run with the wrong crowd, drinking, fighting, and just cutting up. Sarah Ellen tried to talk with him.

Sarah Ellen had been at the school for a few months when Hank came to see her. The rules of the school didn't allow boys to talk with the girls. Even brothers had to get permission to visit with their sisters and then have a teacher in the room. Hank came in the kitchen, where he knew Sarah Ellen worked. She wasn't there that day. Hank was so drunk that some of the girls became frightened and called for help. The night watchman arrested him and took him to jail. In the struggle Hank got hurt. None of the folks on Lonesome Holler understood. They blamed Sarah Ellen. You simply didn't turn your own flesh and blood in to the law.

In her second year she was in a play to be presented in the assembly hall. All the Creek people were invited. Sarah Ellen asked Hank to come.

"I'll be there with bells on," he said. And sure enough, he was. The bells were tied to his mule's bridle, two large cow bells, and he rode the mule right into the hall before anyone could stop him. It took several men to overcome him and get him and his mule out.

"That's what I think of you and yer brought-on friends," he shouted.

And then there was the night Johnnie had come after her. She knew by his face that something was wrong. "It's Rennie, ain't it?" she asked. "Is somethin' wrong with Rennie?"

"No, it's Hank! He got shot. No one knows how, he jest come up on Rennie's porch and beat on the door. When Rennie opened it he fell in. Keeps askin' fer you."

Sarah Ellen would never forget the ride home, but they were too late. "He jest kept on callin' fer you," Rennie told her.

The rap of the president's gavel brought Sarah Ellen's thoughts back to the present. The audience hushed and all eyes turned to the stage. The president looked out at the audience of students and families, and smiled as she spoke. "We have here a group of young men and women who have finished their schooling and are now ready to face the outside world. And, to begin our program, I've asked one of our most honored former students to speak. She has brought pride to the Caney Creek Community School by completing her education in Cleveland, Ohio. She was offered many positions there. They would have brought her much more money than she will earn here, but she has chosen to return and teach in her native region. I'm very pleased to present Sarah Ellen Slone, who will tell us why she made that decision."

Sarah Ellen rose and looked at the crowd. She knew almost everyone in it. How like her mountain friends—all the women together on one side, the few men and boys on the other. She knew that most of the men, including Johnnie, were outside.

"Well, I'll make this speech short and sweet because I know most of you are wanting to go home, kick your shoes off, get back into your old clothes, and be at ease. I've not been gone all that long. I remember the freedom of going barefoot. I'll bet if you looked closely up and down the rocks along Lonesome Holler you could find a whole handful of my toenails that I bumped off when I was climbing." She waited for the laughter to die down.

"Yes, I've been on the outside, which is where some of you who are graduating today are planning on going. It won't be easy. The folks out there don't understand us, our ways, our speech. Our customs are different. Most of them mean to be kind. But, as my father used to say, 'Strange people have strange ways.' Remember that we're as strange to

213

them as they are to us. But also remember not to let them make you feel ashamed of your heritage. You have folks to be proud of. Learn their ways but don't forget yours. When one woman asked me if I was returning to the hills because I couldn't cope with the outside, I just eye-balled her and answered, 'No, I just can't accept the outside.' I love the hills and the people that live here—their friendliness, togetherness, family ties, their true worship of God. I know life in the hills is hard, but it's also beautiful.

"The woman you see here is not just Sarah Ellen Slone. I really represent several women, and if it weren't for them I wouldn't be here. The women who left Ireland to venture into the unknown. Little Granny Alice, who left her family and friends to come to Caney with her husband and sons. Grandma Kate, who didn't know who her own folks were but kept alive the oral history of the Slones. My mother, who gave up her life that I might live. Mrs. Lloyd, who left her safe home in Boston to come to Caney and devote her life to giving us a better life. Most of all, my sister, Rennie, who gave up her own hopes and dreams to raise me and give me an education.

"I just hope that someday some of you can stand here where I'm now standing and say, 'My life was made better and easier because of the work of Sarah Ellen Slone.' I thank you."

Rennie had blushed when her name was mentioned, but her heart swelled with love and pride as Sarah Ellen sat down amid the applause of the audience. She scarcely paid attention to the rest of the ceremony. Raising Sarah Ellen and seeing her educated had been her life's work, and now she knew that work was done.

After the assembly was over, the crowd left Cushing Hall. Rennie waited outside the doorway until Sarah Ellen came out. They walked together down to where Johnnie waited beside his truck.

"Are ye comin' home to Lonesome Holler with us now?" he asked Sarah Ellen.

"No, I have a lot to do here first. I haven't really talked with Mrs. Lloyd yet. I don't know just what she wants me to do. I hope I can teach high school here so that I'll be close to you all. But she could send me to another county."

"I was hopin' that ye'd be teachin' school on Lonesome Holler. I'll soon have three and maybe four ready for ye," Johnnie said with pride in his voice.

"Yes, I know. But for teaching on Lonesome Holler I'm overqualified now, as much as I would love to."

"I know. We can't keep a teacher. One year and they move on somewheres else, and it'll be that way until we get a road. Ever' election year we're promised a county road built, but it's been that way fer year after year."

"When *will* ye be home?" Rennie asked. There was a pleading in her voice.

"I'll be ready by Friday if Johnnie can come and get me. About five?"

"I'll be here with bells on." Johnnie could have bit his tongue, for he knew he'd said the wrong thing before the words were out of his mouth, and he saw the hurt flash across Sarah Ellen's face. They all stood in silence for a moment, thinking of Hank. Then Rennie said, trying to smile, "Well, me and Johnnie are country folks. We go to bed with the chickens, so we must hurry home and get the work done up agin dark." She climbed into the truck beside Johnnie.

"See ye Friday," Johnnie said as he started to turn his truck. By now what few cars and trucks there had been had left, and the folks that had ridden horses or mules were waiting for the truck to get out of their way so they could climb on their saddles and leave also. Sarah Ellen waved her hand and turned back up the hill along the path that ran between two rows of cucumber trees.

"I'd hoped that she would've got over her hurt fer Hank by now," Johnnie said.

"Ye never get over a love like that," Rennie sighed.

"How would you know? You never loved a man." Johnnie wasn't teasing now.

"I read a lot. Ye learn a lot from books," Rennie explained.

"That's not real life, as ye're allus tellin' everbody. I thought at one time that you and Richard Tate might get a love affair goin'. I know that he was struck on you. What happened between you and him?" Johnnie said.

"Well, I guess that I jest ran too fast fer me to catch him," Rennie laughed.

"Whatever became of him? He jest taught that one year. He was a real nice feller. I wouldn't have minded havin' him in the family."

"I don't know. I never heard from him after he left Lonesome Holler. Don't see why ye want to marry me off so bad. If I had a family of my own, who'd help Betsy help take care of yours?"

"What will ye do, now that your life's work is over?" Johnnie asked with real interest and wanting to change the subject.

"Oh, there are lots of things. I'll find lots to do. There's my sewin', more books to read, food to grow. And don't laugh, but I've been thinkin' about writin' down all that I can remember that Ma told me that Grandma Kate had told her about the Slone history. Folks don't set around the fire and talk to their childern about the old days like they used to. So I think I'll write it all down."

Rennie looked at Johnnie's face to see if he was going to laugh as she had expected. But to her surprise he said, "I think that's a great thing to do. And tell it all, not jest the good stuff."

"Yeah, about Pa goin' to prison and yer folks makin' moonshine," Rennie said.

"And don't leave out about Old Kate. She wasn't a Slone, but years from now folks will wonder why she's buried in our graveyard." Johnnie was very interested in the thought of having all those stories written down.

"And another thing that I had planned to do this winter was make three dolls, like the ones Ma made fer me, fer three little girls that I know."

"Why don't ye make some of them dolls and sell 'em to the brought-on folks at the Community Center?" Johnnie asked.

"Ye know how long it takes to make one of them hand-sewn dolls of that size and how much stuff ye have to buy— the cloth, cotton, lace, buttons, elastic, and so on. Why, fer

216

what I could sell one fer I'd be makin' about a quarter a day."
Rennie ran out of breath.

"And ye'd rather make 'em and give 'em away?" Johnnie
smiled.

"Yeah, to those that I love. The happy smile on a child's
face is worth more than money." Rennie meant what she
said.

"I'll never understand ye, Rennie. Did ye know that ye're
an exceptional woman?" There was a quiver in Johnnie's
voice.

"No, remind me ever' now and then," Rennie laughed. By
now they had arrived at the end of the big road. "Let me out
here," Rennie said. "I want to walk up the holler."

"Are ye shore?" Johnnie asked as he slowed down and
pulled the truck over to the side of the road.

"Yeah, I'm shore. I want to get these hot shoes off and
wade in the creek. I have a lot of things to think about, and
there's nothin' more refreshin' than wadin' in the water. As
Hank used to say, I'd druther wear out my feet than have my
head bounced off."

"Okey, if that's the way ye want it. You're the boss. See ye
Friday."

36 _____

It was after dark Friday when Sarah Ellen and Johnnie arrived. There were several boxes in the back of the truck
that Sarah Ellen had brought with her. Johnnie offered to
carry them into the house, but Sarah Ellen told him there
wasn't anything that would be hurt if left on the porch overnight. "Anyway, one of those boxes is full of books that I
brought Rennie, and if she gets into them I won't get a word
from her all weekend." Sarah Ellen smiled at her sister.

"Bring Betsy and the kids over Sunday after church fer

dinner," Rennie told Johnnie as he turned his truck. "We're goin' to have chicken and dumplin's, and there'll be a plenty fer all."

"We'll be here. Anythin' ye want us to bring?" he asked.

"No, jest yer appetite," Rennie told him.

"I never go anywheres without that," Johnnie yelled back as he went rattling down the rough hollow.

Next morning when Rennie awoke she looked over in the other bed for Sarah Ellen. She wasn't there. She was already up. Rennie went to the kitchen. No one there. She looked toward the outhouse, but the door was open. Then she searched the barn, came back to the house, and walked through and out on the front porch. Looking toward the graveyard she saw her sister kneeling by Hank's grave. Rennie thought, "I've heard it said that it's better to have loved and lost than never to have loved at all, but I don't believe that."

After a late breakfast Sarah Ellen went all over the house, even up the ladder stairs into the loft, then all over the farm and garden. Rennie watched her from the front porch. At each stop she would pause and drink in the memories. Sometimes she would giggle, then laugh aloud, other times she would wipe tears from her eyes. Rennie had offered to go with her, but she had said that she wanted to go alone.

After dinner they sat on the porch a long time letting the dishes get dry and cold. The scraps would be hard to get off, but neither thought about that. "Rennie, there's so much I want to ask you, and there's so much that I don't understand. Is the love one has for their kinfolks the same love they have for someone they want to marry? I loved Hank so much." She stopped to wipe the tears away. "There was a boy I met in Canada, a real nice boy. We were together a lot; I enjoyed being with him. He even took me home with him to meet his parents. I know that had I given him any encouragement he would have asked me to marry him. I liked him a lot, but I knew that he would never have been happy here in Kentucky, and I sure was not going to live there away from all my folks and Lonesome Holler. Was this love that I have for Hank . . . for I love him as much now as I did when he was alive . . . is it just because he was my cousin and we

218

grew up so close? Or is it the love that a woman has for the man that she wants to marry?"

"I don't have an answer fer ye. I wish that the English language had more words fer the different meanin's for the word love. Ye can love yer country, ye can love yer friends, we love God, a husband and wife love each other. Ye can even love turnips." At that they both laughed because turnips were one thing that Sarah Ellen would not eat.

"I can see what you mean, but I still don't understand my feelings for Hank. Before I even went to high school he asked me to marry him. We were just kids then. Of course, many of our friends did get married at that age, but I couldn't then nor can I now think of Hank as a husband. Yet I love him so very much. I love him even more than I do you."

"We grew up here where the word love isn't used when ye're talkin' about yer mate, yet when one er the other dies there's so much hidden grief. I think that a friendship love can go as far and as deep as marriage love." Rennie wished she could help Sarah Ellen, but these were questions that she had asked herself many times.

"You and Johnnie have such a beautiful friendship. You're closer than most brothers and sisters that I know. There's nothing that you wouldn't do for each other. If Hank could only have been satisfied with that kind of relationship. But he wanted more. He wanted for us to get married, and I wanted to go to school. I think he was jealous of the school. He thought that was what took me from him. I wonder what I'd do if I had a chance to do it all over again. I just wish someone could give me an answer. I know what you're going to say—that it's only in story books that everthin' comes out right, and this is real life."

Sarah Ellen sighed. She needed more time to understand her own feelings. And she didn't want to go on talking about herself. "Now let's talk about you and what you're going to do with the rest of your life."

Sarah Ellen was pleased with Rennie's plan to write about the family, but she wanted her sister near her. "You know that I could get you a job at the Community Center, and you could come and stay with me. You could be a house mother, or if you didn't like that there would be work in the kitchen or the laundry. Why don't you?" Sarah Ellen begged.

"No, I'd rather stay here and keep busy with my sewin' and readin'. And I do believe that I'm needed here on Lonesome Holler. There's always someone that I can help. Yer plan sounds nice, but please believe me, I want to stay here."

"All right, I'll let you get away with that. But there's one thing that I'm going to set my foot down on. For one time in my life I'm going to boss *you*. First, from now on *I'm* going to pay the taxes. This farm is as much mine as it is yours. And another thing, no more raising corn, no keeping a mule or a cow to have to feed during the cold winter. Maybe a few chickens and a little garden." Sarah Ellen didn't mean to take no as an answer.

"But if I don't raise corn what will I eat fer bread?" Rennie wanted to know.

"You can get used to eating bolted meal bread, just like I have, or better still eat loaf bread." Sarah Ellen went on.

"And where's the money to pay fer that goin' to come from?" Rennie asked with a smile.

"From me, that's where. Now, don't talk back. I'm going to have my say first and you're going to listen. You've spent your whole life doing for me, and now it's my turn to do for you. I'll be drawing enough pay to send you, say, twenty dollars a month. Rennie, if you don't let me do this for you, I swear on Hank's grave that I'll never step my foot on Lonesome Holler again as long as I live." Sarah Ellen's voice was beginning to tremble.

Rennie saw that her sister meant what she said. "Ye don't leave me much choice, do ye? And I know that ye mean what ye say, but it's hard fer me to take money from you."

"It's hard for you to swallow that old Slone pride. But think how I've felt all these years taking from you. Just think of it as a debt long overdue. For that's what it is. Now let's kiss and make up and go catch that old hen and get ready for dinner tomorrow."

That evening they sat on the front porch and listened to the whip-poor-wills and breathed in all the sweet and sad memories of Lonesome Holler.